Denis Dent by E. W. Hornung

Ernest William Hornung was born in Middlesbrough, England on 7th June 1866, the third son and youngest of eight children.

Although spending most of his life in England and France he spent two years in Australia from 1884 and that experience was to colour and influence much of his written works.

His most famous character A. J. Raffles, 'the gentleman thief', was published first in Cassell's Magazine during 1898 and was to make him famous across the world as the new century dawned.

Hornung also wrote several stage plays and was a gifted poet.

Spending time with the troops in WWI he published Notes of a Camp-Follower on the Western Front during 1919, a detailed account of his time there. This was especially close to his heart as his son, and only child, was killed at the Second Battle of Ypres on 6th July 1915.

Ernest William Hornung died in Saint-Jean-de-Luz, in the south of France on 22nd March 1921

Index of Contents

DENIS DENT

CHAPTER I

THE SECOND OFFICER

"Land ahead!"

The North Foreland had been made advisedly snug for the night. In the middle watch she was under her three lower topsails and fore topmast staysail only. Not that it blew very hard, but the night was dark and hazy, with a heavy swell. And it was the last night of the voyage.

At eight bells there had been a cast of the deep-sea lead, with the significant result that the skipper had been the first to turn in; gradually the excited passengers had followed his example, instead of staying on deck to see the Otway light. The second mate had said there would be no Otway that night, and what the second said was good enough for most. The saloon skylight had become a clean-edged glimmer in the middle of the poop, the binnacle a fallen moon; not a port-hole twinkled on the rushing ink; and the surviving topsails, without visible stitch or stick aloft or alow, hovered over the ship like gigantic bats.

Four persons remained upon the poop: the middy of the watch, tantalized by muffled guffaws from the midshipmen's berth in the after-house; the man at the wheel, in eclipse above the belt, with the binnacle light upon one weather-beaten hand; and on the weather side, the second mate in reluctant conversation with a big cigar that glowed at intervals into a bearded and spectacled face, the smooth brown one of the young officer sharing the momentary illumination.

"It's all very well," said the senior man, in low persistent tones, "but if we don't have it out now, when are we to? You know what it will be like to-morrow: we shall land first thing, and you'll be the busiest man on board. As for the rules of the ship, if an owner can't use his discretion he might as well travel by some other line."

The young fellow was smiling pleasantly as the other puffed again.

"Very good, Mr. Merridew! I don't object if the captain doesn't; and of course I must tell you anything you want to know."

"Anything! My good young man, if I am to consider this matter for a moment (which I don't promise) I must at least know everything that you can tell me about yourself first; for what," continued Mr.

Merridew, taking the cigar from his teeth, "what do you suppose I know about you at this moment? Absolutely nothing except that you seem to be a first-class sailor, as they tell me you are, and a very nice fellow, as I have found you for myself—aboardship; but of your shore-going record, of your position in life at home, and of your people and their position, to speak quite plainly, I know nothing at all."

Mr. Merridew delivered himself with a certain dispassionate unction, as one who could do the judicial to a turn, and enjoy it. Yet his tone was kindly, and the periods free from wilful offense.

"You may make your mind easy about my people. I have none," said the sailor, bitterly. A fatherly hand found his shoulder on the word.

"My dear fellow! I am so sorry."

"You mean relieved."

"I mean what I say," said Mr. Merridew, removing his hand.

It was the young man's turn to apologize, which he did with much frankness and more feeling.

"The truth is, sir, my parents have been dead for years; and yet they are nearly everything to me still— they were all the world until this voyage! My mother was Irish; her name would not be new to you, but it will keep. It may not be necessary for you to know it, or anything more about me, and in any case it can't alter me. But I am half-Irish through my mother—though you wouldn't think it."

"I would think it," remarked Mr. Merridew, blowing at his cigar as at a forge, until the red light found him looking wise through his spectacles, but the officer with one eye on his sails and no perceptible emotion in the other.

"My first name," he went on, "is as Irish as you like; it's Denis; and you may say that I've been living up to it for once!"

"Denis!" repeated Mr. Merridew, with interest. "Well, I know that name, anyhow; one of our partners— Captain Devenish's father—he's Denis Devenish, you know."

"Indeed," said Denis Dent, and there was a strange light in his spare eye. "Well, so much for my mother; my father was a Yorkshire dalesman, as his father and his father's father were before him. I am the first of them to leave the land."

"May I ask why?"

"It isn't our land any more. My father gave up everything to take my mother abroad, when her life was despaired of in England, and when her people—her own people—I can't trust myself to speak of them!"

And the young fellow turned abruptly aside, while Mr. Merridew puffed and peered at a massive though clean-cut face, whose only Irish feature was a pair of bright brown eyes, bold and resolute, yet quick to laughter, if quicker still to fire.

The south-easter sang through the unseen rigging; the ship rushed a fathom through the unseen sea. The second had a look at the compass, and came climbing back to windward with his hands in his pea-jacket pockets.

"And yet," said Mr. Merridew, flourishing his cigar, "and yet—you want to marry my daughter!"

"If she will have me, sir," said the sailor, with an uncertainty on that point in becoming contrast to his certainty of himself.

"But whether I will or not."

"I never said that, Mr. Merridew. I should be very sorry to take up such a position, I can assure you, sir."

"You would be sorry, but you would do it," retorted Mr. Merridew with acumen. "You would do as your father evidently did before you."

"I hoped we had finished with my parents, sir."

"But they left you nothing, if I understand aright," rejoined Merridew, changing his ground and his tone with some dexterity. "And you would marry my daughter on the pay of a junior officer in the merchant service."

"I never said that either. I have my captain's certificate, sir, as it is."

The new tone was the tone to take. Mr. Merridew went so far as to give his daughter her name.

"And Nan," said he, "might have ten thousand pounds for her marriage portion. I don't say she would, but for all you know she might have more. Her husband ought to bring at least as much into settlement, even as a self-respecting man, don't you think? And yet you would make her a merchant skipper's wife!"

The young man winced, as though for a flash he saw himself wholly in the wrong. Then his face hardened—all but the Irish eyes—and it was the face of a man who would justify himself with his life's blood. Impulse, initiative, temerity, were in the eyes, indomitable endurance in their solid setting.

"You take it for granted that I will never be anything more!" he exclaimed. "But, sir, once a sailor isn't always one. I've got on well at sea. I'd get on well on land—anywhere—at anything! You may smile. I feel it in me. Mr. Merridew, it may seem what you please, but I'm pretty young even for what I am now. Surely, surely, you would give me time—if she would?"

It was the Irishman speaking, the Irish blood spurting out in words, and Mr. Merridew distrusted the bulk of that race; but his cigar glowed again upon a mouth and jaw that came of harder stock, and for the moment his mind was illuminated too.

Here was this Denis Dent, not one young man, it struck him, but two young men in one, each with a very name of his own. Dents from the Dales, Denis from old Ireland! Mr. Merridew smiled through his spectacles, pleased with his conceit, not altogether disposed to regard it as such, but incontinently interested in a personality to which he had been so clever as to supply the key. The heart of the discoverer warmed toward his own. There was an attractiveness in Denis, a solid worth in Dent. Denis might win the girl. Dent would deserve her. And Denis Dent might have carried her own father with him, had he been the only young man in the case, or even on the poop of the North Foreland as she drove through the haze on the last night of her voyage.

But as the pair stood eye to eye, the pregnant pause between them was interrupted by a loud and startling laugh, and a tall figure loomed through the first gray tinge of approaching dawn. It was that of a young man in a tasseled dressing-gown, with an ornate meerschaum pipe pendent between the bushy black whiskers of the day.

"Well, if that doesn't take first prize for cheek!" cried he, and lurched toward them in his slippers as one who had never found his sea-legs.

"We are having a private conversation, Ralph," said Mr. Merridew in mild rebuke.

"A private conversation that you could hear on the forecastle-head!" jeered Ralph Devenish, who was full of liquor without being drunk. "I suppose he's so proud of it he wants the whole ship to know!"

And the meerschaum pointed jerkily at Denis, who stood the heaving deck as a circus rider stands a horse, his hands still deep in his pea-jacket pockets.

"Captain Devenish," said he, "it's against the rules to speak to the officer of the watch, but you shall speak civilly if you speak at all. Otherwise I advise you to take yourself off the poop before you're put off."

"By God!" snarled Devenish, "but you shall pay for that! Before one owner to another owner's son, on the last night of the voyage! It's your last in the Line, Mr. Officer of the Watch! And you dare to lay a hand on me! Come on. You dare. I know your blustering breed, you damned Jack-in-buttons!"

"And I know yours—you Devenishes! I know you too well to soil my hands on any one of you!"

The concentrated bitterness of this retort had an opposite effect on either hearer; one it stupefied, the other it flooded with a sudden light; but Devenish was the first to find his tongue, and for the moment there was none more foul before the mast. The deplorable torrent was only stemmed by the startling apparition of a square little man in a still more awful, because a more articulate and more righteous, rage.

"I'll teach you to break the rules of my ship! I'll teach you to curse my officers, drunk or sober! Out of my sight, sir, or I'll have you in irons before you're a minute older!"

"Come, come, Captain Coles," said Mr. Merridew, with dignity; "there has been more provocation than you imagine; and this, you must remember, is Captain Devenish."

"I don't care a dump if it's Devenish Merridew and Company lumped into one!" roared the little skipper. "You can have your way ashore, but I mean to have mine at sea; and as for your iron coffin of a ship, I'll be thankful to come off her alive, let alone sailing in her again. No two compasses alike, thirty-six hours since we got the sun, the darkest night of the voyage, and Australia anywhere! Yet this is the night you choose, you owners, to bully and browbeat my officers of the watch!"

But it was no longer the darkest night of the voyage, or even night at all. The group stood visible and divisible in a cold gray haze. The lower topsails were no longer detached from the ship; there was a misty mast to each; and the ship was running dry-decked through the high smooth seas.

It was at this moment that the haze lifted like breath from a mirror; and a subtle new sound was just beginning to insinuate itself upon the ear when the look-out man drowned it with his roar from the forecastle head.

CHAPTER II

SAUVE QUI PEUT

Land was indeed ahead, and in the most appalling shape known to seafaring man: at the last moment, the haze had lifted on a line of jagged cliffs, already parallel with the foreyard, albeit by the muffled thud of the breakers, not quite so near as it looked.

The North Foreland was blessed with a commander who was at his best in an emergency. Little Coles had turned in when he should have stayed on deck, and was no more prepared for shipwreck than if such disasters were unknown; but he rose to the occasion like a lark. His sharp voice cracked like a whip from the break of the poop, and all hands, piped from the forecastle, the petty officers' quarters, and the midshipmen's berth, came running as though the words drew blood.

The spanker was set, with the mizzen and maintopmast staysail, and the helm put down to bring her round; but there was no racing of the cliffs to port. She stumbled a little in her stride; the fresh sails flapped; but there was no getting her on the other tack, though the upper mizzen topsail was pressed into the job.

The skipper waited a minute with compressed lips and fiery eye; then a crackle of musketry from his weatherbeaten throat, and both anchors were let go.

The port anchor had fifty fathoms of cable, the starboard anchor sixty fathoms of chain; in anticipation of their holding, the sails were clewed up, and a man sent into the chains with the lead, for she was drifting inshore every moment. But the lead danced on smooth rock, where the anchors trailed as readily as over ice; the captain had them both up again, but that took longer than letting them go, and meanwhile half the hands were aloft shaking out sail once more.

Coles was showing his resource at every point, and by this time had his ship actually head to wind; in another minute she might have stood away upon the port tack. But at this juncture time was wasted in an attempt to sheet home the topsails, which failing, the buntlines of the mainsail were let go, the port main tack got on board, and the sheet hauled aft. The men were still upon the rope when the North Foreland struck and spilt them like the winners in a tug-of-war.

It was the horrible striking of an iron ship: a terrific crash under the mizzen-chains, and there she quivered like a rat in a terrier's teeth. And the devilish seas that had run with her, hunted with her, how they fell on her now, and swept and trampled her from the moment she was down!

The scene on deck, if it wanted the infinite horror of pitch darkness, was only a degree less dreadful in a pearly dawn that left no doubt about the situation. Every hatchway spouted crude humanity, shouting, shoving, screaming, scolding, covering a chattering nakedness as it gained the deck, and there struck silent at a glance. For nothing was hid, nothing extenuated, for a single moment, to a single eye. There was no learning the worst by humane degrees. It was patent at once to the wildest and the calmest gaze. The sanguine soul was no more help to the stunned community than the born pessimist; there was no chance for the imagination either way.

They could see, every one of them, the towering cliffs—blind sides of houses without an inch of pavement—the rollers running up to them unbroken, for the better sport of leaping sky-high at the impact. They could see her settling, see her bumping, see the top-hamper falling about the deck. There was enough to feel and to hear. The eyes might have been spared a little. Some shut them more than once, as when an upper spar came down like an arrow, transfixing a sailor with incredible neatness, and actually sticking upright through man and deck; but few escaped the sight of blood, and none the dying scream. A worse sight was in store. A steward with the stock of life-belts from the lazaretto touched the captain's arm. And, checked in some hoarse tirade, the valiant Coles stood first aghast and then abject in the sight of passengers and crew—beaten man and broken reed.

The better part of valour was the only part he lacked. Not a boat in davits; the whole fleet docked, inboard, on skids! And exactly six life-belts to go round a ship's company of over a hundred souls!

The second mate was clearing away the port life-boat with five of the hands, one blaspheming, another in tears, more than one vowing with reason that they would all be drowned, and the young officer himself in a consuming agony of his own. At the break of the poop, almost all this time, stood a slender figure in a pink wrapper, between a bearded man in spectacles and a man with bushy whiskers in incongruous silk and tassels. Dent wondered why he did not lend a hand; no, on second thoughts he knew, and cursed the fellow in his heart. He did not mean to leave her side. He meant to have the rescuing of her. Trust a Devenish to play his own game! Denis was too busy to look twice at the trio, but he seemed to see them all the time, and the vision galled him to insensate effort.

"Take your time, take your time," cried the chief officer, all red hook-nose and ginger moustache, an oilskin bonnet fastened under his chin. "The old man's done his part. He'll go down in her. The rest hangs on you and me."

The chief met the responsibility with his own tap of cold profanity, not unaccompanied by shrewd cuff and calculated kick, as he superintended the clearing of the other life-boat. As for the skipper, it seemed that he had recovered his mettle to meet fresh trouble further aft; they could hear him firing oaths and threatening lead; but when Denis looked he could not get his eyes past the two men at the break of the poop, for at that moment they were lashing one of the six life-belts about a forlorn little figure in pink.

The port life-boat was ready first, and the third mate busy marshaling the women and children in a helpless, eager, hesitating, exasperating throng; but Miss Merridew was still detained by her friends on the poop. The gripes had been cut, and Denis himself had sent the last chock flying with a savage kick. He and his crew of five were in the act of hooking the tackles to the thwarts. The chief mate was shouting a timely word of advice.

"When you get her launched, and filled, and stand away in her—"

But Denis did not hear what he was to do then, for at that instant a green sea lifted the port life-boat clean over the side with all six men.

Denis's next thought was that the water was warmer than he should have supposed, and his next but one that somebody was bent on braining him; he was hit about the head, not once but repeatedly; but as soon as he could see he knew the reason, for a dim glimmer was all there was to see. The boat was riding bottom upward. He had come up under her. It was the thwart that had been belabouring him. He caught hold of it, pulled as at a horizontal bar, came up like a cork, and easily wormed half his person between thwart and bilge.

In this position Denis regained breath, immersed to the waist, but with no lack of air, and a bilge-cork handy for fresh supplies, until the real danger occurred to him. The capsized life-boat rode the rollers like a cradle, but at any moment she might shatter herself against the cliffs. It was hardly the work of one for Denis to dive from underneath her at the thought. The cliffs, however, were still far enough away; of the wreck he could see nothing for the swell; but it was now broad daylight.

He went under the boat again, and in about five minutes she righted herself for no apparent reason. Denis was nearly stunned in the process, nor was the advantage otherwise unmixed. The boat had come up full, and Denis had now to bale for his life.

So she floated upon the cliffs, until the big seas began to break, when she instantly capsized again. This time he succeeded in scaling the keel, only to be dislodged as his perverse ship righted herself once more. But the tenacity of the Dents was now uppermost in Denis, if indeed he had any other quality left, and he was back in the boat when she eventually struck upon the cliff. The shock hurled him overboard for the last time, yet was so much less terrific than he had anticipated, that he sought and found the reason as he swam clear. A minute ago the boat had been within a few fathoms of the full face of the cliffs; at the last instant a mouth had opened, and all she had done was to cannon off the perpendicular wall of a strait so narrow as to be practically invisible from without.

It was comprehensible enough. The tide was setting through this tiny channel. The derelict life-boat was not alone; packages bobbed between the towering walls; a table came riding by on its top, three legs still standing, as Denis trod water. And on the table he partly floated and partly swam into a bay which stood to the channel as a flagon to its neck.

It was semicircular in shape, surrounded by cliffs as lofty and precipitous as those without, but mercifully provided with a sandy beach at the upper end. The castaway breathed a hoarse thanksgiving at the saving sight. His smarting eyes had risen involuntarily, and as they rested on the heights, the sun lit up some heath and bracken that overhung the edge a few feet like a table-cloth: thence downward it was sheer for one or two hundred to the beach below. At the base a couple of caves opened romantically upon the yellow sand, but there was no sun for them yet, or for the dancing waves that bore Denis and his table finally to the land.

There in an instant he was staggering and stumbling under the abnormal weight of his dripping and exhausted body. A few yards he reeled, then fell prone upon the warm sand, digging in his fingers to the knuckles, thinking of no mortal but himself, thanking his God for preserving him as though he had made the voyage alone. Indeed the long voyage on the ship was temporarily blotted out of mind by the little one in the boat.

And he a lover! And his love as good as drowned before his eyes!—for not a vestige of the ship had he seen since the original mishap to the port life-boat. It was a terrible reflection to Denis for the rest of his days—but at the time he did not think of her—did not even picture a certain shade of pink and ask himself what it meant and must mean to him till his dying day. He just lay and held on to the warm sand, foot and finger, because the earth heaved under him as the sea had done for thirteen weeks, and his vitality was very low.

Consciousness might have left him altogether; he always wanted to think so, for then he could have forgiven himself; but he was never satisfied on the point. He only knew it was a faint far cry that roused him in the end. But faint as it was, and never so far away, that thin high cry brought the half-dead man to his feet like a gunshot at the ear.

A bar of sunlight slanted through the narrow heads, and in the sun the blue waves were tipped with gold, and across the gold and the blue a black spar floated with some sodden and discoloured rags.

But Denis was in no doubt as to their shade.

CHAPTER III

THE CASTAWAYS

Denis had been a swimmer all his life; how he struck out now every swimmer will know, though none so well as the happy few who have themselves saved life. It is good to think that that noblest of human instincts had its secret place even now in this glowing heart; that Denis Dent would have given himself as unstintedly to the rescue of some unknown person; yet surely the sacred flame alone could have fired those spent members to the last pitch of redoubled endurance. The white left arm, brown as a glove from the wrist down, flew over as white a shoulder in flashing curves; the brown head dipped in the blue, to rise spluttering and dripping a good yard further; but the yards were close on two hundred from shore to spar, and when Denis came up with the latter, it was his love, indeed, but she was already senseless.

They had tied her in a life-belt, and lashed the life-belt to a spar; in time she would have been cast up on the warm sand, dead! She was not dead yet; she should not die. Denis took the hem of her dear drenched garment between his teeth, and swam in, if possible, more strenuously than he had swum out, but with the breast stroke, and in twice the time.

At last she lay where he had lain, only in the sun. Already the sand was gloriously hot to bare knees; and there was still a faint throbbing in the inanimate wrist, though the eyelids lay leaden in a livid face. Denis caught up his scattered clothes, raced behind a ti-tree thicket, and put them on as hurriedly as he had plucked them off.

The thicket grew under the cliffs between the two caves, and Denis delayed some seconds to fill his arms with branches before running back to the girl.

Her pulse seemed stronger. He arranged some of the branches, but left the sun beating on her feet. It was the month of October, and early summer in Australia.

Sundry packages had already come ashore; there was the inevitable barrel of salt junk; there was a box of soap, that Denis spurned, and another box so similar that he left it to the last. Judge therefore of his joy on eventually discovering that here was nothing less than a case of Spanish brandy! He shrieked the good tidings to the girl. She did not stir. He had to run back to her, and lift that leaden wrist once more, before he could bear to open the box.

His sailor's knife was worth a thousand pounds to him in that hour; the great blade made short enough work of the lid, but the heavy haft knocked the neck off a bottle so prettily as to provide a measure with the medicine. Denis filled the inverted neck as he ran, and was soon spilling as much over the marble face as he managed to get between the bloodless lips. Then, for the first time, fear came to him: he retreated a little on his knees. The stuff had caught her breath, her eyelids twitched, and as she coughed the marble flushed to flesh. She did not quite open her eyes.

"I am so cold," she moaned; and the white feet were drawn up a very little, but so stiffly, as though the whole body had been dragged with them.

Denis's blood froze as he remembered some vague saying that the feet die first; even in the hot sun these looked dead enough; they also must be brought to life, and the arch enemy repulsed at every point, at any sacrifice. In Denis, or rather in the Denis who was least a Dent, the act would almost outstrip the thought; this was the Denis who was saving his darling's life without time to realize what she was to him. Quicker than thought he had tipped up the bottle itself, so that the brandy came out in gulps, first over one pale foot and then the other. And now the left, now the right, now with one hand apiece, and anon with both together for one foot, did he chafe and rub, and rub and chafe, until the little lead feet were such pink shells, but so warm, so warm that the tears stood in his eyes. For he had been long enough at it to think a little as he rubbed; but as yet it was otherwise with her; she could only lie there with closed eyes, as meek and unashamed as any other dying soul.

She was not going to die, however, unless Denis dropped dead first. When he could leave her feet he had a turn at her hands, a much shorter journey for the blood, and by the time they began to clasp his feebly there was no more brandy left. Denis went for another bottle, and half the next dose she swallowed properly; the rest she pushed toward him.

"To please me," she whispered: they were her first words, and it his first drop.

Now she was lying with her eyes tight shut, but not in sleep. Her lips moved, first in the faintest smile, then in more whispers.

"I remember—everything. I knew you would come to me. I knew it!"

He could only say her name.

"Nan! Nan! Nan!"

It was as though his heart had broken, it was so full. He had dared to call her his, the other night under the awning; he never dreamed of doing so now. His conception of honour forbade an endearment which she could not repudiate if she would; his own delicacy deplored the vital offices which had been thrust upon him. He had brought the life's blood back to leaden limbs, but he had brought it back at an expense which he already apprehended dimly. In her right senses she might have chosen death. He had taken on himself to give her life, and now she would live to love or loathe him.

Gentle birth and hard upbringing had produced in Denis an essential delicacy underneath a somewhat bluff exterior; but he was not self-conscious on either score. Qualm and pang came upon him as part of the situation, almost as his deserts. He was not aware of any fine feeling in the matter. He was full of feeling, but he did not know that it was fine.

Presently he saw she was asleep, and when he bent to listen she was breathing beautifully; he just touched one hand, with the strange new awe he had for her, and it was warmer than his own. But now he was in a new difficulty; he found time to appreciate his own exhaustion; a stiff pull of brandy alone kept him from fainting, and he foresaw in alarm how it would be. They would both lie sleeping where they were, the almost tropical sun would beat down on them all day, and they might never see another. The nearer cave was not twenty yards away. Denis went to it, and it was lined with far finer sand than outside; he came back and gazed a moment on the girl. She was very young, and so delicately made! He knew that he could carry her, feeble though he now felt: if only it did not wake her. He gathered her tenderly in his arms: he carried her to the cave, he put her down on the cool fine sand, and all she did was to smile on him in her sleep.

If only she would when she awoke!

Meanwhile a pillow she must have before Denis would lay his own head anywhere, and he had seen some rushes in the thicket. He cut an armful, and thin bundle by thin bundle he got the lot under her head at last. Then there was the table. He caught sight of it along the beach, and thought what a fine screen it would make for Nan. It kept him up another ten minutes; but by that time, and thereafter, the sun might stream into the cave, but not a fiery finger would it lay on Nan. So then Denis measured his length at last, outside the screen, as a dog lies across the door.

On finally awaking (for many times he dropped off again deliciously), his first act was to listen on hands and knees; and since the sound he could just hear was as peaceful as it was regular, his next was to go outside and stick a rush upright in the sand. Its shadow was a short finger pointing seaward, so that he knew it was about noon. The tide had gone down. Denis walked to the edge of the surf, and there stood gazing up at the cliff for many minutes. No; there was no way up that he saw or could conceive. Yet the little beach was only as the lees in the flagon of a bay. There was assuredly no way round.

It is fifty years since the wreck of the North Foreland and the second mate's extraordinary climb, but the scene of each remains an object of interest to visitors at the station on the heights above, while the minor incident is unfailing matter for conjecture, contention, and much open incredulity. It has been handed down that the sailor himself failed to identify the place within an hour of his alleged performance. The tradition is so far true. Denis never pretended to know how he had achieved the superhuman: had he been in a condition fully to appreciate what he was doing, the chances are that he never would have made the attempt. He did not mean to make it as it was. But with the brandy in him (and little else) he had clambered a few feet to see whether the thing was as impossible as it appeared. Of course, it was not; but already it seemed safer to climb a little further than to drop at the risk of broken bones; and so in a minute he found himself committed to the ascent. The cliff had beetled by insidious degrees; all at once there was nothing to be seen between his naked feet and the beach far below; one foot was soon bleeding, and the drops falling clear into the sand. To drop clear himself would have meant certain injury now; as well break neck as leg, thought Denis, for all the use he would be to Nan with either. So on and up he went, now flattened for breath against a favourable slope, now swinging by the fingers from some ledge that threatened to saw them to the bone, anon testing tuft or twig with his life, yet all with so light a head that the protracted jeopardy was an exhilaration almost to the last. According to Denis, it was just at the top, when a bunch of bracken came up so slowly as to enable him to grasp a stronger bunch in time, that his gorge rose with the roots.

Remains the undisputed fact that between one and two in the afternoon, a lad on the station, whose boundary was these cliffs, saw an eerie figure approaching through the yellow dust of a mob of sheep which he happened to be driving at the time. It was this lad whom the papers mentioned as Mr. James Doherty; but like Denis he was Irish only by descent, and not for an instant did he imagine that he had seen the devil. He appeared to be a very quick youth, who knew the bush, and a glance convinced him that the ragged wretch had been lost in it and driven to some dreadful extremity; for his face and hands were all bloody, and even his bare feet incrusted with blood and dust. Moreover, his speech was slightly indistinct, as is the case with men who are half-dead with thirst.

This lad Doherty was the first person in Australia to learn the fate of the North Foreland, and the first to discredit the wild finish of the wild man's talk.

"Why, there's stairs right down," he cried. "Over two hundred on 'em, cut in the sandstone."

"What a silly lie," sighed Denis.

"Did you sample the caves?"

"One of them."

"Which one?"

"The one with the big mouth."

"Don't you tell me you never went into the other! It's a nat'ral chimbley at the fur end, and the boss had it shoved right through, and steps cut in the sandstone for bathing."

The sailor's bloodstains were cracking in a ghastly grin.

"So that won't do, old man," added Mr. Doherty, severely.

"Will these?"

And Denis lifted one naked foot after the other; the left sole showed a purple bruise, the right a gash that still dripped as he held it up.

Mr. Doherty supposed that he must be the liar, but only allowed himself to look confounded for the moment; the next, he was emptying his water-bag, from which Denis had already enjoyed a deep pull, over the wounds. The sheep had scattered right and left, but the horse stood apparently fast asleep in the sun.

"Now up you jump," said Doherty. "He's as quiet as a cow."

Denis stared at him.

"Jump up? What for?"

"You're within a mile of the homestead. You struck the right track on top."

"Oh, but I'm not going on," said Denis hastily. "I must go back to—her."

"With them feet and without your tucker?"

And the lean brown lad stood with his bare arms akimbo, a stained statue in a flannel shirt and moleskins.

"At once," said Denis. "I've wasted time enough; and if there are stairs there's no difficulty. Go you back to the homestead, and tell them to send down everything they can think of for a young lady. Food and clothes; mind, she hasn't had a bite since dinner yesterday."

The young Australian doffed his wide-awake with a sweep.

"Why, mister!" he got out, but that was all. "I'm sorry I didn't call you 'mister' before," he added, after the stare of an idolater. "I'll never leave it out again!"

Denis was limping along only a few minutes later when the sound of a gallop made him look round for the rider who had just left him; and the same horse it was, but a different horseman, for whom the stirrups were grotesquely short. In a few seconds he had bobbed and bounded into a blue-eyed man with fair beard blowing and tanned face filled with humane distress.

"Get on this horse," he cried, flinging himself off. "If you don't, I'll carry you myself! There—let me give you a hand; my name's Kitto; this is my run. Everything's following in the buggy, but here's a biscuit to begin on; the beds will be made and aired by the time we get you both back. But only two of you—only two!"

Mr. Kitto had a heart of gold, and wore it on his sleeve; rarer still was a tact almost incongruous in that desolate spot. Not a question had Denis to answer as the horse ambled under him and the squatter strode alongside. But when they came to the mouth of a long stair tunneled through the soft sandstone, it was Mr. Kitto who looked curiously at the rude steep steps.

"Nobody has come up here," said he. "We had a dust-storm yesterday before the wind went round, and the sand on these top steps is as it drifted."

Denis could afford to smile.

"So you didn't believe it either."

"What's that? I could believe the side of a house of you, my brave fellow!" cried Mr. Kitto. "I only mean that your companion hasn't found her way up in your absence."

"Ah, if she could!" sighed Denis. "But she is so weak I am afraid we shall have to carry her up between us."

The squatter smiled, but said nothing.

"If only she is no weaker—if only she has slept right through!" Denis went on, and repeated himself all the way down; but at the base he button-holed his guide.

"Do I look very awful, sir? Is my face as bad as my hands? Wait a bit, then—stay where you are."

And his injured feet could still dance him down to the water's edge; but he came stealing back, one index finger to his lips, signing with the other to Mr. Kitto to let him go first; and the smile on the cleansed face told that good man a tale.

The mouth of the greater cave was just as Denis had left it. He crept on all fours between the table legs, and listened. There was no sound. He leaped up and looked over.

The cave was empty.

CHAPTER IV

LOST AND FOUND

Mr. Kitto saw the ragged figure shoot from the cave as though propelled by some unseen power within; and for one second he imagined the worst. He was relieved when the shipwrecked sailor raised his voice.

"Nan! Nan!" he yelled. "Miss Merridew! Miss Merridew! Nan! Nan! Nan!"

The squatter, running up, alone interrupted him.

"She's gone!" cried Denis in terrible excitement. "Gone clean away—God knows where! Look for yourself, if you like; with the sun pouring in you can see to the very end. Do you think I would miss her if it were ten times the size? See, there's where I left her lying; that was all the pillow I could give her; you can almost see the shape of her head!"

And the hoarse voice broke piteously; but such a firm, kind hand had him by the arm, that Denis bit his lips and blinked the tears back to their source.

"Come, now," said Kitto, "there's nothing wonderful in this; the only wonder is that we didn't expect it. Why should she have slept so much longer than you? She had done far less; and they are tougher than you think. She would wake up and find you flown—"

"Poor Nan! Poor Nan!"

"And having the vitality she must have, to say nothing of the pluck, you wouldn't expect her to sit still and wait, would you?"

"I suppose not," said Denis, gloomily. "I only know I would have died to save her what she must have gone through alone—alone."

"You have done your best to die for her," retorted Mr. Kitto, with his kind smile. "Were her people on board with her?"

"Her father, yes; she has no one else."

"Then you may have to live for her," the older man said gravely. "So don't commit any more of your follies, and above all don't make yourself ill without a cause. She is probably trying to find her own way to the station, and it's safe to be the wrong way."

"But you said no one had been up those stairs."

Mr. Kitto stood confounded in the sun.

"She may be about the beach somewhere," he said hurriedly. "After all, it's not so little that you take in every cranny at a glance. Come and let's look. There are all sorts of holes and corners under the cliffs," he added as they went, "where my children play hide-and-seek at picnics. It's our favourite place for them; in fact, that's why I cut those steps. No harm could come to her here."

But his voice had lost something of its cheery confidence, and in spite of him it lost more as they sought together, but sought in vain. As for Denis, there was an end to his lamentations; he was past that stage; but his dumb eyes plumbed the pit.

"Can you cooey?" asked the squatter. "No, you're too hoarse; don't try. But I can, like a blackfellow, thank God!" And he arched his sun-burned hands about his mouth.

"Cooooooooo—eeeey!"

It was long enough and loud to reach the one top-gallant mast of the North Foreland that they descried between the heads, at a certain stage of their wanderings, standing out of the waves for a monument to those beneath: had a single sailor been clinging to it, he must have heard so penetrating and so sustained a call: but from the lost one on shore, as from the drowned multitude without the gateway of sparking blue, not a sound, not a sign.

Doherty and another arrived with blankets, clothes, coffee, mutton, damper, billy-can, everything that kind thought could send, with a sweet message from her who sent them; but this fell on deaf ears. Denis would touch nothing till she whom he had lost was found again; so the squatter thrust him down into the sand, and between them they forced him to make a meal. And being at last in a more reasonable frame, he would have ended by putting on the shoes which he had cast off in the morning, and forgotten or despised ever since; but now his feet were so swollen, he could not get them on. But as for letting them send him back to the station in the buggy, and leaving the search to them, as Mr. Kitto had now the temerity to suggest, it was as much as Denis could do to hear him out civilly.

The survivor went his own way after this, and it led him first to the summit of the cliffs, to see for himself whether there was no trace up there; for he had been incredulous on that point all along; but now so many had been up and down that he had still only one man's word for the absence of foot-marks in the beginning, and he roamed far afield in vigilant circles. He had been lost himself but for a fire they made on top of the cliff; and when he came shambling back to the brink, down below there was quite a galaxy of lanterns moving in different directions, a constellation of creeping stars. So they had not found her yet; and now it was black night.

In the utter heart-break of the hour, and the last stage of physical distress, Denis had half a mind to fling himself over and be done with it all; but only half a mind, and not a hundredth part of the heart. Instead, as he went down gingerly in the dusk, one painful step at a time, he reviled himself from top to bottom for the unnecessary climb which is not wholly credited to this day. It was already at the root of everything in the climber's mind. Had he only explored the smaller cavern, he had been back with succour in one hour instead of three.

Mr. Kitto meanwhile had made up his mind. "We shall never find her alive," he whispered to his overseer, who arrived upon the scene a little before Denis's return. "But for that poor fellow's sake we must keep up the pretence a bit longer. I can see there was something between them; and when we find her body it will probably kill him; and after all every soul will have been lost. Did you know the bodies were beginning to come ashore? There's a little chap I take to be the skipper: last to leave and first to land."

"But you aren't looking for this girl among them?" the overseer exclaimed aghast.

"Not yet; but it will come to that," whispered Kitto. "I cooeyed till I was hoarse; that's why I can't raise my voice above a whisper now; and all the rest of us are in the same box. Mark my words, it's a case of suicide, and a fearful case: the poor thing was so terrified at her position when she awoke and found herself deserted on this desert coast, that it drove her clean out of her mind. I almost hope he won't live to realize it was that—though he's the sort we want in this colony—if he gave up the sea."

"Was there no tracking her?"

"Scarcely a yard from the mouth of the cave, and he doesn't know I did that; the sand is so heavy outside. But the tracks I did find pointed straight to the sea. I grant you there were not enough of them to mean anything in themselves."

They chanced to be passing close to the ti-tree clump as they conversed. Suddenly the overseer stood still.

"You've looked in there, I suppose?"

"In there? What would be the good? It's not above a dozen yards thick, though so dense; if she were alive in there she'd have heard us long ago; if she's dead she's in the sea. Why do you ask?"

"I thought I heard something. That was all."

They moved on a few yards.

"I say, Mr. Kitto, I do hear something! Listen, sir—listen to that!"

They heard the voice distinctly, faint and feeble though it was.

"I am dying!" it moaned. "Oh, Denis, where are you?"

Mr. Kitto almost choked.

"Thank God—but if she does die!" he croaked and whispered in one breath. "We're coming! We're coming, my dear, dear young lady! But," in his whisper, "who's that hobbling toward us—dot-and-carry-one? It's Dent, man, it's Dent himself; go and tell him like a good fellow—only don't raise too much hope." And deeply agitated, the squatter thrust his lantern among the outer branches of the thicket.

In an instant came the faint voice, immeasurably stronger, and poignant with a nameless agony:

"Take it away! Oh, take it way, or I must die—I must!"

Kitto flung his lantern far behind him: he had seen a terrified face among the branches, a burning face that told him all.

"And you have been here all day!" he cried, but chiefly to himself, in the inward glare of his enlightenment. "And I cooeying till I could cooey no more!"

"I thought it was savages," the voice in the clump faltered unconvincingly. "I—I never heard it before—"

"We have everything ready for you," continued Kitto, cheerily: "hot coffee, plenty to eat, dry clothes, and our best bed when we get you to it. Here, take this to go on with." His coat came off with the words, and was thrust through the branches until he felt she had it. "Now I'll get you the rest," he said, and was hurrying off.

"Wait! Wait!" she called to him, and even more strongly than in her last alarm. "Where's Denis—Denis Dent? He was the second officer, and he saved me, he alone. I must speak to him first ... to thank him ... while I can!"

And her voice broke for him, as his had broken for her, but with more reason than Nan Merridew could dream; for Denis was lying close at hand on the beach, with the station overseer stooping over him.

CHAPTER V

A TOUCH OF FEVER

Denis awoke between clean sheets in the widest berth and the largest cabin he had ever occupied: it was a matter of moments to realize that he was really on land, for the bed still heaved a little as the beach had done yesterday, or whenever it was he had been washed ashore. He felt as though he had been asleep a week; he could not have imagined so delightful a lassitude of limb and spirit. It was a small room without pretense of paper upon its weather-board walls, but the toilet cover on Denis's left was as snowy as the sheet under his chin, and a sunlit blind flapped soothingly behind it. Silence reigned, but it was the peculiarly drowsy hush of hot weather, only the deeper for its innumerable tiny sounds: one could have heard that it was hot. But there was so little on him, that little was so light, and so sweet a draught blew through the room, that in his own person Denis felt deliciously cool.

He tried to remember how he had come there, but the final stages were a painful farrago. He beheld a bandage on either hand, and could feel one on head and foot; but they led him too far back. He had an impression of the stars as he lay upon the beach, and another of interminable steps with a handbreadth of starry sky at the top, but there was something far more important that he was seeking in his mind without avail. He certainly had not found it when the blind was pushed aside by a sun-burned face, which vanished instantly, to reappear with its appertaining shirt and moleskins in the doorway opposite.

"Awake at last, mister!"

"Only just," said Denis, feebly, but with his first smile, and the lad entered staring curiously.

"You couldn't look like that whilst we was seekin' her," said he, drily. "Why, what's wrong now?"

Denis had shot upright in bed.

"Didn't we find her?" he cried. "Yes, yes, of course we did! I remember now. I'm so grateful to you; that's exactly what I was trying to remember. Well? Well? And how is she?"

"Right as the mail, mister, so they all say; but I haven't seen her yet."

"You're sure they say so?"

"Sure as my name's Jimmy Dockerty."

Denis fell back with a whispered thanksgiving.

"What did you say your name was?" he asked presently.

"Dockerty," replied the boy. "Christian name of Jim."

"Well, Jim, I don't forget you. It was you I clapped eyes on first, and I'm almost as glad to see you again. Where am I exactly?"

"Merinderie Station: the barricks."

"The what?"

"Where the parlour men camp," explained Mr. Doherty, darkly. "You've got the tooter's room; he has his schoolroom next door."

"It's very quiet."

"They've all cleared out for the day, apuppus; and you ain't in the house, you see, though nice and handy. But I'll have to go over to the house, to tell 'em you've waked up. There was something ready for you the moment you did. But, I say—mister!" And the boy stood wistfully beside the bed.

"Well, Jim?"

"Ask for me to come back and set along of you! Say you feel lonely like, and ask for me to look arter you, mister. You needn't take no notice of me, and no more won't I say nothink, if you don't want."

"But I shall want, Jimmy. I shall want you to tell me heaps of things. Go and say so for me, by all means; and bring me anything they like to send, though a cup of tea is all I fancy."

But when a chop was sent in characteristic conjunction it was eaten with its slice of damper, and so heartily as to exclude immediate conversation.

"One thing at a time," said Denis, "and the next thing is a wash; but I don't mean to get up yet a bit."

"I wouldn't," said the boy, removing the tray and flourishing a towel. "The young lady, there ain't any signs of 'er either; I'll give you the word when there is."

Meanwhile the subject nearest Denis's heart was the one on which he could extract least information. Doherty did not warm to it as he did to other topics. And yet Denis could not help liking the lad; in the first place, the lad was openly enamoured of him, and the present Denis far too languid a hero to object very strenuously to his worship. There was nothing slavish about it; hardly a word was employed in its expression; but in the pauses the boy's eyes would remain upon the man's, and once he said he had been to see the place, and continued gazing at Denis and his bandages with redoubled reverence. It appeared that many bodies had been washed ashore, and Mr. Kitto with nearly all his men was down there now. Mrs. Kitto was at the other bedside, and had sent word that she preferred not to leave it in case her patient, who had been asleep many hours, should wake and miss her. Doherty suddenly remembered the message; it drove Denis back into yesterday's inferno, and he lay with such a pained face that the boy darted in with his own details. It was four o'clock in the afternoon: Denis had slept nineteen hours, but Miss Merridew was beating him. And they were the only survivors; not another soul had been saved.

Denis thought of the hundred souls on board, above all of Nan's father, her all in this world, to whose loss she would awake now any moment. And that was a thought which brought tears to the second mate's eyes, yet it was one with several facets, and presently his eyes were shining in quite a different way; then he caught himself, and little Jim saw the marine bronze deepen on the heroic cheek. But at last it was Jim's turn, for Denis turned to him as though impatient of himself.

"Now let's hear about you," he said. "How long have you been in Australia, Jim?"

"Only since I was born, and a bit before, and ever after, amen!" said Mr. Doherty; and the teeth displayed by his grin were certainly worthy of an aboriginal.

"And how long is that?" asked Denis, smiling, too.

"I don't know. They say as I am a good seventeen, but I don't look it, do I?"

"What! Don't know your own age?"

"Not to a year or two."

"Didn't your parents tell you?"

"I never had none, mister."

And Mr. Doherty grinned again.

"You don't remember, them?"

"That's what I mean. They were—I don't mind tellin' you, mister, though I'd rather bite my tongue out than tell another soul on the place"—and little Jim came sidling from his seat at the foot of the bed to an easy distance from Denis's ear, a dead secret in his astute young face. "But you'll think no worse of a cove," he went on, whispering, "and you won't split either; so it's a bit of a relief to tell you—they was both old hands."

"Old hands?"

"Lags!"

Now Denis understood. "Of course I don't think the less of you," he said, gently; "we are what we make ourselves, at any rate there's no credit in anything else we may be. I, for instance—"

But Denis had strength enough left to control his tongue, and his parents' memory was too sacred for association with that of transported felons, however little there might be to chose between their sons.

"It might be worse," the lad went on, with an elderly air the more pathetic for its unconscious humour: "they was married at Parramatta factory, and my mother let me know it when I was as high as this bed; it's the one thing I recollect her by, keepin' on tellin' me that; but 'im I never see as I remember. Parramatta factory," he continued, lifting his shrewd eyes once more, "was the place where they kep' the women prisoners, up on the Sydney side in the convict days; you could go and take your pick as long as you married her." The boy's stare grew into a contemplative grin, and Denis prepared for a familiarity. "There'll be need for you to go there," said Mr. Doherty.

Denis was not offended; either he was too stricken to be readily ruffled, or the young monkey had a way with him. He only rolled his head on the pillow, and questioned whether such an establishment existed still.

"It doesn't," rejoined Jim; "but even if it did, eh? You're all right, you see, so you can go on shaking your head till you loosen it! I seen, whether or no, last night when you couldn't."

"I don't want to know what you saw," cried Denis, vehemently enough; and lay quite agitated between the sheets.

"I suppose," the imp pursued, with a precocious union of tact and tenacity, "you'll go and get married straight away, and never let us see or hear from you again."

Denis set his teeth, not because the boy jarred, but at the gulf between this fancy picture and the possibilities of the case as it now stood. It was characteristic of him that for the first time they seemed impossibilities. He had saved her life, and now they were alone in the world, he and she: how could he trade on such things, how avoid the suspicion of trying to trade on them? If only another had saved her! If only others had been saved!

"Don't speak of it," he groaned. "I am far too poor."

"Too poor, are you?"

The boy had brightened.

"And she is too rich."

"Then what more do you want, mister?"

"What more? It should be the opposite way; we should both be one thing or the other. Anything but as we are!"

There was a brief intermezzo of the tiny summer noises. The blind flapped; a mosquito sang an ominous solo in the sick man's ear; from without came the faint hacking of an axe at the wood-heap. Denis looked up at last, and there sat Jim with a startlingly wise face upon his narrow young shoulders.

"Do you know what I should do, if I was you, mister?"

"Well, what?"

"If I felt same as you," said Mr. Doherty, "I'd make a fortune same as hers."

Denis smiled tolerantly; the urchin amused him.

"Well, and how would you do that?"

"I should go up to Ballarat, and peg out my claim, as sure as my name's Jimmy Dockerty!"

"It would have to be a lucky one," said Denis, dryly, though not until he had paused to think.

"Then it wouldn't be the only one," retorted Doherty, with the readiness of their common race.

Denis could not help dallying with the idea.

"Have they been doing such good business up there, then?"

"Good! Why, haven't you heard? There's never been such doings as they've had on Ballarat this year. I thought it was all over the world," the boy added, with shining eyes.

"It may be," said Denis, "but I've been at sea since June, and it isn't exactly in a sailor's line."

"Isn't it!" laughed Jimmy. "You wait till you see the empty ships in Hobson's Bay! Some of 'em been stuck there since the last day of January, when the fun began. Do you mean to say you never heard of the big finds in Canadian Gully?"

"You tell me, Jimmy. I want to hear."

Denis was leaning on an elbow. Jimmy had long been on his feet.

"There were some coves had a claim in Canadian Gully, on Ballarat," the boy began, a wild light in his face, a light that Denis had never seen before. "They were doing well, but not too well, and they offered to sell the hole for a matter of three hundred. Then one of them went down and came up with a nugget weighing sixty-six ounces!"

"At how much the ounce?"

"About four guineas."

"Well, that wasn't quite the three hundred."

"Stop a bit!" cried Doherty, a perfect fever in his eyes, a fever as new to Denis as the light upon the lad's face. "That was only the beginning of it. Of course they wouldn't sell after that. And before night they'd got a nugget of a hundred and twenty pounds. Troy weight—whatever that is—perhaps you can turn it into the other pounds, for I can't."

Denis sat forward, pressing the lint upon his forehead with his hands. When at length he looked up there was the same light beneath the bandages, the same fever in the still blood-shot eyes, as Denis himself had remarked in the face and eyes of his companion.

"Six thousand pounds!" he whispered almost aghast.

"Six thousand golden sovereigns!" shouted the lad, capering about the room. "Think of that, mister, think of that! I had it read to me out of the papers. I got it off by heart. It was one big, solid, yellow lump of gold, and they had to carry it between them slung to a pole. It wasn't the only one, neither; as they went tunneling on it stuck out of the sides, like bunches of grapes—at twenty pound a berry! There was only four on 'em in the party; they made their fortunes in less than no time; and two on 'em was new chums, same as you'd be if you went up and—and—"

"And what, boy?"

"And took me along with you!"

Denis only wondered that the little brown face, thrust so near him in its eagerness, did not burst into actual flame; it never occurred to him that his own was perhaps presenting the like phenomenon.

"You talk as though you'd been there already, Jimmy," said he.

"But I haven't. I'd only give my two ears to go. The boss won't let me. He says I'm too young; and he's been such a jolly good boss to me, I haven't the heart to go agin him, especially when he's promised me my kit if I wait till the Noo Year. But I b'lieve he'd give 'em me to-morrow, mister, if I was going up with you!"

It was a strange talk for Denis on the day after his deliverance, in the bed where they had laid him more dead than alive, but the manner of its ending was the strangest part of all. In the fever that was so new to Denis, that he had a touch of it before he dreamed there was such a disease, he not only forgot the perils through which he had passed, but his every sense turned blunt by comparison with the intensely keen edge put so suddenly on certain of his desires. He had not heard the voices outside; neither had Doherty; and the feet upon the threshold fell upon four equally deaf ears. It was not until Mr. Kitto opened the door, and entered first, that the one looked round and the other up.

"Here," said the squatter, "is a gentleman whom I know you will be heartily thankful to see again."

The gentleman stood forward with outstretched hands and a quivering lip.

It was John Merridew.

CHAPTER VI

NEW CONDITIONS

The following were the facts, as Denis grasped them by degrees.

Not many minutes had elapsed between the mishap to the port life-boat and the resolution of the North Foreland into so much wood and iron at the bottom of the sea, with a single top-gallant mast standing out to mark the place. But during those few minutes the minor disaster had caused another.

The loss of the first boat augured ill for the rest; and, indeed, only the chief officer's lived to salute the sun; but before it was launched, Miss Merridew had been swept overboard through the little faith of her own friends, who had lashed her life-belt to a fallen spar, only to give a gratuitous handle to the next great wave.

It was Captain Coles whose last remembered act had been to prevent one or both gentlemen from diving after her to their death—some said with his revolver at their heads; and, as if because neither seemed to care any longer for his life, these were the two male passengers to be saved. They were dragged into the mate's boat. The boat was successfully launched by a mixture of good management and better luck. But it was entirely to the mate's credit that she immediately stood out to sea, and so continued until picked up by a coasting vessel, which landed the party in Melbourne before night. The post-haste journey to the landward scene of the wreck, all that night and nearly all next day (it was a matter of a hundred miles up and across country), was only such as any father would have undertaken in the circumstances, and most men in Ralph Devenish's position would have taken with him.

But Captain Devenish did not accompany Mr. Merridew to the little outbuilding in which Denis lay; nor did Jim Doherty, or his master, remain even so long as to see the older man take the bandaged hands, tenderly, tremulously, in both of his.

The interview which followed was an affecting one; but Denis had done too much, too recently, to take a very emotional view of his exploits. In his heart he took little credit for them. It was not he who had saved Nan Merridew's life, but a merciful God who had merely used him as His tool; and while, perhaps, more thankful than he now knew for that supreme preferment, the prostrate man was almost morbidly alive to its disadvantages. Thus, when Mr. Merridew led the conversation back almost to the point at which their last had been interrupted, it was Denis who created the awkward silence. He was touched by the uncontrolled revelation of a hard man's soft side, by the contrast between the exceedingly deliberate and rather irritating voice that he remembered on the poop, and the voice that still broke with very tenderness. But his own voice was so much the more dispassionate, and apparently perverse.

"I unsay every word," said Mr. Merridew, for the second time, and more pointedly than ever; for, even in his really generous emotion, he could not help feeling that it was unsaying a great deal.

Denis nodded from his pillow, but only to signify that he heard. "You are very kind," he answered at length, with no ironic intent; "too kind, I almost think. You might live to regret it."

"No, no; never, never! Now I know what you are."

"I am a junior officer in the merchant service—with a captain's certificate."

Mr. Merridew was genuinely pained. "Dent," said he, "I take back my words twice over, and still you throw them in my teeth! Surely you must see that everything is altered now?"

"But it might have happened to anybody else," urged Denis, with gentle tenacity. "You should look at it in that way, Mr. Merridew. Suppose it had been one of the stewards; for all you knew, or seemed prepared to believe, I was no more eligible than they, the night before last. I have been infinitely lucky—no, blessed, blessed!—but that's all. It doesn't give me ten thousand pounds to put to hers."

Mr. Merridew jumped up from the bedside. It was partly with temper that he was trembling now.

"Have you changed your mind already, Mr. Dent, or is all this so much affectation on your part? Did you mean what you said to me that night before we struck or did you not?"

"Every word of it," answered Denis, in a whisper that brought the other back to his former position on the bed, only now he was peering into eyes averted from his own.

"You do love her, don't you, Dent? I can see it—I can see it—whatever you may say!"

Denis could only nod. His weakness had come upon him very suddenly. But by an effort he was able to prevent it from rising to his eyes. And soon he was sufficient master of himself to attend to what Mr. Merridew was saying with so strange an eagerness of voice and manner.

"You must come back with us. That's what you must do. Melbourne's a perfect pandemonium: street upon street of tents, teeming with the very sweepings of the earth, and ship upon ship without a man on board. But there's a fine clipper, the Memnon by name, lying ready for sea at Geelong, and we'll all go home in her together. She's bound to be under-officered, and I suppose you would be happier so than as a passenger; but let this voyage be your last. You said you were as good a man ashore as at sea, if my memory serves me as well as yours. Well, now I can believe you, and in you, as I shall show you— as I shall very soon show you! I have no one to follow me in the firm, Denis—that's your name, isn't it?— and you don't mind my calling you by it, do you? But if you became my son, Denis ... can't you see ... can't you see?"

The man's tongue had run away with him, as the unlikeliest tongues will, under strong emotional strain: so we prattle of our newly dead, magnifying the good that we belittled in their lives. But here the strain was far greater; for she who had been dead was alive again; and this, this was her saviour, for whom nothing, not even the girl herself, was now too good.

"There is one thing you have forgotten," said Denis, without withdrawing his hand from the nervous grasp that now hurt considerably. "I had not got my answer—the other night. And how can I press her for it now? Don't answer yourself, sir, till you have thought it over, if I may ask that much of you, alone; and then I know you will agree with me. She ought not to be allowed to give me her answer now. And I—I ought to go away without seeing her again—until I have really shown myself—" He could not finish. His weakness and his sincerity were equally apparent: deeply moved, the elder man took his leave, with but one more syllable, and that to promise Denis, from the door, not to repeat a word of their conversation to Nan.

But Denis had not said all that it was in him to say, for in the first place he had not the heart, and in the next he was not too proud of his latest resolve; but it was a resolve no less, and already it might have been the resolve of his life.

"This is not the real man," he lay saying to himself. "The real man had his say on the poop—and the sounder man of the two. I won't take advantage of either of them. Let me make that money. I can, and I will. Then she shall give me her answer—not before."

And yet he had an uneasy conscience about his new resolve, plausible as it became in words; but the qualm only hardened it within him; and he lay in the twilight with set teeth and dogged jaw, quite a different Denis from the one who had leaned forward to listen to Jimmy Doherty, but every inch a Dent.

Doherty came stealing back with the face of a conspirator; his worldly wisdom did not as yet include a recognition of the difficulty of picking up broken threads, even when they are threads of gold. Denis would not promise to speak to Mr. Kitto, would hear no more, indeed, of Ballarat; all he seemed to care to know now was what Captain Devenish was doing with himself.

"Him with the whiskers?" said Jimmy. "I can't sight that gent!"

"What do you mean?"

"Beg yer pardon, mister, but I don't like him. He speaks to you like as if you was a blessed dingo. That sort o' thing don't do out here; we ain't used to it." And young Australia shook a sage old head.

"But what's he doing with himself, Jimmy?"

"Oh, lookin' at the papers an' things, an' yawnin' an' smokin' about the place."

"And Mr. Merridew?"

"With the young lady. She ain't a-goin' to show up to-night, the young lady ain't; and you can take that as gospel—for I had it from the missus herself."

The boy's eyes were uncomfortably keen and penetrating. Denis got rid of him, and lay thinking until it was nearly dusk. Then they brought him his first solid meal; and presently Mrs. Kitto paid a visit to a giant so refreshed that nothing would persuade him to keep his bed without a break. He must have a breath of air: he was quite himself. So early evening brought him forth in a pair of Mr. Kitto's slippers.

The very first person he saw was Ralph Devenish, reading by lamplight in one of the many rude verandas which faced and flanked one another under the bright Australian stars. Denis went limping up to him with outstretched hand.

"I am glad to set eyes on you, Devenish," he said gravely.

"Really?" drawled the other, with light incredulity; but he could hardly refuse the bandaged hand.

"Ralph Devenish," pursued Denis, chilled but undeterred, "I make no apology for the sudden familiarity, partly because we've both been so near our death, and partly because we're cousins. My mother was a Devenish; you may open your eyes, but I would drop them if I came of the stock that treated her as her own people did! I never meant to tell you, for there can be no love to lose between your name and mine, but I blurted it out in a rage just before we struck. I want to say that I'm heartily ashamed of the expressions I made use of then; that I apologize for them, and take them back."

"My good fellow," replied Devenish, with engaging candour, "I don't recollect one of them; the fact is, I was a little drunk. As to our relationship, that's very interesting, I'm sure; but it's odd how one does run up against relations, in the last places you'd expect, too. I can't say I remember your name, though; never heard it before, to my knowledge. If there's been anything painful between your people and mine, don't tell me any more about it, like a good feller."

"I won't," said Denis, secretly boiling over, though for no good reason that he could have given. It certainly was not because Devenish continued occupying the only chair, leaving the lame man to stand. Denis was glad to have so whole a view of him as the lamplight and the easy chair afforded. Save for the patent fact that his clothes had not been made for him, the whiskered captain looked as he had looked on board, a subtle cross between the jauntily debonair and the nobly bored. As Denis watched he produced the same meerschaum that he had smoked all the voyage, a Turk's head beautifully coloured, with a curved amber mouthpiece, and proceeded to fill it from the same silken pouch.

"Another soul saved, you see!" said Ralph Devenish, as he tapped his Turk affectionately; it was the acme of sly callousness, even if intended so to appear. Denis turned away in disgust, but turned back for a moment in his stride.

"Are you going home with the Merridews?" he asked.

"I don't know," said Devenish. "Are you?"

"I don't know," echoed Denis. "But I think—not."

"Really?" drawled Devenish. "Well, as a year's leave don't last forever, I'm not so sure."

And as Denis saw the last of him under the lamp, he had not yet resumed the filling of the Turk's head.

CHAPTER VII

DENIS AND NAN

Miss Merridew continued prostrate, yet so exempt from bodily mischief that her case began to baffle all except the other woman, who had charge of it.

Mr. Merridew allowed himself to be dissuaded from obtaining indifferent medical advice at exorbitant cost, but his anxiety increased with his perplexity, and was only allayed by his instinctive confidence in Mrs. Kitto. That lady proved as practical and understanding as she was good and kind. Yet even Mrs. Kitto was puzzled just at first. They had to deal with one singularly reserved—who could lie for hours without closing an eye or uttering a word—and the father's way was to force her to say something, at the pain of his own passionate distress. But Mrs. Kitto would bring in her sewing, of which she seemed to have a great deal, and sit over it, also by the hour, in a quietude as grateful as her sparing speech. She was very observant, however, and the one thing that puzzled her only did so in the beginning. This was the anomaly presented by a patient whose face was often in a burning fever while her head and hand kept perfectly cool.

The wreck was never mentioned in the sick-room, nor did Nan guess that an inquest on the bodies was held within a few yards of where she lay. Yet it was she who eventually broke the ice.

"Is Mr. Dent still here?" she asked, but in a tone so magnificently offhand that a less astute person than Mrs. Kitto would have detected its anxiety as soon.

"He was this morning," replied Mrs. Kitto, smiling.

"Do you mean that he isn't now?" the girl demanded, half-rising on an elbow.

"No. I think I should have heard of it if he had thought of leaving us to-day."

Nan Merridew fell back upon her pillow.

"I wish he would go on board," she said petulantly, "if he is going."

"On board?" queried Mrs. Kitto; and she set down her work.

"Isn't he to be one of the officers on the ship we are all going home by?"

"I didn't know of it," said Mrs. Kitto, with equal embarrassment and surprise.

"But he is," declared the girl, with all an invalid's impatience. "I understood that from papa the day he came; he had spoken to the agents, or he was going to speak to them, and Denis—I mean Mr. Dent— was to have the best berth they could give him. I do wish he would go on board. I—I almost wish he hadn't saved my life!"

And she tossed her face to the wall, for it was burning as it had burned so often since her deliverance.

"It's meeting him again," said Mrs. Kitto to herself; "and she does care for him, or she would mind less." It made it all the harder to ask aloud, "Did your father say he had succeeded, dear?"

"We have never mentioned Mr. Dent again," said Nan to that, quite haughtily.

"Because I don't think he's sailing in the Memnon at all," continued Mrs. Kitto, gently. "I think he's going to the diggings instead."

"Going where?" the girl asked after a pause. The first sentence was all that she had heard.

"To Ballarat or Bendigo—to make his fortune."

"I hope he'll succeed," said Nan, after a pause; but her voice was a sweet bell jangled, and an hour went before she turned her face from the wall. It was still red, but there was a subtle difference in the shade. And in the hazel eyes, which were the most obvious of Miss Merridew's natural attractions, there was a crude, new light.

"I am going to get up," said she.

Mrs. Kitto proved not unprepared for the announcement; it appeared that all her needlework had been for Nan, and now it was as though the last stitch had just been put into everything. It was all a surprise to the girl, who had not given the matter a thought. She was to get a fresh outfit at Geelong, before the ship sailed, but Mrs. Kitto insisted on sending her so far equipped by herself. And the dress which the kind soul had been so busy altering was almost the last remnant of her own trousseau, and some years behind the fashion.

In point of fact it was what used to be called a "double robe" of lavender cashmere; and it was trimmed with braid of the same colour, but the braid was a shade darker than the rest, and its criss-cross pattern as unlovely in its way as the voluminous skirts it was intended to adorn. But the fabric was soft and fine, and the delicate tint happened to suit Nan Merridew, who had a singularly clear and pale skin, and dark gold ringlets almost the colour of her eyes. For she was of the type dear to the pre-Raphaelites, with rather more flesh and blood, and a much more conspicuous spirit of her own, perhaps a little too conspicuous when Nan reappeared in the sunlight, with quite another light in her eyes, on the fourth day after the wreck.

It was near the close of a radiant afternoon, and Mr. Merridew was absent for the day; but Captain Devenish had been seen strolling toward the cliffs, and Nan thought that she would stroll after him in spite of the direction. No one must think of accompanying her; she would so enjoy finding the way for herself. To this Mrs. Kitto pretended to make no objection, but expressed a belief that Mr. Dent was with Captain Devenish, thinking she had named the last deterrent. On the contrary, it only decided Nan to go quickly; and go she did with that peculiar light stronger than ever in her eyes.

Now the way led through a belt of young pines, by which the station was almost surrounded, and in the middle of them Nan met a man in moleskins and a red shirt. Him she was approaching with downcast eyes, as one who must regard her curiously, when his voice thrilled her at close quarters.

"Nan! And you'd have passed me without a word!"

Denis was standing in her path, a common wide-awake drooping from one hand, the other reaching out for hers.

"I didn't recognize you," she said, scarcely touching his hand. "And I was looking for Captain Devenish—can you tell me where he is?"

"He has gone down to bathe," replied Denis with some reluctance. To bathe where a ship's company had been drowned that week! No wonder Nan winced. "Can't you spare me a few minutes instead?" he added as she was about to turn.

"Oh, yes, if you wish it."

"Of course I wish it!" exclaimed Denis. His shoulders looked very square under the coarse red flannel; but they were heaving, too.

Nan was her own mistress on the spot. "I couldn't know," said she. "You see, you never sent me any message—not one word."

"I shall tell you why."

"And then I understood you were going to the diggings."

"So I am," said Denis. His voice was preternaturally deep and vibrant. She looked up at him with the odd light in her eyes.

"And why haven't you gone yet?"

"I wanted to see you first."

"That was very kind."

"To tell you why I was going at all—to tell you everything, Nan, if you will let me—if you aren't determined to misunderstand me before I open my mouth!"

Their eyes were together now, his dark with passion, in hers a certain softening of the unlovely light that hurt him more than her tone: and her eyes were the first to fall, to wander, to espy a stump among the pines.

"I must sit down," she faltered. "It's my first appearance, and I tire directly. But I'm not too tired to listen to you—I want to."

Yet already a change had come over her, and either she was physically weaker or else softer at heart than she had been but a minute before. At all events she took his arm to the stump, which was one of several in a little clearing lit and checkered by the slanting sun. And she sat there almost meekly in his sight, while Denis planted a foot upon one of the other stumps and said what he had to say with bare arms folded across a moleskinned knee.

"In the first place," he began, "I saved your life."

Nan's smouldering spirit was in flames upon the word, and her face caught its fire.

"And you remind me of it!" she cried in red scorn. "Is it the sort of thing one forgets? Is it a thing to thank you for like any common service, and are you the one to put the words in my mouth?"

Denis did not wince.

"I am wrong," he said, quietly. "In the first place, I asked you to marry me; it was only in the second place, and before you had time to give me an answer, that I was so unfortunate as to save your life."

"Unfortunate!"

"Most unfortunate to be the one to save you, Nan, because if it had been any one else it would have made no difference between us; as it is it makes all the difference in the world."

"I don't understand," she said, trembling because she was beginning to understand so well. "I only know how brave you were—how brave!"

And she raised her sweet face without restraint, for now she was thinking of nothing but his bravery.

"Most men are that at a pinch," said Denis, with a twitch of his red shirt: "but I was luckier than most. I won't make too light of it. I can swim. But you don't suppose I was the only strong swimmer on board. And which of the rest, I should like to know, wouldn't have made as good use of my chance?"

"But it wasn't only the swimming!" the girl cried without thinking, to break off with her bent face in its besetting fever.

"If you mean the climbing," he continued equably, "there was still less merit in that, for it was absurdly unnecessary, as you probably know, besides which I was full of Spanish brandy at the time. Not that I'm ashamed of that," added Denis with the absolute candour of the dales. "I believe that brandy was the saving of us both; but it was another piece of pure luck."

Nan said nothing for a minute. She was trying to see his hands, and he showed her with a shrug the only finger that was still in rags. His wounds had not been serious; he was scarcely walking lame; the scratches had skinned over on his face. She could look in it again, steadfastly, simply; she was even beginning to like it better between a wide-awake and an open throat than in the spruce cap and collar of the voyage. Her own scarlet she had conquered in a tithe of the time it had often taken her in secret: it was not so dreadful to be with him after all. And if he loved her nothing mattered: not even her long agony in the ti-tree thicket. Yet he had hurt her by belittling himself, and by something else of which his last words reminded Nan.

"But you don't look on it as luck. You aren't a bit glad you saved my life!" And her eyes fell once more, if this time not involuntarily.

"Glad!" he cried out. "Gladness is no word for my feeling about that—for what I feel every moment of every hour."

"Yet you wish it had been some one else."

"I don't!"

"But you said you did, Denis."

"Well, and I have felt it, too, when I couldn't send you a single message—couldn't make a single sign—for fear you should think—for fear you should misunderstand!"

Nan had not raised her eyes again; his tone made it difficult now. He was leaning toward her, almost bending over her, and yet his foot clung to the pine-stump as though by conscious effort of the will, and his face was a fight between set jaw and yearning eyes. But Nan could not see his face; she could only see the sunlight and the shadows in the lavender skirts that spread about her as she sat, and a few inches of hard yellow ground beyond. She was beginning to believe in his love, to understand his position before he explained it to her, to see the end of her own doubts. His halting voice was more eloquent than many words.

And yet for words she was constrained to probe.

"So you determined to go up to the diggings?"

"I did."

"And to leave me?"

"Nan, I must."

His voice reconciled her more and more.

"Must you, Denis?"

"To make some money, Nan dear! And I will make it—I will—I will!"

She felt that he would. His voice only stirred her now.

"And then?" she asked.

"And then," he cried, "and then I sha'n't mind pressing you for an answer to what I dared to ask you on the North Foreland."

There was a silence in the little clearing among the young pines. Only near at hand the hum of insects, and in the distance a cloud of cockatoos shrieking the sun into the sea, and the sea itself faintly booming upon the base of the sandstone cliffs. Before either spoke there was indeed one other sound, but it fell on ears doubly deaf; for Nan had flung back her dark-gold ringlets in a way of hers, and from the bold pose of her head none could have imagined the warm bloom upon her cheeks, or the tender film that dimmed the hazel eyes.

"Suppose I prefer to give you your answer first?"

"Nan! Nan! I would have you think it over, and over, and over again!"

"But suppose I refused you after all?"

"I would sooner that than be accepted in haste and—and repented of—you know!"

It was as though he was maintaining his balance for a bet, and near the end of his endurance even so. Nan watched him with a smile touched by the last beams of the setting sun, but as she rose the red glory beat full upon her.

"Very well!" said she. "Then if you won't come to me for your answer, I must bring it to you."

Night falls like an assassin in that country, but the purple tints were only beginning when in his very ear she implored him not to leave her any more, and he held her closer, but said he must. It would not be for long. Others were growing rich in a day; he would make one more. He knew it; something told him; and again, something else told her.

Yet she was vexed with herself for her impulsive appeal against a decision to which she had felt reconciled but the moment before; and vexed with him for scarcely listening to her appeal, unpremeditated as it was, unreasonable as it might be. He might have wavered; she would not have had him yield. His resolution was fine, heroic; she only wondered whether it was quite human, and wondering, lost the thread of his defense.

"Think, think!" he urged. "Think what it would be for me to go home in this ship and marry you as I am, on my poor captain's certificate and nothing else; and then, only think, if I followed in a few months with a few thousand of my own behind me! You may say I ought to have thought of this before. But I did. I told your father so a few minutes before the wreck. I wanted you to wait for me—I was selfish enough for that from the beginning!"

The disparaging epithet pricked Nan to interrupt him and take it on herself. But Denis persisted without a smile.

"Darling, I am selfish about it still; for if I am not worth waiting for, I am not worth having; but if you can wait only a few months—not a day more than a year—I will come to you as I should come if it is to be— but come I will, rich or poor, if I am alive! Nan, darling, I have everything to gain, only these few months to lose; but I will gain all the world in them. I will, I will, I will!"

She could not but be infected with his confidence, his enthusiasm, and his ideal. There in the dusk were the eager Irish eyes glistening and burning into hers, but there also was the strong north-country jaw set for success as the needle to the pole. And yet—and yet—she was weeping on his shoulder as the purple turned to deepest blue.

"I could have helped you, dearest," came her broken whispers. "But no, not here. It's an awful country. It will break my heart to think of you in it. I thought, if you loved me ... after all we have been through ... you would never, never leave me again! But, dearest, I do believe in you, and I will wait, for you know best."

So after all it was a brave face, bright as her will could make it, though still wet with tears, that she held away from him, for Denis to look upon it for the first time as his own. But it was a very terrible face that hovered over the same spot but a minute later, when Ralph Devenish came crashing through the young pines to curse the very ground where they had stood, and the sea that had not swallowed one or both.

CHAPTER VIII

COLD WATER

The Merridews sailed for England about the middle of October. They had been less than a fortnight on dry land; and it was with a heavy and uneasy heart that Denis watched their new vessel to a speck from the highest point commanding Corio Bay.

With all his candour, there were one or two things that he could not hide from himself, but that he had hidden from the girl to whom he was now engaged. He was a very young man. He loved adventure for its own sake, and though he had been through much, he felt to the very bone that he was only on the threshold of an exciting and successful career. There could scarcely have been a more sanguine temperament, or a character with more right to one. But the young man's confidence in himself was neither blind nor overweening, and in his heart he was under no illusion as to his own motives. It grieved his soul to see the ship sailing away with all he loved on earth, yet he knew how bitterly he would have felt sailing in her, with never a sight of Bendigo or of Ballarat. Then he was inordinately independent. It was in the blood. He must make his own way. And here he was frank, yet not so frank as to tell his Nan that her father had definitely offered to put him in a position to make his way quietly at home; and the father was not so incontinent.

A little incident had contributed to Denis's depression; and he was not one to make much of little incidents. But the first person he had encountered on the Memnon, when he had gone on board to see the last of them, was another survivor of the North Foreland—a diseased being named Jewson, who had shipped in her as chief steward, only to be disrated for an incompetent sot before the voyage was a month old. The disrating had been largely due to the second officer, who did not hesitate to ask the fellow in what capacity he saw him now.

"Captain Devenish's servant," was the answer, with a grin that maddened Denis, but it was the fact that rankled. He had said no more. It was too late; and the man had been saved, he deserved a fresh start; but that Devenish, of all people, should give him one, in that vessel of all vessels! It was a sign of more than Denis had time to realize until Corio Bay lay blue and bare at his feet, and the tiny sail on the horizon had vanished forever from his view.

He sat in the sun with his face hidden in his hands. His heart had filled with prayer, his eyes with tears; he dug his knuckles into them, and missed the bloodstone signet-ring that he had worn since his father's death. There had been no time for an engagement ring, but Nan was to wear this one until they met again. And she had given him one of hers—a ruby, a diamond, and a sapphire—that jammed in the middle of his little finger nail; but he was to wear it day and night about his neck instead, on a tiny lanyard that she had plaited for it out of her own warm hair. Denis could not trust himself to look at it yet; he could only press the ring to his heart until it hurt, as holy sinners press the scapular, but that was enough to nerve him. He could even smile as he remembered the absurd injunction which had accompanied this sweet talisman. Still smiling he looked down again through the sunshine upon the empty bay; but now the first thing Denis saw was a separate shadow on the grass.

"Cheer up, mister! All board! It's getting on for fifty knots to Melbourne, and the Lord knows how many bells!"

Jimmy Doherty was standing over him, and his dark skin beamed as he rolled the nautical phrases on his tongue. Denis got up without a smile.

"Don't remind me of the sea, Jimmy; help me to forget about it. And as for Melbourne, we shall never see it to-night."

"Sha'n't we though!"

"What! Fifty miles between midday and midnight?"

"It's not so much, and I've got us a lift half-way."

"But we can't afford that, Jimmy."

A shifty grin from Doherty betrayed a sort of guilty pride in his arrangements.

"I've got it for love, mister, from a hawker as only wishes he was a-goin' all the way, for the honour and glory o' carryin' a gent that's done what you've done and got himself in all the papers."

Denis was divided between natural satisfaction and annoyance.

"Very well, Jimmy, and I congratulate you; but, once and for all, never another word about that unless you're asked! We're mates now, remember; I might as well brag of it myself. Besides—but it's a bargain, isn't it?"

Mr. Doherty said he supposed it must be; but for once his spirit was under a cloud, for he had appointed himself sole minstrel of his hero's praises, foreseeing both honour and profit in the employment; but on reflection the embargo only made him think the more of Denis, and his first care was to whisper it in the hawker's ear.

The hawker was waiting with his wagon outside an inn in Moorabool Street, and Denis was relieved to find the man less palpably impressed by his exploit than Jimmy had represented him. He was a little flint of a fellow, sharp but surly, who accepted an eight-penny glass of porter with a nod and drained it without removing his eyes from the sailor's face. But in a mile or so his tongue loosened, as the trio sat abreast under the wagon's hood, and the scattered buildings of the budding town melted into the unbroken timber of the bush track.

"So you're bound for the diggings, are you?" said the hawker. "And what may you think of doing when you get there?"

"Well," said Denis, to enter into the man's humour, "we did think we might dig."

"Oh, dig!" said the hawker, and relapsed at once into his former taciturnity.

"What would you do, then?" inquired Denis, nudging Doherty, who, though he had plenty to say when they were alone, was a respectful listener before a third person.

"Bake!" said the hawker, without a moment's hesitation.

"Bake?" echoed Denis in amused dismay.

"It's four-and-six the half-loaf at this moment," said the hawker. "Same price as a quarter of sheep. On the diggings, that is. Yes, sir, I'd bake, that's what I'd do, if I had my time over again, and capital enough to make a start."

"And if you hadn't enough?"

"If I hadn't enough, and if they were full-handed in all the publics, and I couldn't get a job in any o' the stores, and the Commissioner wouldn't give me one, and if I could borrow a license, beg some tools, and steal enough to eat, well, I might have another dig myself. But not till I'd tried everything else. You've heard what they got in Canadian Gully, I suppose?"

"I have," said Denis.

"So had I," said the hawker.

"And what did you get?"

"Not enough to eat bread on; not one in a thousand does. But you go and have your try. You may have a bit of luck in the end, and manage to bring your bones away with the flesh on 'em, like me. That's the most I can wish you, and it's hoping for the best. But you take my advice, and when the luck turns, never wait for it to turn again. You get rid of your claim for what it'll fetch; mine fetched what you see—a hawker's wagon, horses, and whole stock-in-trade. I just jumped in and drove away, and he jumped into my claim. And I will say I'm doing better at this game than I was at that."

"And how is he doing?"

"I don't know," said the hawker, "and I don't care."

"Prices must be good," remarked Denis.

"Among the middlings," said the hawker with a sidelong glance at Doherty, who, however, was looking the other way. "I can let you have a nice pair o' boots for a five-pound-note, and a spare shirt like what you've got on for thirty bob. But it's not what it was when I came out last year. I wouldn't come into the hawking business if I were you; you could get twenty-five bob a day as a carpenter, and three-pound-ten to four pound a week at bullock-driving. But I'd rather be a labourer on the roads, with two crown certain a day, and wood, water, and tent supplied, than peg out another claim."

Denis had heard enough. He was not easily discouraged, but he found it a relief to turn his attention to the scenery. They were intersecting a forest of rather stunted trees, all blown one way by the wind, which made music of a peculiar melancholy among their branches. Doherty said the trees were she-oaks, answering Denis's question with great zeal. Similarly Denis learned the names of the various parrots that perched by the flock amid the dull green foliage, or fled from tree to tree with a whirr and a glint of every colour in the rainbow. Then a pond must be called a water-hole, it seemed—a beck a creek, and the curly-bearded aboriginals blacks or blackfellows—but not niggers. It was the earliest and most elementary stage of Denis's colonial training, and he would have relished it if only for his mentor's intense satisfaction in his task, to say nothing of a capacity to teach not inferior to the will. But the hawker had a last word left, which he kept, as though by demoniac design, for one of their glimpses, depressing enough to Denis as it was, of the sparkling sea never many miles distant on their right.

"Ah!" said the hawker, pointing with his whip, "if I'd been one hour earlier in Geelong, I'd have sold lock, stock, barrel an' ammunition for a berth in that ship that cleared out for Old England this forenoon. Ship from Melbourne you can't get. It was a chance in a hundred, and I'd have given all I have for it, as you will for such another before you've seen half as much as me."

It was about three in the afternoon, at a place called Wyndham, that the pair took their leave of this dispassionate pessimist, with as little regret as may be supposed, and found themselves afoot for the last twenty miles. And almost from the first step Doherty was loud in his denunciation of every word the hawker had uttered, not one of which was Denis to believe for an instant. But there was no Denis left to embrace this view; the leave-taking of the morning and the hawker in the afternoon had reduced him between them to unmitigated Dent, a dogged fellow ready for the worst, though more than ever bent upon the best.

"There are two sides to everything, and give me the dark side first," said he; "besides, a lift for nothing is a lift for nothing. But what's that you've got in your pack, Jim?"

"What's what?" asked Doherty, changing colour as he trudged.

"There's a box of some sort showing through your outer blanket."

"Oh, that's my revolver."

"Your revolver! You hadn't one this morning. Who's given it to you?" demanded Denis.

"No one," the boy confessed. "I bought it from the hawker while you were on the ship."

"And how much did you give for this?" asked Denis, as they squatted by the roadside, with a neat oak case open between them, and a great five-chambered Deane and Adams twinkling in the sun.

"Ten guineas, mister."

"Ten guineas! More than half the wages you drew from the station, for a second-hand revolver? He didn't say it was first-hand, did he?"

"No, but he said it was worth more."

Denis sprang impatiently to his feet.

"Well, it may save our lives, and then it will be," said he. "But I like your notion of a lift for love!"

CHAPTER IX

THE CANVAS CITY

The travelers had been variously advised as to their best road to Melbourne from a certain point; but what they did (by pure accident) was to come out on the Williamstown promontory and get a second lift (by sheer luck) in a boat just leaving for the Sandridge side. They were even luckier than they knew. The gain in mileage was very considerable. And there was sun enough still upon the waters for them to see with their own eyes the derelict sail of all nations and of every rig, swinging forlornly with the turning tide, their blistered timbers cracking for some paint, and all hands at the diggings.

But the sun was sinking when the two friends landed at Liardet's Jetty, and came at once by the Sandridge Road to the first thin sprinkling of the tents which formed the Melbourne of those days. The track ran in ruts through sand and dust as fine as tooth-powder; they trudged beside it over scanty grass, with here and there a star-shaped flower without the slightest scent. Gum-trees of many kinds, some with the white bark peeling from their trunks, others smooth and leafless as gigantic bones, made amends with their peculiar aroma. There was a shrill twittering of the most unmusical birds, the croak of bullfrogs from a neighbouring lagoon, a more familiar buzz of flies, a tinfoil rustle of brown grass at every step. Once the grass rustled before Denis's foot came down, and in a second he had stamped the life out of his first snake—a long black fellow with a white waistcoat and pink stripes. Doherty held it up in horror.

"That's not the way to kill a snake," said he. "Jump out of the road if you haven't a stick. It's lucky for you that you came down on his right end, or he'd have been up your leg like a lamplighter, and in a few minutes you'd 'a' been as stiff as him. Poisonous? I believe you, mister! You thank your stars, and don't do it again."

And Denis went on with a cold coating to an active skin, but without a syllable until Doherty drew his attention to a marquee under the trees, with a brass plate stitched to the canvas; and when they got near enough to read the legend it was ESTABLISHMENT FOR YOUNG LADIES, in tremendous capitals; there was even a blackboard nailed to a blue gum, with benches fixed to stumps, and every accessory but the young ladies themselves. Denis was prepared to meet them two-and-two in the next glade, but the multiplication of tents soon put this one out of his head, and their infinite variety became apparent as they drew together into streets. There were canvas cones, canvas polygons, canvas in every figure defined by Euclid and in more that baffle definition. A cricket tent had a publican's sign swinging from an overhanging branch. A red lamp surmounted the nearer of two uprights which carried a pole with a sheet stretched across it; the doctor crawled out of this his surgery, and lit up with a brawny arm, as the travelers passed. Denis thought it still quite light, but when they came to the first bricks and mortar, as it seemed but a few yards further, there was just enough rose in the dusk for good eyes to glean from the notice-board in front of the house that its three rooms and its strip of yard were to let at £400. And in another minute it was night.

An unpleasant feature of these canvas streets was that slops and refuse were hurled into the middle of them, while cast-off clothing literally lined the sides; but as a light twinkled at one tent, and a fire blazed up outside the next, the picturesque contrasts afforded by the firelit faces, the inconceivable jumble of grades and races, blinded Denis to all else. Now it was a drayman with a single eye-glass, now a gentle face at the wash-tub and a diamond flashing through the suds. The peoples might have been shot by the shovelful from their respective soils; yellow Yankee, gross German, suspicious Spaniard, sunny Italian, burly Dane and murderous Malay, there they all were, so many separate ingredients newly flung into the pot. A noticeable link was the hook-nosed Jew who spoke every language and hailed from every clime. And either there were more Chinamen even than Europeans, or their blue breeches and their beehive hats brought them oftener to the eye. But the usually drunken blackfellow and his invariably degenerate gin were already becoming scarce in their own land.

Denis and Jim drifted with this cosmopolitan crowd across a bridge, into a region of fewer tents, better lights, more weather-board walls, and not a few of bricks and mortar. A veranda where a free fight was raging turned out to be that of the General Post Office; the flag flying over it celebrated the arrival of an English mail, and it was for their letters that the poor folk fought. One shook himself clear with his letter in his hand, and an indescribable look of happiness on his face, as Denis looked on enviously. In an innkeeper's yard hard by, the horses of a bullock-team scratched the panels of a resplendent brougham; and though this was evidently the fashionable quarter, judging by the numbers of regular shops, the gutters were swollen to such rivers that in places drays acted as ferry-boats across them. In some of the shop windows the things were marked VERY DEAR to tempt the plutocratic plebeian; but in nearly all there was a legend which went to one head at least—the legend of GOLD BOUGHT IN ANY QUANTITY.

"There must be plenty going after all," said Denis, "or you wouldn't see that at every turn."

Doherty agreed without enthusiasm; it was what he had always held; but the surface excitement of his years was not proof against a ravenous appetite, whereas Denis could have gone on and on without a bite. Yet they were really in search of modest fare, and were actually reconnoitring a large and flaring shanty, which rather chilled the frugal blood in Denis, when a choice harangue was poured into them from the veranda; and there sat a gorilla of a man, his shirt half-hidden by his beard, dipping a pannikin in a bucket between his knees, and spilling the contents as he waved it to the pair.

"Come in, ye cripples!" roared he. "Come and have a pannikin o' champagne with ole Bullocky, or by the hokey you'll be stretched out stiff!"

And with that the true gorilla fell to pelting them with the empty champagne bottles that surrounded him, until Denis cried a truce and led the way in, laughing, under a storm of drunken banter from the successful digger and his friends.

"A new chum, I see!" said Bullocky, rolling an unsteady eye over Denis when he had handed him the pannikin. "Another blessed 'Jack ashore,' by the cut of ye; deserting orf'cer, I shouldn't wonder! All the more reason listen me: none of your damn quarter-deck airs here, you know. There ain't no blessed orf'cers aboard this little craft. We're all in the cuddy or afore the mast—w'ich you please—so you can just sweat all the notions you ever had. And if you don't empty that there pannikin down your own gullet—"

A huge fist finished the sentence with a terrifying shake, as Denis was in the act of handing the tin mug to the open-mouthed Doherty.

"We haven't had our supper yet," he explained. "It's dangerous stuff on empty stomachs."

"Not had your suppers?" thundered Bullocky; a lurch took him to the tap-room door, where he gave the order in a roar. "Now you drink up," he went on, with ferocious hospitality, as another lurch brought him back. "It cost five pounds a bottle, and if it ain't good enough for scum like you, I'll stretch the two of ye stiff till your grub's ready."

And the genial brute bellowed with laughter until the veranda shook, and flinging off a wideawake garnished with an ostrich feather, stuck his great head into the bucket of champagne and drank like his betters of the field. As a result, Denis and Jim had their meal in peace, for it was but lukewarm mutton and sodden duff, and while they ate, one of his friends informed them that "Bullocky" was the short for Bullock Creek, Bendigo, of which the great man was patron sinner, having made several fortunes there that year, and spent them in the way they saw. "Which isn't so bad," added his friend, who did discredit to a better class, "for a gentleman from over the way."

Denis asked him what he meant.

"An old hand from Van Diemen's Land," the man answered in a despicable undertone. And Denis felt inclined to tell the old hand, who now returned to crown his hospitality by forcing a nugget apiece upon the two beginners.

"But it must be worth fifty pounds!" exclaimed Denis, in vain protest, as he handled his.

"Fifty smacks in the mouth!" thundered Bullocky preparing to administer them. "You ain't on your dam' quarter-deck now!"

"Very well," said Denis, "we'll keep them for luck, rather than come to blows about it; and we really must thank you—"

"You dare!" interrupted Bullocky, with another flourish of his hairy fist. "It's no more'n wot I'd do for any other scum with all their troubles ahead on 'em. I ain't got no troubles fore nor aft; I'm Lord God o' Bullock Creek, I am, and I ain't done with you yet; you come along o' me."

So saying, he led the way toward certain sounds of revelry which had begun to fill the lulls between his detonations. And in a marquee crowded with diggers, and reeking with the fumes from pipe and pot, the trio were in time for the last lines of a song from a buffoon on the platform at one end:

"And when you think it's all serene— Pop goes the weasel!"

It was the latest song from England, and was vociferously encored; but not for the first time, it seemed, and the mountebank would only bow and scrape. In an instant the rank air was yellow with flying orange-peel. But Bullocky handed Jim a nugget to throw for him, which Mr. Doherty discharged with such effect that it hit the performer on one leg and sent him hopping round the stage on the other, until the nature of the projectile was discovered, and the song given yet again. At its close the plutocrat's party were accorded a table in front, and more drink ordered to Denis's embarrassment. "Careful, Jimmy," he contrived to whisper, and received a reassuring kick under the table by way of reply.

A poor painted girl, with a voice that had some little sweetness left, and a pathos all its own, came next with a song just old enough to have associations for some of those who heard. It was, however, a sweet song in itself, and in a few bars a hush had fallen on the audience; even Bullocky sat back in his chair, his huge beard leveled at the singer.

"You are going far away, far away from poor Jeannette; There's no one left to love me now, and you too will forget; But my heart will be with you wherever you may go— Can you look me in the face and say the same, Jeannot? When you wear the jacket red, and the beautiful cockade, Oh! I fear you will forget all the promises you made. With a gun upon your shoulder and a bayonet by your side, You'll be taking some proud lady and be making her your bride— You'll be taking some proud lady and be making her your bride!"

So it ran; and Denis caught himself pressing his dear new amulet to his heart. He was so saddened that he did not see Bullocky until he heard him roar, "No, he won't, my dear! I'll stretch him stiff and stark if he do!" at which one behind gave a laugh, and so brought that formidable fist within an inch of his nose, while with the other paw the gorilla dashed away a tear that ought to have filled a wineglass. Denis lost half the next verse in watching him. Bullocky was now sprawling across the table, his great face hidden in the hirsute folds of his powerful arms.

"Oh! if I were King of France, or still better Pope of Rome, I'd have no fighting men abroad, no weeping maids at home. All the world should be at peace, or, if kings must show their might, Why, let them who make the quarrel be the only ones to fight— Yes, let them who make the quarrel be the only ones to fight!"

Bullocky's shoulders were heaving with vinous sobs. He did not join in the tempest of applause, and before the last verse had been repeated his emotions reached their anti-climax in a sounding snore. Denis gave Doherty a nod, and they deserted under cover of the final furore.

Near the exit of the marquee a degenerate sailor reeled into them; and it shocked Denis slowly to identify the blurred features of his late shipmate, the chief officer of the North Foreland. It was but a week since he had given evidence as clear as it was creditable at the inquest in Mr. Kitto's wool-shed.

"Seen you come in," said the mate. "Thought you was in blue water by this time."

"How so?" asked Denis.

"Homeward bound," hiccoughed the mate.

"I'm not going home yet," said Denis. "I'm going to try my luck on the diggings first."

The chief swayed incredulous. "Thought that was all plain sailin'?" said he. "Thought you was to go home with 'em, an' marry her at t' other end if not at this? Well, well, you might just as well have taken my advice!"

"What advice?" asked Denis, coldly.

"It was just as you was swep' overboard," explained the mate. "You didn't hear it; and if you had it wouldn't've been no use without the boat; but I was goin' to tell you to stand out to sea like I did; and you might as well, don't you see? Drawn your pay at the agent's yet?" he added as Denis was turning away.

"Not yet; that's what I've come for; but I only got here to-night."

"Ah," said the chief, "I have! I wish I was you!" And Denis left him with the tears in his eyes.

Outside the marquee a crowd had collected, and with reason, for in the centre stood a blacksmith with a shod horse whose four hoofs he was displaying in turn; and it was shod with pure gold, which he rubbed with a leather until the horseshoes shone again in the glare of the naked flame that lit the entrance to the booth. Denis knew it must be Bullocky's steed, and they had not to ask a question to gather that it was.

"How about the dark side now?" whispered Doherty, slipping an arm through his hero's as they walked away.

CHAPTER X

THIEVES IN THE NIGHT

Where they were to sleep was now the question. Doherty, who had still some sovereigns in his pocket, was strongly in favour of good beds at any reasonable price; but this did not commend itself to the son of the dales, whose hard head was always less sanguine for the day than for the far event. Dent was to draw his due next day; he was not very certain how much there would be to draw. He had assured Mr. Merridew that he had plenty of money, when he was really at his last gold piece. The squatter, on the other hand, had insisted on giving each adventurer a pair of blankets with his blessing; with these in tight rolls about their shoulders, they had made their march; and Denis now announced his intention of sleeping under a tree in his as soon as he had found the bed for Doherty. Their first quarrel nearly ensued. The boy had to shed a tear before Denis would hear of anything different; and then they had to find their tree.

After a fright from a spurred police cadet with drawn sabre, who threatened the pair with a five-pound fine apiece for attempting their ablutions in the Yarra, back they went across the river to the chartered squalors of Canvas Town; but instead of keeping as before to the main streets of tents, struck off at a tangent for the nearest open country. And this led them through worse places still; now wading knee-deep in baleful filth, and now through its moral equivalent in the most rampant and repulsive form. In these few dark minutes they saw much misery, more selfishness, and very little decency indeed. Jim slipped his hand through Denis's arm with a timidity that spoke volumes in his case; and Denis drew his deepest breath that day when the lights lay all behind them, save a single camp-fire far ahead in the bush.

Dent and Doherty were wandering toward this light, neither actually intending to go so far, nor yet knowing quite how far they would go, when a mild voice hailed them from under just such a tree as should have met their needs.

"I say," it said, "you fellows!"

"Hullo?" cried Denis, stopping in his stride.

"Steady!" returned the voice in an amused undertone. "Mum's the word—if you don't mind coming nearer."

The pair stole up to the tree. A slight young man stood against the trunk in the shaded starlight; it was his voice that conveyed his youth; they could barely see him at arm's length.

"Thanks awfully," he went on. "I have no idea who you are, but I should like awfully to shake hands with you; unfortunately, I haven't a hand at liberty—feel."

What Denis felt was a coil of rope, and another, and another, as he ran his hand up and down.

"Tied up!" he whispered.

"And robbed," added the complacent young man.

"Of much?" asked Denis, getting out his knife.

"Only the result of five months' hard labour on Bendigo; only my little all," the young man murmured with a placid sigh. "But it might be worse: they sometimes truss you up with all your weight on your neck, and then you can't make yourself heard if you try. Isn't there a fire somewhere behind me?"

"A good way off there is."

"It's not so far as you think. I heard them light it. But it would be just as well not to let them hear us."

"Why shouldn't they?" asked Denis, as he worked a flat blade between the young man's middle and the rope; whereupon Doherty put in his first word in an excited whisper.

"Don't you savvy? They're the blokes what done it, mister!"

"Exactly," said the mild young man. "And that's about all I know of them, though I've been in their company all day. But my name is Moseley; you might make a note of it, in case anything happens. My father's Rector of Much Wymondham, in Silly Suffolk—as you might expect from his imbecile son."

"I don't see where the imbecility comes in, much less what can happen now," said Denis, encouragingly; as he spoke, he loosened the severed coil, and the late captive stumbled stiffly into the open.

"I ought to be ashamed to own it," he went on in whispers, squatting in the grass to bend his limbs in turn, "but I met these chaps on the way into town—with my poor little pile, heigho!—and took them for father and son, as they professed to be. I thanked Providence for putting me in such respectable hands, and stuck to them like a leech till they lured me out here to camp with the result you found. As for nothing happening now, they swore they'd murder me if I uttered a sound; they've camped within earshot to be handy for the job; and I give them leave to do it, if I don't get even with them now."

Doherty rubbed his hands in glee; but Denis was quite unprepared for this spirited resolution, voiced as it was in the spiritless tone which distinguished the other young man; and he asked Moseley whether he was armed.

"I should be," was the reply, "but they took my pistol with my pile, confound them."

"Then how on earth do you propose to get even with them?"

"Oh, I may wait till the blackguards are asleep; I shall steal a squint on them presently, and then decide. But don't you fellows bother to stay. I'm awfully obliged to you as it is."

It did not require this generous (and evidently genuine) discharge to retain their services to the death. In Denis the Celt had long been uppermost, and, like Doherty, he was in a glow for the glowing work. Apart from that, Denis was rather fascinated by the rueful humour and the chuckle-headed courage of a temperament at once opposite and congenial to his own.

"Either we stand by you, Moseley," he muttered, "or we all three run for it; and I'll be shot if we do that just yet! Luckily, one of us can supply the firearm, and the other can use it if the worst comes to the worst."

Doherty was already at his pack. The polished oak case shone in the starlight like a tiny tank, until the lid stood open and its contents gave a fitful glitter. Wadded bullets, percussion caps and a powder-horn had baize-lined compartments to themselves; in their midst lay a ponderous engine with a good ten inches of barrel. Denis was some time capping and loading it in all five chambers, while one companion watched with languid interest, and the other in silent throes of triumph.

A minute later they were all three creeping on the fire, like Indian scouts. The two rascals sat over it still. One had his back turned to the advancing enemy; and it was so broad a back that they caught but occasional glimpses of his vis-a-vis, who had a rather remarkable face, pale, shaven, and far more typical of the ecclesiastic than of the footpad.

"That's the dangerous one," whispered Moseley. "The other beggar's twice his age."

"Wait, then," said Denis—"what a hawk he looks! Hadn't we better work right round and take them in his rear?"

"As you like," said Moseley, light-heartedly.

And they had decided on this when quite another decision was rendered imperative by the younger robber suddenly bounding into the air and flinging something from him with an oath. For one cold instant the three imagined they were caught. They had halted unwisely, where there was little cover, some fifty yards from the fire and perhaps a hundred yards from Moseley's tree. It became immediately apparent that there was only one thing to be done.

"Why, it's more than half silver!" the rascal shouted, white with rage. "It's a cursed fake; he's got the rest somewhere else—I'll hack his head off for this!"

A clump of bushes lay nearer the fire than the crouching trio. "Run for them!" whispered Denis, and led the way with his nose between his knees. They reached the cover just in time. The man passed within a yard of them. His mate remained squatting over the fire.

"Now you take this," said Denis, handing Jimmy a length of the cut rope which he had brought with him, "and you this," giving Moseley the Deane and Adams. "Now both follow me—like mice—and do exactly what I tell you."

So they crept up to the fire in the formation of an isosceles triangle.

"Where are you? Where's your tree? If you don't answer I'll carve your head off!" they heard one ruffian threatening with subdued venom in the distance; his voice was at its furthest and faintest when Denis leaped on the other from behind and nipped an enormous neck with all ten fingers.

"I'm not going to choke you, but you'll be shot dead if you make one sound. Here, Moseley, stick it to his ear. You understand, do you? One sound. There, then; now you'll be gagged. Jimmy, the rope."

Denis felt rather sorry for his man as he went to work; he was such an elderly miscreant, so broad and squat (rather than obese), as one who had been pressed like a bale of wool. But he held his peace with stolid jowl until gagged by a double thickness of the rope that soon held him hand and foot.

"Now for your mate," said Denis. As he spoke, the fellow could be heard shouting that their bird was flown; thereupon the three withdrew behind trees. "And remember," said Denis, who went last with the revolver, "if you make a sign to send him back you'll be the first."

They had not a minute to wait. Their second victim came back cursing their first for sitting so unmoved over the fire. Denis peeped and saw the lean, ascetic face advancing white-hot with passion; in the last ten yards he stopped, suspicious, but not yet of the truth, for the untended fire had declined to a mere red and white remnant in his absence.

"Good God, man, are you dead?" he cried, and then came running at the thought. At the same instant Denis stepped from behind his tree.

"Throw up your hands before I fire!"

And up they both went, but one barked and flashed on the way, and the ball whispered in Denis's ear as he took deliberate aim and shot the scoundrel down.

"Take care!" he shouted to the others, rushing up. "I aimed low. He isn't dead. Don't trust him an inch!"

But the man had been drilled through the sciatic nerve, and he leaped where he lay like a landed fish. He had let fall the pistol in his pain, and Moseley had the pleasure of picking up his own.

"Has anybody any brandy?" asked Denis, for the wounded man looked ghastly, writhing in the starlight, and he was bearing his torments without a word; but when Moseley produced a flask, and Denis held it to him, the unbeaten brute only seized the opportunity of snatching at the revolver in his other hand.

"The blackguard!" piped Doherty, as Denis disengaged without a shot. "I'd finish him for that!"

"No, you wouldn't, Jimmy; but if he wants to grin and bear it, why, he's welcome—till they come for him! Come on, Moseley," added Denis, as that placid person characteristically took his time, under the gagged man's nose, over his stolen belongings. But in a few moments the three were off at the double, and in a few more the contents of a third revolver followed them without effect.

"I expected that," said Denis as they ran. "But what a fine villain! Not a word in his pain. Educated man, I should say."

"Mean to put the police on 'em to-night or in the morning?" called Moseley, with languid interest, as he jogged along last.

"Not at all," said Denis.

"Not at all?" panted Doherty.

"We want to get to the diggings, not to cool our heels in this nice place. We've winged one and taught them both a lesson, and wasted quite enough time on such carrion as it is."

They were now in full view of the lights of Canvas Town. Moseley, far behind, petitioned for a more civilized pace in the most strenuous tone the others had yet heard from him. And while they waited Denis returned the revolver to its rightful owner.

"I'm heartily ashamed of myself, Jimmy," said he: "first I blame you for buying the one thing we want more than another, and then I take it from you and use it myself! But the credit's every bit of it yours; but for you those villains would have gone scot-free with this fellow's fortune; but for you he would be a poor man to-night, and he's got to know it. I hope you recovered everything?" added Denis, as Moseley came up with them at his leisure, and all three proceeded toward the lights.

"I don't know," was the reply. "I ought to have thirty-eight pound, twelve and six, but there's over a pound of it in silver, and you didn't give me time to count it."

A few paces were covered in silence; then Denis gave a grim little laugh. "So we've all risked our lives for thirty-eight pounds odd!"

"It was my all," said Moseley, rather hurt. "I never said it was much, and never asked you to risk your lives."

Denis took his arm with a heartier laugh.

"My dear fellow, we weren't going to let you risk yours alone, and I wouldn't undo it if I could. It wasn't a question of amount, either; if you had told us the figure it would have made no difference. But you did say it was your pile, you know, that you were taking back to England!"

"It wasn't much of one, certainly," the other admitted on reflection, with his own ingenuous candour. "I am not so sure, now, that it would have paid my passage home. I never thought of that before. So you two are going up to the diggings, just as I come down?" he added rather wistfully, after a pause.

"We start to-morrow if we can."

"Much capital, may I ask?"

"Not much more than half your pile between us, I'm afraid."

"It needs more capital than you'd think," said Moseley, in a pensive way.

"I dare say."

And Denis sighed.

"Ballarat or Bendigo?"

"I thought of tossing for it."

They were back again on the foul fringe of the sail-cloth suburb. Moseley stood still in the mud. And the bright southern stars discovered a pleasing diffidence in a wholly amiable face.

"Have you really no choice?" he asked.

"Absolutely none."

"Well, then, I hardly know how to put it," stammered Moseley; "but I've some experience, if I haven't much to show for it; and if Ballarat would do for you—I should be sorry to turn up again in Bendigo; I'm afraid I did pretend I'd done a little better there—but Ballarat's really the place, and if you could do with a third—well, there's my poor little pile, it would go into the pool, and—well I don't mind saying I should be proud, after the way you've stood by me to-night."

"So should I!" cried Denis, seizing Moseley's hand. His warm heart was touched. "So would Jimmy," he added, for the lad was standing aloof as he always would when they were three. "It's the natural thing, and your experience will be more valuable than even your money, not that we can take more than your share of that. Come, laddie, and give him your hand on it, too; and then for the best three beds we can afford, and three good glasses of ale to seal the partnership."

Doherty turned to Denis rather quickly when he had shaken the new partner's hand. "You see," he said, "it is a case of beds, after all!"

But his tone was reproachful rather than triumphant, as though Denis might have listened to him before.

CHAPTER XI

STRANGE BEDFELLOWS

The firm of Dent, Moseley, and Doherty, gold-diggers, was formally established next day, in a clump of trees a few miles out of Melbourne. Denis had experienced no difficulty in obtaining his paltry dues from the shipping agents, but even so he and Doherty could not muster twenty pounds between them. Moseley, on the other hand, was for putting in nearly double this amount, and yet only receiving his one-third of the profits. He argued that but for the others he would have had nothing to put in at all. It was long before Denis would listen to him, and Doherty took no part in the discussion. But eventually a compromise was agreed upon, and thus entered by Denis in a new pocketbook purchased for the nonce:—

October, 19, 1853.		£	s.	d.
Dent and Doherty	Cash	19	12	10
Moseley	Cash	19	14	6
Moseley	Loan to Company	18	10	0
		─────		
		£57	17	4
		─────		

This pocketbook, with its blue-lined sheaf of glorious possibilities, represented Denis's one disbursement in Melbourne beyond bed, board, and the glasses of beer overnight. A rigid economy was his watchword; they must walk to Ballarat; so let their packs be light, and if kits were dearer on the diggings, they would still have saved.

Doherty agreed with every word; but as they resumed their journey, and Moseley fell a few paces behind, he reminded Denis of the nuggets which Bullocky had forced upon them at the inn.

"I said we'd keep them for luck," replied Denis; "but, of course, I could only speak for myself; you must do what you like with yours."

"I do what you do," said the boy.

"And you both do well!" added Moseley, catching them up. "I'm all in favour of a fetish; that's what I never had on Bendigo. But nuggets—decoy nuggets—set a nugget to catch a nugget, eh? That's a fetish and a half! I suppose they're only little bits of things? Do you mind letting me see them?"

When he did see them, he changed his tune.

"Good heavens! But these must be over a pound between them, if not getting on for three figures in the other kind of pounds; do you mean to say you had these given you? I say, I'm not sure that my affection for a fetish would hold out against one of these."

"Well, mine will," said Denis, smiling with set teeth. "I don't turn presents into money, Moseley, till the devil drives!"

"But who on earth made you such presents as these?"

"Oh, a rough diamond with a beard to his middle, and a voice like a bull, who did his best to stand on his head in a bucket of champagne."

"By Jove! I believe it must have been old Bullocky himself."

"It was. Do you know him?"

"Know him? No one was ever yet on Bendigo without knowing old Bullocky; he's cock of the walk in Ironbark Gully, finds gold every time, by a sort of second sight, as some of these chaps find water. Why, the first time I ever saw him he was sitting picking nuggets out of a lump of earth like plums from a pudding!"

And Moseley beguiled a mile or more with tales of the great gorilla; he had, indeed, a very passable gift of anecdote, and an easy, idle, fanciful wit which made up in rarer qualities what it lacked in brilliance and virility. He had not a foul or an unkind word in his vocabulary; and Denis had been too long at sea to undervalue either merit. Moseley was not only a gentleman, but a man of refinement and no little charm, whose companionship might well be prized by such another at that wild end of the earth. And yet Denis forgot to listen as one entertaining tale led light-heartedly to another, for it was only the humours of the life that Moseley seemed to have absorbed.

"But I might as well save my breath," said Moseley, with more truth than he supposed. "It's bound to be the same on Ballarat, only more of it; the one thing I can promise you is plenty of compensation if the fetish doesn't do his duty."

Denis smiled without replying. "I suppose you don't know what sort of soil it is at Ballarat?" he asked at length.

"At Ballarat?" cried Moseley, greatly amused. "Why, my dear fellow, I couldn't tell you what sort it was at Bendigo!"

"But you were digging there five months."

"Digging, exactly; not studying the soil."

"They seemed to you to find it anywhere, did they?"

"Anywhere and everywhere, my dear fellow! Are you a geologist, Dent?" The question came after a pause.

"Not as yet," said Denis; and Doherty, who had no notion what a geologist was, glanced at him sidelong as at one who could soon be it or anything else he chose.

So the time passed, and the miles were mounting up when Moseley, who ought to have known the way to a certain point, found that he had overshot it by as many miles again. It was a trying moment for the height and heat of the afternoon; but so savage was the mild Moseley with himself, so unusually animated with his contrition, that Denis slapped him on the back, and they turned back laughing to an inn where they had drunk beer a couple of hours before. This beer-drinking was an extravagance resented by Denis, yet not a point on which he cared to oppose the man who had contributed so freely to the common fund. Nothing could have been more wholesome for active young fellows, but their beer alone cost them eight and threepence the first day, bread three and six, billy-can two and six, tea and sugar two and six, and their beds at this inn six shillings. One pound two and nine-pence for the first nine miles.

Denis did not grumble, but in his heart he resented the beds almost as much as the beer; there was more to be said for them, however, especially in a country teeming with desperate characters; and the beds at least were cheap, few travelers breaking their journey so near its beginning or its end. Denis, however, sat late in the bar, listening to the conversation of all and sundry who stopped to drink, and learning much in an unobtrusive way: he had never in his life been quite such a Dent, so canny, so calculating, and so cool. As a first step toward the accomplishment of his great resolve, he had already overcome the romantic spirit of its inception; thus the next night, at Bacchus Marsh, he thought nothing of foregathering with an odious little man, who consulted Denis as to the best place to get a "white 'igh 'at and a diamond ring" immediately on landing in London, but who gave him much valuable information in return. And the night after that, when they were fifty miles from Melbourne, there was a landlord with gold-dust sticking to the palms of his hands, who only needed plying with his own liquor to talk by the hour. By this time Moseley was keeping them all back with a sore heel; and the nearer the diggings, the greater each day's expenses; but Denis no longer grudged the money, for he was gaining much that money could not buy.

Often they were overtaken and left behind by more dashing adventurers, aggressively mounted and armed, and what was more galling, once or twice by swifter pedestrians than themselves; but Moseley preferred hobbling with his companions to boarding the scarlet coach which passed them, pitching like a ship on its leather springs. The partners met with no moving accident on the road. Rumours of bushrangers were never followed by their appearance. It was not the less delightful to meet the Ballarat gold-escort coming down, in its sparkling cordon of sabres and lace, for it made the braver show in those sombre wilds, and left a reassuring sense of law and order in its yellow wake.

The fourth night they camped out but ten miles from the diggings, where they hoped to arrive by noon next day; but the blister on Moseley's heel broke and bled, and though either Denis or Jim carried his pack thereafter, while the other gave him an arm, the last and most exciting stage of their journey was also the slowest. The deep-cut bullock-track led them all morning by open flat and shallow gully, between low hills timbered like an English park; from noon on, as the track converged with others, the party received more than one cheery invitation to drain a pannikin of tea at wayside encampments; but even the lame man would not stop again, and the light in his eyes was as bright as any. The three drew close together as they walked. It was as though each made it a point of honour neither to lead by an inch nor to keep the others back; it was also as though all three had lost their tongues and found new eyes, for the gold-light was in them all.

"Hush!" exclaimed Denis, stopping suddenly.

A deep though distant hum came to their ears, faintly at first, but in a steady boom as they stooped and listened without a breath between them.

"It's like the streets of London, from the docks, after a voyage," whispered Denis, raising a puzzled face a little.

"It's a creek," said Doherty. "I never knew they had a creek like that."

"Nor I."

And as one man they turned to Moseley, to stand upright on the spot; for so he was standing, and grinning at them both from ear to ear.

"That's not traffic, nor yet a creek," said he. "It was the same when you got near Bendigo. It's the gold in the cradles. It's the gold!"

The broad brown track rose before them, scored by a myriad wheels, backed by hard blue sky. In an instant they were racing skyward between the ruts. Jimmy had given a whoop, and Moseley his light-hearted laugh, but Denis led without a word until the deep hum had risen to a rumble. Then he looked round, and Jimmy passed him with a yell. Moseley was running very lame. Denis waited for him.

"Jump on my back!" said he. "I won't leave you, and I can't wait."

"You certainly can't carry me."

"We'll see."

"Then you sha'n't."

"Come on!"

And Denis was soon staggering in Doherty's steps, a lean shin protruding from the crook of either arm, a good ten stone upon his back. As he stumbled on, in the last hundred yards, the rumble resolved itself into the roar of ten thousand cradles rocking as one. And on the hill's crest Doherty stood waving his wideawake against the blue.

Denis reeled up to him, breathing hard, with Moseley still protesting on his back. But for the next few minutes it might have been a bronze group that crowned the hill.

Under their eyes, in a single smooth green basin of the sere and wooded ranges, were the tents and earthworks of all nations, joined for once in unnatural war upon the earth that bore them. White were the tents of that unparalleled encampment, gleaming coolly in the sun, and pitched in patches like the scent from a paper-chase; and for every tent there was a red-lipped shaft, with men like ants crawling out and in, and muddy pools here and there between the heaps, with more ants busy at their brim. Here a few cradles rocked, like great square-toed shoes; but they blackened either bank of the yellow stream that picked its way between the tents and the ant-heaps of gravel and of clay; and thence the noise, as of a giant foundry, which could be heard a mile away. The squeak of a windlass was a variation at closer quarters; the deeper claims were thus distinguished; the deepest of all had windsails, too, that rose from the earth like tall ghosts, with lantern jaws and arms like fins.

"Anything like Bendigo?" whispered Doherty to the seasoned digger, who was standing between the other two.

"More compact," replied Moseley. "And not half the trees."

"This must be Black Hill Flat, this open ground on our right," said Denis. "And that should be Bakery Hill over there on the left."

His tone made the others look from the landmarks indicated to Denis himself; and he was consulting a dirty bit of cardboard.

"What have you got there?" asked Moseley, edging up to him.

"A map, a map!" cried Jimmy, who had run round to his other side.

"Where on earth did you get hold of that, Dent?"

"Aha!" chuckled Denis. "I suppose you don't remember the man I told you about at Bacchus Marsh, who wanted the white hat and the diamond ring? He gave it to me, and I'd rather have it than the fifty pounds he said he'd give for his ring! I make that the Gravel Pits right ahead across the stream; you can see the sun on the pools of water; they say it's the wettest bit on the diggings. And you see the trim tent to the right on the green mound? That's Commissioner's Flat, where we shall go first thing on Monday morning for our licenses."

"You've been here before," said Moseley, with an amused shake of the head. "You were here last voyage—don't tell me!"

"My last voyage was to Calcutta," said Denis, laughing as they walked on; "but if you like I was here most nights on the way up, more especially the one we spent at Bacchus Marsh."

The first pair of diggers actually at work in their hole thrilled Denis none the less, and it was he who led the way to have a better look at them. They were quite close to the road on Black Hill Flat, which was an attractive part for new hands, with fewer claims and more trees than there seemed to be further on. These men's tent stood out of the grass like a roof in a flood; and beyond the tent a red night-cap bobbed above ground, as one man plied the pick while the other leaned on the shovel awaiting his turn. The new chums halted at a respectful distance, but the man with the shovel made them welcome with a friendly oath, and chatted good-humouredly in the Tyneside tongue as they all stood looking down into the hole.

"You'd bettaw come and peg out alongside of us," he said. "We come from Newcassel, and we're new chums ourselves."

"And why did you choose this place?" asked Denis.

The man with the shovel gave a happy-go-lucky shrug.

"Howt!" said he. "One pudding's as good as anothaw until you eat it;" and Moseley added, "Quite true," with an experienced nod.

"But we'd gotten a good account o' 't," put in the man with the red night-cap, burying his pick in the upper earth, and scrambling out of the hole with its aid. "The wash-dirt's close to top, an' dry as a slag-heap; what's more, a parcel of Frenchmen have made their fortunes here this very year; an' it's a queer thing if we can't do as well as them beggaws."

The man with the shovel was now doing his part below ground with great vigour. Shovelfuls of a hard conglomerate of quartz, ironstone, sand and clay, were flying in all directions. As the newcomers withdrew, Moseley took Denis by the arm.

"We might find a worse place to camp: what do you say to that gum-tree further on toward the hill? I tell you what—I'll borrow an axe from these chaps, and cut fire-wood and tent-poles if you two will go for some rations and a dozen yards of canvas. It'll be dark in another hour; don't be much longer, and you'll find a fire on, and everything ready for pitching the tent."

"We don't want to settle on the first place we come to," said Denis, between dubiety and a natural attraction to the spot.

"Or anywhere else, in a hurry," agreed Moseley; "but we've got to spend the night somewhere, and a quiet Sunday while we look about us; and for that I don't think you could do better."

So the site of their first encampment came to be selected; it was marked by a solitary and rather stately blue gum-tree, of which Denis took due note as Doherty and he regained the track.

CHAPTER XII

EL DORADO

On the road they fell in with a long-legged digger, in the muddy remnants of a well-cut pair of trousers, which telescoped into top-boots of a more enduring excellence; the man was further distinguished by a certain negligent finesse of beard and moustache, a very quiet blue eye, and a voice as quiet when he stopped in his stroll to address the pair.

"Surfacing, I suppose?" said he, with a slight but sufficient indication of the Tynesiders' claim.

"I beg your pardon?" said Denis, out of his depth at once.

"I ought to beg yours," the tall man responded, opening his blue eyes a little wider, and regarding Denis with quiet interest. "I merely saw you come away from that claim over there, and I take rather an interest in Black Hill Flat. That is it, you know."

Denis nodded.

"You aren't a new chum, then?" the other added, smiling over the term.

"Oh, yes, I am. This is our first sight of the diggings."

"Then it's no use asking you a technical question; but surfacing, of course, means going no deeper than the surface—some ten or twenty feet, don't you know. Very few do go deeper, and I am not sure that it would pay on this flat."

Denis explained that the Tynesiders had only got about five feet down.

"So many of them give it up at that," said the tall man, with a faint smile, and would have gone on with the least little nod; but Denis quickly asked him how deep he would go himself and what he thought of Black Hill Flat.

"I'm a deep-sinker," was the reply; "but if I wasn't, and was one of a party, there's nowhere I would sooner try my luck than over there. The drawback is than you can't go very near the water, because the lead doesn't; so you have a long way to carry your wash-dirt, and it wants three or four to keep the pot boiling. On the other hand that's what keeps off the average digger, who's the most impatient person in the world, and so you have the place more or less to yourself. Still, of course, the fewer there are to seek the longer they will take to find, unless some one is very fortunate. A lucky man, though," said the tall digger, looking back toward the Tynesiders' camp—"a lucky man with two hard-working mates might make his fortune there as soon as anywhere."

"Didn't some Frenchmen?" asked Denis, remembering what he had heard at the claim.

"Ah, that was on the hill, and quartz; how they crushed it I can't conceive; for the ordinary man it would be more ruinous than deep sinking, which is saying a great deal."

The tall digger was turning away again, with rather more of a smile, but Denis's eager face detained him a little longer.

"Then which do you recommend," asked Denis, "surfacing or deep-sinking?"

"Oh, come," laughed the other, "I'll be shot if I recommend either! It depends on yourself and your resources. One's quick and cheap and easy, but nearly all a matter of luck; the other's far slower and more expensive, but also far surer for a man of intelligence, as I can see you are. If you go in for surfacing, you might give Black Hill Flat a trial; but I shouldn't tackle it less than three strong."

And with a last good-humoured and yet distant nod, a mixture of courtesy and condescension alike inbred, the tall man went his way, as it might have been down Pall Mall—at the same pace, and with the same carriage—in his deplorable trousers and his long-suffering top-boots.

"I wonder who he is," said Doherty, on whom the still blue eyes had not rested for a moment.

"I wonder where he is," returned Denis, "and how much good he's doing there." Nor would he discuss the man, with Doherty, as a man at all, but only as the most superior digger thus far within their ken. It was nevertheless a new type to Denis; he did not belong to it himself, neither did Moseley, nor yet Ralph

Devenish with all his airs. But it was as a digger of transparent parts that the tall man returned to a mind from which the general impression soon blotted the particular.

The general impression on the banks of the Yarrowee was a strident chaos in extreme tints. The rocking of the countless cradles made a distracting chorus at close quarters. The vividness of the picture helped to daze a newcomer. The sky was bright blue overhead; the mud on all sides was the very brightest mud; the tiny patches of green were as bright as emeralds. Grass and mud sparkled with a rank dew of empty bottles. Nearly everything was wet and glistening in the level sunlight. The hairy miners shone with their own moisture and their own sunshine of enthusiasm, for the gold-light lit up every face. Nor was it an ignoble face as Denis saw it over and over again. It was full of the hearty virile hope that expanded his own soul. And it was every vivid tint of red and brown, as the mud was every bright shade of brown and yellow; and to each red face there was a redder shirt, and to every red shirt a pair of moleskin trousers, often snow-white, never the less picturesque for the clots of splendid mud that plastered and spattered it. For to Denis the mud was gold at first sight, molten gold that should have nipped off his foot when he sank ankle deep in it, as it was liquid gold that wound in and out among the tents, and was seen piecemeal through the strings of moleskin legs and rocking cradles, between the banks of the Yarrowee.

The famous cradle really was like a great wooden boot on rockers; the ankle was a raised and perforated tray into which they threw a bucketful of earth and then a balerful of water; the foot was a trough which received the muddy fluid and its precious sediment. As Denis watched the operation for the first time, he imagined the gold-dust pouring through the perforations like pepper from a caster; yet all that was ultimately taken out of the toe of the cradle, and good-naturedly thrust under the new chums' noses in the hollow of a horny palm, would have been a small helping of salt. Denis could have taken his hat off to it, nevertheless, and in another moment Doherty did throw his into the air.

"Not a bad tub," the digger had informed them. "Very near an ounce, I'll wager, or four good quid while you've been watching."

Some claims were so near the water that the newcomers saw exactly how the labour was divided in parties of three. One man was busy in the hole, digging and filling bucket after bucket; another carried the buckets to and fro, emptying the full one into the tray of the cradle; the third did the rocking and supplied the water. The deeper claims were crowned by a windlass mounted on a framework of logs; and Denis supposed it was a fourth man who stood thereon to raise and lower the buckets. But nothing was more fascinating to watch than the most primitive operation of all, namely the use of the tin wash-pan by certain old diggers who still preferred it to the cradle: there was downright legerdemain in the whirlpool of earth and water that they made in a mere hand-basin, but especially in the way they got rid of both, slop by slop, until only the gold-dust tinkled in the tin.

The pair picked their way between the heaps of mud and gravel known as the Gravel Pits. They walked up to Commissioner's Flat, and saw the Commissioner himself, in his gold-lace cap, seated at a table in his tent, like an ordinary general in the field. On the table were a pair of scales that Denis undertook to trouble before long. "Those are what they weigh it with," he whispered to Doherty; and they watched a happy miner go in with a leathern bag and come out gloating over his receipt. This was the most populous part of the diggings. There was some speaking sight or some striking face at every turn. All the men were bearded like the pard; they might have lost a nugget while they scraped a chin; and the community seemed devoid of women. On one claim, however, a whole family were at work, the father digging, the mother rocking as she nursed her babe, an elder infant toddling with its share of grist, the eldest pouring water into the mill.

As man and boy wandered and looked on, oblivious of their errand, the day's work ended as by a miracle at six o'clock to the minute. Perhaps they had missed some warning shot or signal in their absorption; it certainly was as though a second Big Ben had clanged the hour from which no man might rock a cradle or fill a tub. One minute the cradles roared their loudest; then, a lull that grew into a widespread human hum; and within a quarter of an hour, a thousand crackling fires, each with its wreath of bluish smoke, its steaming pot for the centre of the firelit circle. The bewildered pair had meanwhile set about their business by an effort; and it tided them into a world of yellow and translucent tents, a simple world presently enlivened by blurting cornets, squeaking fiddles, and the ubiquitous concertina.

It was a Saturday night, and the scene was very like a gigantic fair; here was a small, ill-lighted tent, sibilant with the suppressed excitements of sly grog; but here, there, and everywhere were large, well-lighted, over-crowded store-tents, with flags flying honestly against the stars. Yet even in these a Hogarth might have reveled. Diggers of the stamp of Bullocky pitched bank-notes right and left, nor ever counted the change; or instead of change, lengths of calico or bars of soap were tossed across the counters. Yet Denis had managed at last to get more or less of what was wanted at comparatively reasonable prices. He paid only eighteen pence a yard for thirteen yards of canvas, three shillings for a pound of cheese, tenpence a pound for potatoes, and four-and-sixpence for a hindquarter of mutton. He was struggling out of the tent, holding the meat aloft, with Doherty at his heels, when a cold thrill ran down him. Two other men were struggling in, and the four met so fairly as to block each other's way. One of the newcomers had a grayish beard badly dyed, and little eyes under a peaked cap; the other was smoking a meerschaum pipe with a Turk's face, as unmistakable as his own, yet Denis had to hear him speak before he could believe his eyes.

"Well met, Dent! I suppose I'm about the last person you expected to see here, eh?"

"You are."

"Why, I passed you on the road, man, passed you in the coach, and you never saw us! I changed my mind before the pilot left us; didn't see why you should do all the fortune-making, Dent, my boy; so here I am." And the bold eyes of Ralph Devenish gleamed with a sudden malice that pierced the man's gay crust, while those of his companion seemed smaller, closer, and yet merrier than before.

"Good!" said Denis, looking his cousin steadily in the face. "I hope we may both make our fortunes, Devenish—and then go home together in the same ship!"

CHAPTER XIII

THE ENEMY'S CAMP

Ralph Devenish was the eldest son of doting parents who had done their duty by him according to their lights. They were well-to-do folk, though the homely epithet would have insulted the blood which was their boast; they were not, however, really wealthy, and they had the vast family of their generation. It was therefore something of a sacrifice to send Ralph to his public school, and a distinct one to support his subsequent commission in the Guards. It is true that the sacrifice fell principally upon a long line of younger brethren, who could scarcely have filled the parental eye less if they had stood all their lives in Indian file behind the first-born. But many was the time the father paid some debt with hardly a murmur, or the mother pinched herself to make surreptitious additions to the gay lad's allowance; for man and boy he was the first consideration in their minds, and consequently the sole consideration in his own.

In return this criminal couple had a brilliant and successful son, who was a favourite wherever he went, especially among strangers, and who fraternized to their satisfaction with the more direct issue of families almost as old as their own; the only disappointment was that Ralph was nearing his thirties without having married into one or other of them. It was time, for many reasons, that he made the marriage that was only to be expected of him, and settled down. The marriage that was only to be expected of Ralph Devenish declined in brilliance as the years went on; but the prospect finally resolved itself into no regrettable alliance with a beautiful and charming girl, who was also quite a little heiress in her way. Then Ralph and Nan had known each other all their lives. The families were allied in business. There was nothing in the world against the inferior family, except that invidious juxtaposition. It was therefore a sound choice, if it was nothing more.

Yet Ralph became a company officer without getting engaged even to Nan Merridew. Some said she had refused him. Mr. and Mrs. Devenish could afford to smile. Nevertheless, the attachment became obvious on his side and not on hers. Then Ralph had an illness at Portman Street; it developed into a malignant typhus which nearly killed him; and the shattered officer was given a year's leave in which to recruit from the day he got about again. It seemed certain that this episode would bring matters to a crisis; and when the convalescent was ordered a health voyage in one of the firm's vessels, and Mr. and Miss Merridew accompanied him, it was quite understood that the engagement would be announced on their return.

Nan alone did not so understand it; and in exceptional circumstances already set forth, her father was the next to relinquish an idea which he had cherished as much as anybody. Devenish, however, was naturally no prey to the sentiment to which he attributed his reverse in one quarter and its acceptance in the other. He had never regarded it as a defeat, and he was certainly not the man to do so as he saw the last of Denis against an Australian sky from the Memnon's poop. On the contrary, the gallant Ralph had never been nearly so much in love as with the ardent and disheveled girl, nobly careless of appearances, who wept and waved within a few feet of him until the last.

His tact, however, was not equal to his passion, and it was a breach of tact that sent Ralph Devenish ashore with the pilot.

"Ah, well!" he had said at last. "He has the best of it, after all!"

"What do you mean?" cried Nan, as she turned on him with fiery tears, but not one in her voice.

"He has all the fun of the fair," replied Devenish, lightly. "They say it's the biggest fair ever held on earth."

"You mean the gold-fields, I suppose?"

"Yes. I shouldn't blame him for wanting to have his fling on them."

"I don't understand you," said the girl, very coldly. "Pray who is blaming him?"

"Well, Dent is rather in Mr. Merridew's bad books for insisting on staying out, you know; and I thought he might be in yours, too."

"Did you, indeed! Then let me tell you I am proud of him—for what he has done, and for what he's going to do. But if he were here now, standing in your shoes, though I would give anything to have him here, I should still be ashamed of him in my heart!"

Devenish winced, and his dark, clear skin was stained a deeper shade; as for Nan, she was so heated that every tear had dried upon her angry blushes.

"If you are thinking of me," he said, "you certainly aren't thinking of what you are saying, or you would remember that a year's leave is a year's leave."

"And that yours isn't up till May," she added with ironic levity. "It's no business of mine, of course; only you shouldn't start comparisons between the man who stays and the man who turns back."

"I am also in less need of money," he told her through his teeth.

"Money!" she cried in unrestrained contempt. "I wasn't thinking of the money—I was thinking of the fun and adventure and romance that would have enticed every man worth calling a man, once he had got so far—except you!"

"From their sweethearts even!" he hissed out, with a devilish nod—"from the girls they pretend they want to marry!"

Nan was stung in her turn; and hers was a poisonous sting. The blood drained from her face. It was some moments before she could speak.

"That is their business," she whispered at last. "At all events you know what I should have thought of Denis if he hadn't stayed; but if you want to know what I think of him now, you shall." And with trembling lips, before Ralph, before the man at the wheel, before the officer and the midshipman of the watch, Miss Merridew kissed the bloodstone signet ring upon the third finger of her left hand. That was what happened on the Memnon while Denis watched her dipping out of sight.

What happened next was that Devenish nearly knocked his servant, Jewson, from top to bottom of the companion hatch; the man just managed to clutch the rail, and was called roughly into his master's cabin forthwith.

"Sorry I upset you, Jewson, but you should have got out of my way. You were listening, of course?"

"I couldn't help hearing that last, sir."

"No, I suppose the whole ship heard that. Nice, isn't it?"

"I know what I'd do in your place, sir."

Devenish looked fiercely into the cunning, elderly face, with the dyed beard and the foxy eyes.

"You do, do you?"

"I do, sir; but don't look at me like that, Captain Devenish, sir, or I shall never dare to tell you. There's something else I'd as lief tell you first; but how can I when you look like giving me a horse-whipping if I so much as open my mouth?"

"Go on, you old humbug," said Ralph, relaxing a little; "give me some brandy and water, and let's have it."

Jewson gave him the brandy and water first. Ralph took a gulp, and nodded for the news.

"Well, sir, you see what he give her; but do you know what she give him?" asked Jewson, in a vile undertone, half-gloating, half-afraid.

"No. What?"

"Another ring."

"He's not wearing it."

"That's just it; he is, round his neck. And what do you suppose he's wearing it on?"

"Out with it."

"It's one of her own rings," said Jewson, bringing his small eyes so close together that they seemed to touch. "And he's wearing it round his neck on a lanyard she made him out of her own hair!"

Ralph's comment did him some credit.

"You brute!" he said at last.

"Captain Devenish, sir, it's the four gospels."

"But you've been listening to them too."

"I couldn't help it, sir; really I couldn't. She only give it 'im to-day when he come aboard to bid good-bye. They went into the after saloon, and I was only in here with the door open. I couldn't help hearing every word."

And the wretch displayed his obvious longing, with the cunning light in the little eyes and the grin amid the dyed hair on the wizened face; but with all his faults Ralph Devenish was still something of a gentleman, and, Nan notwithstanding, even more of a man.

"You will never dare to repeat one of them," said he. "If you ever do, and I hear of it, you will get what you yourself suggested just now. That'll do, Jewson; not another word about that."

The old steward accepted his rebuff with aplomb.

"Very well, sir. Of course my feelings ain't like a gentleman's; a gentleman wouldn't expect it. But this I do promise, never to tell anybody if I don't tell you. And now, sir, I should like to tell you, if I may make so bold, what I'd do in your place."

"If it amuses you, by all means."

"It does, sir; but it'd amuse me more if you'd do it, and there's time enough still. I'd take Miss Merridew at her word, and ashore I'd go with the pilot, and to Ballarat by the first coach!"

Ralph sipped his brandy on the settee. It was finished before he spoke.

"I should never make my fortune there," he said.

"You might if you took me with you. I was in CaliforNY in 'forty-nine. And I'd cook for ye," added the steward, his face shining with its least evil light; "I'd cook as not many can in Australia, let alone the diggings. That's what I used to ship as; but it's heart-breaking work at sea."

"If I did make my pile," added Ralph, shrewdly, "it wouldn't alter matters one way or the other."

"Perhaps not. But you'd be able to see whether he made his!"

That was all Jewson said; that was all Devenish heard. But the words were spoken with so subtle an intonation that the tantalizing prospect held out sounded the most solid satisfaction in the world; and they turned the scale. Captain Devenish's portmanteaux were not even unstrapped; within a few hours he had bag and baggage aboard the pilot's cutter, with Nan's last ironic wishes ringing unkindly in his ears, and the chief steward of the North Foreland, whom the second mate had been instrumental in disrating, at his elbow. The next day but one they passed Denis and his companions on the Ballarat Road, and had pegged out a claim in the palpitating heart of the Gravel Pits before the week was out.

The encounter in the crowded tent was not a solitary experience of the kind in Ralph's case; being a public-school boy, he had not been an hour on the diggings before he recognized an old schoolfellow. It was, indeed, the old schoolfellow who first recognized Ralph Devenish; but that was not Ralph's fault. Nigger Rackham was the very fellow whom his old friends would have expected to find up to the bare neck in wash-dirt, but perhaps the last whom they would have looked for in spruce uniform at the head of a jingling mob of mounted troopers. He came of an old West Indian stock, thickly tinctured with native blood, and had been expelled from school for a hearty, natural blackguard who was only good at games. His present employment suggested extensive reformation, but that impression was soon removed over a bottle of brandy in Rackham's tent, and the pair cracked another in Ralph's on the Saturday night.

"You ought to join us," says Rackham. "Talk of me being out of my element! I'm more in mine than ever you'll be in yours as a licensed miner. You've neither the turn nor the patience, as I remember you; and what do you want with a few extra thousand, which is all you'll make with the luck of the devil?"

"They will come in very useful when I get back to town. You breathe money in the Guards, Nigger."

"But you won't make enough to feel the difference. I know you won't. You're not the sort. Whereas, if you were to join us, I could promise you the best sport on earth, better than fox-hunting, and plenty of it."

"What's that, Nigger?"

"Digger-hunting!" says Rackham, his white teeth gleaming in a grin, his bright eyes brighter than ever in his cups. "You look upset: we won't hunt you; but you want to be one of them, and I want you to be one of us."

"But how and why do you hunt them, Nigger?"

"To see their licenses; half of them don't take a license out; you did, because your man knows the ropes. But of course I wouldn't have let an old chum get into trouble."

"But what trouble can it get you into?"

"If you're caught digging without a license on you, whether you have it elsewhere or no," said Rackham, with a gleam and a glitter from his negroid teeth and eyes, "you may get run down and run in, and shut up in the Logs till all's blue. The Logs is the camp lock-up. You sha'n't see the inside of 'em—unless you want, out of curiosity—but that's what happens to the ordinary digger-devil. I've had a fine fellow chained up to a tree all night for his cheek. I rather like 'em like that. But when they don't go to ground in their claims, and break for the bush with you after them, boot and saddle, spurs and sabre, then you know what hunting is!"

"It seems a bit unfair," said Devenish, blowing a reflective cloud from the Turk's head.

"Unfair as you like," says Rackham under his breath, "but the best fun going! I'd rather put up one well-nourished digger than all the foxes in Leicestershire; but there you are, and now you know, not that it applies to you; only, if you should happen to make any enemies (and they're a precious rough crowd to do with), you pass the word and I'll do the rest for the sake of old times."

Devenish coloured a little, and looked to see whether Jewson was within earshot outside the tent; and he was; but just then a diversion was caused by a pistol-shot in the distance, then another, and then so many more, both far and near, that it was as though battle and murder were taking place on no small scale.

"You'd better empty yours, too," said Rackham, pointing to Ralph's revolver in answer to his look. "Some do it most nights, but every mother's son does it on Saturday night, to load up again and start the week with fresh powder and shot. Now's your time, old fellow, while the night's young and your hand steady; then fill up my can, for to-morrow's the Day of Rest!"

The brandy had been obtained at a sovereign the bottle from one of the numerous sly-grog tents at which a digger-hunting constabulary was delighted to wink. But neither Devenish nor Rackham was a drunkard; they were merely congenial and convivial spirits whose incongruous environment promoted a mutual warmth. And the guardsman's contribution to the common fusillade, which still continued, was heard with the rest not a mile away, in the other new tent on Black Hill Flat, where Moseley was making the like explanations to his equally inexperienced comrades, and the redoubtable Deane and Adams was duly emptied in its turn.

CHAPTER XIV

THE FIRST CLAIM

Moseley had amused himself, in the absence of his mates, by pegging out a supposititious claim, twenty-four feet by eighteen, just to let them see what they might expect between them elsewhere. He was much astonished, and withal as elated as his easy nature would permit, at Denis's decision in the morning. Denis found the pegs almost in the shadow of the blue gum-tree, beneath which they had pitched their tent, and he declared that they could not possibly do better. The tall digger was duly quoted on the possibilities of Black Hill Flat. Its merits as a residential quarter were already obvious. The Tynesiders' camp was the nearest, and it was not within speaking distance. As for Moseley, it entirely suited him to settle down with the least trouble and delay, in the first peaceful spot; and the party spent a happy Sunday in re-pitching the tent and carefully arranging the whole encampment.

The day was an experience in itself. It was kept wonderfully holy, for that community, in those wilds. Dent and Doherty took a morning walk; it did not interest Moseley, who had also volunteered to cook. But Denis was much struck and a little touched to meet the string of Sunday promenaders, all in their best and cleanest, as at home, and to realize that the average digger was a really law-abiding creature after all. Outside every tent the Sunday dinner smoked or hissed on fires all but invisible in the strong sunlight; one or two had been turned into canvas church or chapel, and a familiar hymn, heard in passing, was only the more moving for the gruff voices which groaned it forth. On one point Denis satisfied himself: not a hand was put to the cradle or the spade; and so peaceful was the impression left in his heart, that not even Moseley's cooking, which was very disappointing, could spoil an hour of that first auspicious Sabbath.

The gold license at that time cost thirty shillings; it had to be renewed monthly at the same tariff, and it carried with it as many vexatious restrictions as were ever put in print on document of the sort. But the three new diggers, who were the first to obtain theirs on the Monday morning, did not wait to read the regulations. Two of them rushed back through the heat to Black Hill Flat, where Doherty had turned the first sod, and Denis many more, before Moseley rejoined them at his leisure.

Rather more than a foot's depth of black soil was soon turned up, and then rather less than another foot of reddish-coloured clay, much harder to work upon; by the time he was through this layer, Denis perspired freely, and was inclined to be irritable with Moseley, who was for "trying a tub" already, and seemed for once to have Jimmy with him.

"The wash-dirt's from six to twelve feet down," Denis objected. "Everybody says so; and we shall hardly get as far to-day. Besides, where's the cradle to try your tub in? I thought we would pick one up this evening."

"We might have tried some in a tin," said Moseley, who, like many a mild being, had no slight gift of opposition. "The way to paddock is to keep on trying it all the way down. That's what we used to do on Bendigo."

"What's paddocking?"

Moseley smiled, though with perfect amiability.

"Do you mean to say you don't know?"

"I wasn't on Bendigo."

"Well, it's the most superficial form of surfacing. But I'm not set on it," added Moseley, with obvious sincerity. "I only thought as it was cold tack for dinner, and three of us can't work at the hole, it would be something for me to do; but it really doesn't matter."

"My dear fellow, of course do as you like," urged Denis, as Moseley's tone made him critical of his own. "You're the experienced man, after all, and we're mates, not skipper and mate. Try a tinful by all means."

"No; on second thoughts, it's a long way to the water; but I'll tell you what I might do," said Moseley, brightening. "I might go and buy the Long Tom while you two work at the hole. That's a thing I could do, for it won't be the first I've bought."

Denis felt constrained to consent to this, but with misgivings, for his comrades' notions of economy were not his own. It was Moseley who had bought the pick and shovel, of their neighbours from Newcastle, with other articles of which the Tynesiders had duplicates, on the Saturday night, when, for all he knew, Denis might have returned with those very purchases; and the canny north-countrymen had found a customer after their own shrewd hearts. Now the fellow said he would not be gone an hour, which augured another incontinent bargain; and Denis dug on grimly into an eighteen-inch layer of stones and sand. He was not particularly pleased with Jimmy either; the little fool had looked so confoundedly eager at the prospect of a premature test, so ridiculously disappointed when Denis put his foot on it. However, he had not said a word, nor did he now that they were alone, which was more unusual. He merely looked on rather wistfully, because Denis would do all the work; but presently he began looking even more wistfully toward the tent; for a long hour had doubled itself, and still Moseley did not return, and still Denis wielded pick and shovel by untiring turns.

At last came Moseley, strolling with a huge cigar, and a box of them under one arm, but no cradle.

"I've got it," said he. "It'll be here directly; a couple of Chinamen are bringing it slung on a bamboo pole. I got it you for thirty bob. But look here what I have brought—a box of the best—but they're out of my private pocket, and better not ask the price."

That day they got down four or five feet, and tried two or three tubs toward evening, walking over half a mile with each, first and last, and extracting altogether one pennyweight of gold precisely, or about four shillings sterling. And the expenses of the party to this date were £18 10s.

The first week's record was bad enough to make them laugh and too bad to continue. Washing everything after the second day, they had exactly half an ounce of gold dust by next Saturday night, while their further expenses amounted to several pounds. Everything but meat was at a fancy price, and in the beginning some new appliance was wanted every day. Denis held out against the dearer items as long as he could in decency, but it did not grow easier to restrict the partner who had contributed the lion's share of capital. The second week realized three ounces (£12 1s. 6d.), and cost less, though Moseley insisted on laying in fifty pounds of flour as a bargain for £2 15s. Denis for one, however, refused to be comforted by the second week. It was not bad, but to him a total and immediate failure would have been more acceptable than the prospect of a run of such insignificant success. The second week raised neither high hopes nor a laugh; the third began better, with an ounce on the Monday, but dropped at once to three or four pennyweight a day. This was worse than Moseley had done on Bendigo, and he was soon advocating a new claim on some lead that held good to the water's edge; but Denis was not so readily deterred, much less since at the outset he had invented a contrivance which reduced to a minimum the natural disadvantages of the flat, in the shape of a hand-barrow to hold as much wash-dirt as half-a-dozen tubs, and so save as many journeys to and from the river. It was only a couple of saplings with a few feet of canvas nailed across, which it took two to carry when full, but nobody happened to have thought of it before, and it was a success when nothing else succeeded.

These beginners had begun badly in every other way. There was really nothing romantic in the life as they found it. It was only fascinating to the spectator, or to the exceptionally successful performer. They had ceased to be spectators with the turning of their own first sod. There were many discomforts in the life. Moseley was quite an infamous cook, yet it was the one direction in which he exerted himself at all. He was still rather amusing, and would have been a capital companion in triumphant times, but Denis was no longer easily amused. Doherty was also disappointing; he had not been the same bright boy since Canvas Town. Denis himself was seen to have a temper, and not unknown to lose it; but they had drifted into a belt of unromantic experience not innocent of the actively abominable. One morning Denis woke itching; and in the leaden light he thought it was oatmeal on the rolled blanket which was his only pillow; but minute movements betrayed a nauseating form of life; in a word, the whole of his scanty bed-clothes were most thoroughly fly-blown. The day went in boiling them in salt and water, which carried the offense to heaven, and during this horrid task Denis did talk of pastures new, which Moseley at once went to seek. After a discreet interval he returned with glowing accounts of a disused hole near at hand on the Native Youth, and before sundown the three started off with ropes and spars to place across the top for a preliminary descent; luckily one of them threw down a log to stand on, the bottom being under water; for in another instant the pit was more alive than Denis's blankets, but with writhing bodies and red eyes enough to furnish forth a reptile house. Denis cut a slip from one of the spars, penciled the word SNAKES on both sides, and planted it like a rose-label as close as possible to the brink of this dreadful hole. Nor was the unfortunate day complete until they had tried a tub at the old place without getting a grain. It was the twelfth of November—in all fitness a Friday—and this is its candid record.

Moseley began to talk seriously of throwing the whole thing up. It was plain that he regretted his second innings on the gold-fields, yet he was not the man to desert his mates, and this soon became the greatest embarrassment of all. There was much that was lovable in Moseley. He was the cheeriest member of the party, and in happier circumstances might have been its life and soul. As it was, some ready conceit would often turn aside that wrath which indolence and inefficiency were peculiarly calculated to excite in Denis; yet Moseley was naturally indolent, and his inefficiency seemed nothing less than catholic. He might have been a genius, but if so it was at nothing that counted on the diggings. There he was unstable, indecisive, happy-go-lucky, a trifler, a procrastinator; hopelessly unpractical himself, and what was much more tiresome, a consistent caviller at the practical in others. His equally consistent good-humour was his saving merit; it also made him in a sense incorrigible, for one must be more of a brute than Denis could ever have been to blame with any bitterness a man who was at all times unaffectedly prepared to blame himself. There was, however, one occasion upon which even Denis felt inclined to say exactly what he felt and rather more. He had at last written a letter, and on returning from the creek with Doherty, had found it gone from the rack which a few stitches had made in the canvas over the place where he laid his head.

"Where's my letter?" he asked at once. His tanned face was pale as well as blank.

"It's gone," replied Moseley, with a reassuring nod.

"Gone! Who sent it?"

"I did, with one of my own. I say, I hope I haven't done wrong, Dent? It's English mail day, you know, and I thought you'd forgotten it."

"I knocked off early on purpose to take it myself."

"I'm awfully sorry, Dent, but I happened to see that it was already stamped."

"It's all right, Moseley," said Denis, conquering his displeasure, "and of course I'm really very much obliged to you, though I came back on purpose to post it myself. It was very good of you to trouble."

Moseley was beginning to look embarrassed, and not merely because he had meant well and done ill. He had not taken so very much trouble after all, and he was too good a fellow to retain more credit than his due.

"There was an old soldier came along," said Moseley, colouring: "not a bad old chap, but a bit of a gossip; he had a look down the hole, and asked how we were doing, and drank a pannikin of tea. As he was going to the post-office, and offered to post my letter for me, I let him take them both."

Denis could hardly believe his ears.

"You gave my letter to a strange digger?"

"And my own with it, Dent."

"A man you'd never set eyes on before?"

"I certainly never had; but we had quite a long chat first, and he seemed a decent soul enough. I saw no reason to distrust him, at any rate. I know what you're saying to yourself," added Moseley, as Denis smiled sardonically; "but I've been more careful since the lesson I had the night we met. Even if I'm still the worst judge of character in the world, what object could anybody have in tampering with simple letters like ours?"

The ingenuous question gave Denis an idea.

"What was the fellow like—to look at?" he asked in his turn.

"Oh, just a respectable elderly man, not much of the old soldier about him, but the diggings must be crawling with them, and how many look the part?"

"Then how do you know he was one?"

"He told me, of course."

"Had he a beard?"

"That goes without saying." Moseley and Denis were each growing one.

"But was his beard dyed?"

"No—gray."

"It should be gray," said Denis, grimly. "Did he tell you which diggings he came from?"

"Sailor's Gully."

Denis breathed again. He knew that Devenish and Jewson were at the Gravel Pits. He had really no reason to connect the man who had taken the letters with the man whom he had in mind; and further questioning finally relieved him of the idea, partly because Moseley was unconsciously anxious to make the best of his emissary. But the altercation had stirred the emotions of both young men; neither spoke in his natural voice; each resembled an unpleasing portrait of himself. So much had been said, however, that it was an opportunity for saying more.

"You know, Dent," Moseley went on, "I've had enough of the whole thing. I made a mistake when I turned back with you, instead of taking the first ship home as I had intended."

Denis said nothing. The sentiment expressed was too identical with his own. Doherty reduced the considerate distance to which he had withdrawn, and there was no doubt he was beginning to listen.

"But I hadn't written to say I was going home," continued Moseley, "so I'm expecting my money at Christmas. It won't be much—thirty pounds—but it's sure. You see, my father wasn't so sanguine as I was when I came out, and he's allowing me sixty pounds a year."

Moseley smiled a little sadly. Doherty drew a few steps nearer. Denis had become a picturesque study in sympathy, framed in the opening of the tent.

"I wish I could persuade you to come home with me after Christmas!" said Moseley, wistfully enough.

Doherty looked tragically at Denis, but could have flung up his wide-awake at the way Denis shook his head without a word.

"Then I'll be shot if I go either!" cried Moseley, with a noble tremor in his voice.

"My dear fellow!" urged Denis, while Doherty spun round on his heel.

"No," said Moseley, "you stood by me, and I'll stand by you as long as you stay on Ballarat. It's no use talking, because I won't listen to a word. You went through fire for me, Dent—you both did—and I'd go through fire and water for you! And look here, Dent, I'll never do another silly thing, and I'll work harder and cook better—you mark my words!"

They were such as neither listener had ever heard from him before; but, Doherty was no longer listening with any interest, and Denis was too much affected to perceive that the humourist of the party was surpassing himself when least intending it. All he could do was to drop his two hands on Moseley's shoulders, and shake him affectionately until the fellow smiled.

"But what about the thirty pounds, when it comes?" asked Denis, with presence of mind and some sudden eagerness.

Moseley's face lit up with the sacred flame of loyalty.

"It goes into the Company!" said he. "I'll back you with my last stiver as long as you stay on Ballarat!"

CHAPTER XV

A PIOUS FRAUD

So the little Company continued its existence, and on Black Hill Flat, because Denis was more and more against sinking a second hole until there was no more gold to be got out of the first. It was like his thoroughness and tenacity of character, but was inconsistent with his original attitude as a digger. A moderate success was of no use to him; it must be a small fortune, or it might as well be nothing at all. So it had been in the beginning, and it was obviously still the case. Yet there was no shifting Denis while there was a pennyweight to the tub, and once there was nearly an ounce, and one day in November yielded two ounces four pennyweight. He was further fortified by the opinion of one whom he instinctively regarded as an expert. Passing with Moseley through Rotten Gully, on the Old Eureka Lead, to look at one of the many sites which his companion fancied in these days, Denis became much more interested in a very well-built hut in juxtaposition to an evidently deep hole with a capital windlass atop. A fellow with trim whiskers and an expression of splendid disgust was turning the handle, and as they watched a very muddy digger came up standing in the pail, from which he stepped with as much daintiness as a lady with a dress to spoil. "Thank you," said this one in an off-hand way to the other, but Denis he favoured with a stare, followed by the shortest of nods, for it was the deep-sinker who had recommended Black Hill Flat.

"Did you try the Flat?" said he.

"I've been trying it ever since," returned Denis, and soon added with what result. He was furthermore able to answer one or two technical questions in such a way as to interest the deep-sinker, who seemed quite struck with the simple device of the hand-barrow.

"Well," said he, as the partners were taking their leave, "I can't help my opinion, and I've got it still. I believe there's gold on Black Hill Flat, and plenty of it; what's more, it's the sort of nice dry place where it should be pretty near the surface, if it's there at all. But, of course, you might prick about for a year without finding it. I'm sorry I said so much about the place the other day; if I hadn't I'd give you another piece of advice now, and that would be to take your time and go in for deep sinking. You're too good a man for surfacing. Good-afternoon to you, and better luck." And he ducked into his hut with a last least nod.

The upshot of this conversation, and of another between Denis and Moseley upon the obvious quality of the deep-sinker, was that Moseley went "pricking about" the flat while Denis persisted in the old hole, and Jim Doherty oscillated between the pair. Nothing more came of it. Moseley was a poor digger, who scarcely pricked skin-deep. He soon went back to his evil cooking, which, however, had been less evil since the little scene with Denis. His chops oftener hit a medium between the blue-raw and done-to-a-rag extremes; but his bread would still have murdered a dyspeptic, and the lean but hungry Doherty was laid up for forty-eight hours after one of Moseley's duffs. Denis himself little knew how many of his sleepless nights he owed to the same devastating cause; and on Black Hill Flat he slept the sleep of the lost.

Early to bed was the digger's natural law, but if Denis kept it he would be wide awake by the smallest hours, and so lie tossing till the Flat was astir. He found it a lesser evil to sit up late over a lonely camp-fire, and beguiled these vigils with congenial employment. He was making a new map of the diggings. This one was in ink on a clean piece of cardboard cut to fit the jacket pocket. It grew out of odd scraps marked in pencil on Denis's walks abroad; some of the latter were taken on purpose during these very sleepless nights. So the map was his own, correct or incorrect, and it was made on his own plan. It was largely geological. There were the depths of sinkings where Denis could ascertain them, and the various leads flowed in rivers of bold red ink, which made up for any lack of academic accuracy by a rather stimulating appeal to the imagination. But that was to come; as yet it was a spy's map, which even Jimmy had not seen.

And sometimes when it had been put away for the night, and there was enough fire still to kick into a redder glow, or a great white moon in the sky, then Denis would loosen the shirt that he buttoned higher than most, and there was the little ring his Nan had given him, the red-white-and-blue of its ruby, diamond, and sapphire, twinkling and glittering as it had in the light of day upon her finger; and there was the lanyard of her beloved hair; and it, too, shone as though still upon her sunny head: and so he thought she told him she was well. But what had he to tell her? He had stayed behind to do something that was not yet fairly begun, and already two months were up. There were times when Denis did not regret the letter which might never arrive. Its unredeemed tale had cost him much in the unvarnished telling on which his nature insisted; what if it were to cost him as much again in her sight? There could be, after all, but one excuse for his separate existence at Ballarat. And when he realized this, it was a hard, dark face that Denis turned to great white moon or little red fire; it was dark with disgust of self and circumstance; it was harder than ever with a determination which had never wavered.

After one such night in the middle of December, the beginning of the end came quite quietly and naturally at the following evening's meal. Moseley had received his remittance, days before it was due, and, as Denis said, it could not have come at a better time. At this the moneyed partner had looked up from his platter in somewhat anxious inquiry.

"Because I'm going to take your advice," explained Denis, "and give in—and clear out!"

"Home to England?" cried Moseley, while Doherty stayed the hand that held a loaded fork.

Denis shook his head, and Moseley's face fell a little; but Doherty sat munching with a satisfaction as solid as the morsel in his mouth.

"Eureka?" inquired Moseley, putting a brave face on it.

"No."

"Canadian Gully?"

"No."

"The Gravel Pits?"

"No, thank you."

"I know!" chimed in Doherty. "Sailor's Gully!"

"No, Jimmy."

"Little Bendigo, then?"

"No."

Jimmy said he gave it up. But Moseley had an idea.

"Not the other Bendigo, Dent?"

Denis smiled. "From what you've always said," he went on, "it's the better diggings of the two."

"I believe it is," said Moseley, doubtfully.

"Not quite so over-run and overdone, you know."

"No; that is so, I'm sure; but—but, I say, Dent, I don't want to show my face there again, I don't really!" said Moseley, with a manifold anxiety more droll than he supposed. "You may laugh," he went on, smiling himself, "but I didn't commit a crime there, though you might think it. I didn't even tell a lie. But I did pretend that I had done pretty well. I let them think I was on the point of sailing, cock-a-hoop, for England home and beauty!"

"And so you are," said Denis at length. He spoke very quietly, but with a conviction that turned Moseley's blushes to an almost passionate glow. Yet in an instant the loyal creature was fighting his heart's desire.

"I don't want to desert you," he said. "I don't—and won't!"

"Then you keep us here."

"I don't want to do that either. Yet you see my position about Bendigo?" And his troubled glance included Doherty, whose brown face was also awry with mixed feeling.

"We see it perfectly, my dear fellow," Denis answered; "and if we ever have another mate" (Doherty looked up quickly), "may he be half as staunch as you! We have done our best, but so far we've made a mess of it. You had had enough in October, and you've wasted these two months on our account out of the sheer goodness of your heart; my dear Moseley, you sha'n't waste another week. You've tried Bendigo, and we haven't; you go home with as good a conscience as you leave us, and in three or four months I shall follow you."

And they really parted in three or four days, and at a point not very much further than that from which they had first beheld the tents and mud-heaps of Ballarat; only Jimmy looked his last on them with a sigh, and even he had recovered his spirits when it came to clasping hands. But all three had light hearts at the end, and shoulders to match; for they had sold their entire kit at the very fair figure of £11 3s. They had also cash in hand to the tune of £2 11s. 6d., so that the Bendigonians had nearly £10 as their share, to take with them to the new field, but as Denis said, at least a hundred pounds' worth of experience to put to it. He it was who had kept the accounts, all through, and he who would not hear of Moseley's generous but unfair proposals at the end. It may be added that the Company's debt to the latter had been duly, if not forcibly, discharged; but after all, they had taken some thirteen ounces of gold out of the maligned hole on Black Hill Flat, and sold the same for over £50.

Denis and Jim stood without speaking while Moseley hurried away from them down the Melbourne road; but it may have been that their hands ached more from his than did their hearts. When he had waved his wideawake at the bend, and they theirs for the last time, it is certain that from that moment the original pair were more to each other than they had been for two wearisome months. They had almost as much to say as if they had been separated for the same period. But it was not Moseley that they discussed; it was their own new prospects, ways, and means. Nor had Denis long to wait for Mr. Doherty's earlier manner, which got up like a breeze in the free expression of his opinion that ten pounds was not enough to "see" them to Bendigo, "let alone starting of us when we gets there."

"Perhaps it isn't," said Denis, slackening a stride which had lacked something since the parting of the ways. "Let's sit down under that gum-tree and talk about it. If you are right," continued Denis, paring a slab of tobacco when they were duly seated, "it might be better to turn back to Ballarat instead of going on to Bendigo."

The matter-of-fact tone in which Denis made this startling suggestion betrayed him to Doherty without more ado. "You meant to do it all along!" said he.

"It was the only way to do it," returned Denis, rubbing his tobacco between both palms, "without hurting anybody's feelings. Now he need never know. He had a heart of gold, Jimmy, but it was the only kind we should have got with him; and that's the last word about him now he's gone, poor chap! Back he goes to Silly Suffolk, and back we go to Ballarat with nine-pound-three between us! But no more nice dry games on Black Hill Flat, or anywhere else where the chances are big and the certainties next to nothing; we're going to sink deep and wet and dirty, Jimmy; and we're not going to sink on chance again."

Jimmy's eyes were wide open in all senses at once.

"Sink deep on nine-pound-three, mister? And you've been studyin' the 'ole game all this time?"

"There's this," said Denis, producing Bullocky's nugget. "I believe you still have its fellow."

"And many's the time I've thought of it," cried Jimmy; "but you said we was to keep them forever—for luck!"

"A lot of luck they've brought us," said Denis; "on the other hand, I've learned a lot since then, and even now I don't propose to part with them altogether. No, but since the devil drives we must raise our fresh capital on them, and so let them bring us luck after all. If they do we can soon redeem them; and I mean them to, Jimmy, this time. Come a bit nearer: I've something to show you," continued Denis, drawing out his new map. "I've made this at odd times, some of it when you and Moseley were fast asleep. I don't say it's accurate, but it's given me a better grasp of the diggings as a whole than ever I had before, and I should like it to do the same for you. You see the double lines straggling from top to bottom like a bit of loose tape?"

"Yes."

"That's the Yarrowee."

"And the little squares sprinkled all over?"

"Fancy tents."

"And the blots in between?"

"The holes belonging to them."

"And the centipedes, or whatever they are?"

"The Seven Hills of Ballarat, Jimmy! Bakery Hill, Specimen Hill, and all the rest."

"And the hanks of red ink in between the hills, twisting all over the place, under half the tents and holes; you must have put 'em in first, mister; they look like rivers of blood. I'm blessed if I know what else they do look like!"

"They're rivers of gold, Jimmy, and I did put them in first."

Jimmy looked up very quizzically, for, of course, he felt he was being quizzed, and made a scathing inquiry as to the green that was or was not in his piercing eye. But Denis swore to his golden rivers, and then admitted they were underground, which heightened Jimmy's interest while it restored his faith.

"They're the leads, of course," continued Denis; "and the leads are neither more nor less than rivers of gold, flowing on the bed-rock at heights varying with its height, or, if you like, frozen where they flowed a million years ago. On the whole they flow thin, and you only get so much to the tub; but like other rivers they have their thicker backwaters, and here and there their absolutely stagnant pools; those are their 'pockets' and their 'jewelers' shops,' as they call them—and as we shall call ours one of these days. But it will take time, Jimmy, perhaps weeks and months, before we sink deep enough to begin driving right and left as all the deep sinkers do. If it wasn't for that I should have shown Moseley my hand. He never could have held out, and he would have hindered us who can and will. He was longing to go, and he may be back in Silly Suffolk before we get down deep enough to do much good."

Doherty began to feel consoled for a prospect which could not but chill his younger blood a little. He did not wish to be months in getting to the gold; at any rate he would have preferred not to know that they might be months; but still less did he want Moseley back. He was content therefore to inquire how Denis could know before he went to work that he was sinking in the right place. And in a moment their heads were together again over the map.

"You remember what the squares and blots are?"

"Tents and holes."

"Then don't you see how they follow and fill the red rivers?"

"There's nothing else from bank to bank."

"Well, we've only got to squeeze in between any of them, on the lead we decide on, say Eureka, or Sailor's Gully, wherever there's room to peg out a claim and pitch a tent. Now look up to the top of the map, and tell me if you see that square and blot all by themselves."

"I see them."

"High and dry on the banks of one red river, instead of on the river itself?"

"Yes."

"That was our old claim."

CHAPTER XVI

A WINDFALL

The pair had passed the place where they had waved farewell to Moseley, and were in sound but not quite in sight of all that one of them had never expected to see or to hear again, when a voice hailed them in the rear, and they found that a buggy and pair had crept upon them while they talked. Doherty was filled with apprehension. He had not been so happy for two months. But Denis was much interested in the driver of the buggy, who drove alone, and who looked as though he might have been got up in Bedford Row, what with his black silk stock, his high hat still shining through its layer of yellow dust, and his spectacled face clean-shaven to the lips.

"May I ask if you are Ballarat diggers," said he, "or new arrivals like myself?"

"We are diggers," replied Denis, "and Ballarat's just over that hill."

"So I should suppose," observed the gentleman from afar, and proceeded to weigh the couple with a calculating eye. "Been at it long?" he added as one who did not find them altogether wanting.

"A couple of months."

"H'mph! Not so long as I should have liked, but there's just a chance that you can help me, as I am sure you will, sir," nodding at Denis, who nodded back, "if you can. Perhaps the lad will be so kind as to hold my horse. Thanky. Not that it's mine at all," the incongruous gentleman went on, as he flung down the reins and addressed himself to the contents of a small black bag. "I couldn't afford twenty-four hours in Melbourne waiting for the coach, so I had to hire, with all sorts of arrangements for changing horses on the way. But my coachman was in liquor before midnight, and when I left him, appropriately enough at Bacchus Marsh, early this morning, I wasn't going to trust myself to another. If you have a tongue in your head, sir, you can find your own way from Lincoln's Inn to John o' Groats. Ah, now I have it!" and he produced a photograph, of the carte-de-visite size then alone in vogue, and shook it playfully at Denis before putting it into his outstretched hand. "There, sir!" he wound up. "If you happen to know that face, just say so; and if you do not know it, have the goodness not to pretend you do. The answer to the question is Yes or No."

Denis looked upon the full-length presentment of a very tall gentleman, in a frock-coat, a white waistcoat, and an attitude as stiff as the heart of early Victorian photographer could desire. An elbow rested on the pedestal of a draped pillar, and the thumb of that hand in the watch-pocket; but the handsome face looked contemptuously conscious of its own self-consciousness, only it was the very gentlest contempt, and Denis recognized the expression before the face. Strip off his muddy rags, re-apparel him thus, shave his chin and nick his beard into flowing whiskers, and there was their friend the deep-sinker, hardly a day younger than when Denis had last seen him on his claim in Rotten Gully.

"The answer is Yes," he said, returning the likeness.

"You are sure of that?"

"Quite."

"You don't want the lad to confirm your view?"

"As you like; but he has only seen him once, and I have twice. It's the deep-sinker, Jimmy," added Denis over his shoulder.

The shaven gentleman pulled a wry face.

"May I ask if that's the only name you know him by?"

"I have never heard his name; but that's what he is, and the most scientific one I've come across."

The wry face went into a dry smile.

"And do you know where to find him?"

"Well, I know his claim."

"Would you very much mind getting up beside me and directing me how to drive there?"

"I should be delighted to have the lift."

"Thanky. There'll be room for your young friend behind. This is one of those happy coincidences which almost give one back one's childish belief in luck!"

The diggings were in the state of suspended animation which was their normal condition from twelve to three. The latest pilgrim blinked about him through his spectacles, more interested than impressed with what he saw. Denis took the reins, turned off the road at once, found a ford in the northern bend of the Yarrowee, and drove straight into an outpost of windsails and windlasses hidden away behind the hill. In another minute the buggy drew up beside the deep-sinker's solid little hut, in whose shade his soured assistant sat asleep, with his eyebrows up and the corners of his mouth turned down, even in his dreams.

"Where's your master?" demanded the visitor, causing Denis and Doherty to exchange glances; but the other merely opened a long-suffering eye, pointed indoors, and had closed it again before the gentleman descended.

At his request, the partners remained in the buggy, where they spent an interval of a few minutes in covetous admiration of the neat hut with its bark roof, the iron windlass, the stack of timber slabs for lining the shaft, and the suggestively solid opening of the shaft itself. They agreed to look down, if not to descend, with the deep-sinker's permission, before departure. Meanwhile his quiet voice was not to be heard outside, but the visitor's was, and eventually the pair emerged.

"But I'm just going to touch bottom," the tall digger expostulated. "After weeks and months I'm all but on it, and now you want to carry me off!"

The visitor whispered some smiling argument, which elicited a shrug of familiar and restrained contempt.

"It isn't the money," said the tall man. "It's the fun of the thing, don't you know."

The visitor took out his watch as though they could just catch a train.

"I've arranged for fresh horses all along the road," said he. "These have only done ten miles, and they can do the same ten back again. I hope I made it plain about the first ship. It may sail the day after to-morrow."

The digger sighed inevitable acquiescence. He looked rather sadly, yet with some quiet amusement, at his rude little home, at the good windlass on its staging stamped against the sky. His assistant had meanwhile risen from his slumbers, and was standing respectfully at hand.

"Charles," said the digger, "I've got to go home. Are you coming with me, or will you stay out here and make your fortune out of the hole? I'll make you a present of it if you will."

But the look of splendid disgust had vanished as if by magic from the assistant's face. "I'll go home with you, sir!" he said emphatically, and then looked from one gentleman to the other, as though he might have committed a solecism. He was forthwith ordered into the hut to put his master's things together, with a grim smile on the master's part, who proceeded at last to notice Denis, or at any rate to record such notice with his fraction of a nod.

"So it's to you I owe my prompt discovery," said he. "'Pon my word I'm not as grateful to you as I ought to be! Doing any better on Black Hill Flat?"

"I've left it," said Denis, rather shortly.

"Where are you now?"

"Nowhere. We have sold up and are going to start again. Your friend has given us a lift, for which we're much obliged, but I think the horses would stand all right without us."

"Would you like to take over this claim and hole?"

"I have no money," said Denis. Behind him Doherty had given a gasp, followed by something like a sob of disappointment. But the deep-sinker wore the broadest smile they had ever seen upon his languid countenance.

"My dear good fellow, I don't want money for it!" cried he. "I want a worthy inheritor with energy and ideas, somebody a cut above the stupid average, and by Jove you're my very man! Come on: if you don't the whole thing will be jumped by the nearest ruffian. I don't say there's much in the hole; but it's a good, sound hole as far as it goes, and it can't have to go much further. We've worked through the light clays and through the sand, and we're well in the red; when you get through that you can start washing, and I wish you the luck you deserve. Thank me? What for? If you don't come in some one else will. I am only too glad to leave the little place in such good hands. It was pretty carefully chosen, and if it isn't plumb over the gutter it ought to be."

So the reconstructed firm of Dent and Doherty became possessed of one of the deepest holes and best-appointed claims on the celebrated Eureka Lead, and all within a few minutes; for it took the man Charles no longer to collect such chattels as were worth his master's while to take away with him. Thus, ere the diggings were astir again for the afternoon, the new owners were alone in their unforeseen glory, and one of them at least was still capering and singing in his joy. But over Denis a cloud had already fallen; and there was a blacker cloud on Jimmy when he grasped the cause.

"It's Moseley," said Denis. "This is horribly unfair on him."

"Unfair! How?"

"Suppose we should have as good luck here as we had bad luck on the flat!"

"Well? Didn't he want to be out of it? Wasn't he longing to go home?"

"I don't like it," persisted Denis. "I played a trick on him, but I never thought it would turn out like this. I thought we should spend months doing what we've after all had done for us." He raised his brooding eyes from the ground, and there was the buggy still in view, labouring in and out among the tents. "Jimmy, you stay on the claim!" he cried, and dashed after it on the spur of the moment.

"What's happened?" asked the late sinker, pleasantly. "We haven't forgotten anything, have we?"

"No, but I have," panted Denis, "and if you can help me I'll be as grateful again to you. There's a chum of ours who left us only this morning. He was sick of it; but he little knew the luck that was in store for us. His name's Moseley, and he was going home in the first ship, which will be your ship, but you will probably overtake him on the road to-night."

"What's he like?" asked the spectacled gentleman, who no longer drove; and when Denis told him he was sure he had met Moseley in the forenoon, and felt confident of recognizing him again.

"Then will you tell him exactly what has happened to us, and that he shall come in on the old shares if only he'll come back? Say we changed our mind about Bendigo; and say we must be two men and a boy, and we'd far rather he was the other man than some stranger, especially if there's a fortune in it. Tell him there probably is; and if you will tell it him all from his friend, Denis Dent, gentlemen, I can't say how grateful I shall be to you!"

Denis had an odd reward for his trouble and this outburst. The tall digger shook hands with him for the first and last time.

But the climax of the business was to come long before Moseley's answer. Denis had not been five minutes absent, yet on his return to the new claim it was surrounded by a fringe of diggers embellished by a posse of mounted men in spruce uniform.

"What on earth is it?" cried Denis, rushing up in alarm.

"The old story," answered a digger. "Joe! Joe! Joe!"

"Traps," added another; but Denis had not been on the diggings two months without learning the meaning of both words. Either was the diggers' danger signal, and signified a raid by the police in search of their licenses; in fact, that very sport whose praises Lieutenant Rackham had sung in the ear of his old crony Captain Devenish.

And it was Rackham who led the present field; dismounted, he had run his man to earth in the bark-roofed hut; and his man was no more of a man than the unfortunate Doherty, who was clinging tooth and nail to the door-post, while Rackham himself, a full-blooded negro in his rage, tugged like a terrier at his ankles.

"Stick to it, little 'un!" cried one in good-humoured encouragement. "If you don't, the claim'll be jumped afore your mate gets back."

"Hold your row," growled another with an oath. "It's a fine deep hole, and I have a jolly good mind to jump it myself."

Denis burst through them at that moment.

"What's the matter?" he demanded of Rackham; but he had the sense not to lay a hand on the fellow's uniform, and the black devil let go one of Doherty's ankles.

"He's not got his license, and he's going to the Logs," says Rackham, showing his white teeth in the sun. "Who are you?"

"His mate," said Denis. "Do you mind letting go his other leg?"

"And where's your license?" added Rackham, turning on him as he complied.

Denis was feeling in his breast pocket with a smile; before quitting the flat Jimmy had proposed to destroy his Ballarat license as of no further use, but Denis knowing better had got it from him on some pretext.

"Here is my license and his, too," said he, and handed both to Rackham, who now stood livid and trembling with mortification, under a derisive cross-fire of "Joe! Joe! Joe!" from all sides of the claim. "If you will examine them," added Denis, with the politeness he could afford, "you will find that they both have about a week to run; and after this you may trust us to take out the new ones in very good time."

CHAPTER XVII

HATE AND MONEY

Nigger Rackham had the freedom of the tent on the Gravel Pits, where he would appear sometimes at dead of night, brandishing a bottle and demanding the Welsh rarebit or the savoury omelette at which Jewson had shown himself an adept. Many an impromptu carouse was thus initiated, and it was after one of them that Rackham distinguished himself by whistling for a hansom outside the tent. He was a man of violent appetites, whose every vein was swollen with sufficiently savage blood. But he had a crude vitality and a brutal gaiety very bracing on occasion, as when he told of Denis's fortunes in one breath, but undertook his ruin in the next. This was a night or two after their collision at the new claim; the bottle was getting low, and the lieutenant's eyes were like living coals.

"I'll take it out of him! I'll have him at the Logs yet, never fear," said he. "There are only two of them; some fine morning there'll be only one, and no license to show. Then away he goes, and if you like you shall jump the claim. But it won't be for another month."

"Another month!" echoed Devenish with a blank face.

"The brutes have taken out their new license a good two days before they need," explained the lieutenant. "That I happen to know, but they don't know I know it. They've had a fight, and we are ready for another raid; if we let them be they won't take such care when this next month's up. But we must wait till it is up, and we must chance your poor relation growing rich in the time."

Ralph Devenish sat up smoking for an hour when the bottle was empty and his companion gone. He was much the more temperate man of the two, but patience was not one of his virtues, though it had become a necessity of his protracted suit. That only left him with less than ever for the ordinary incidents of life, and his experience as a digger had not made Devenish more patient. He had been as lucky at the start as Dent had been unlucky. In these few weeks he had actually netted some three hundred pounds sterling, out of a chain of shallow workings whereby he and others had been tracing the Gravel Pits Lead down its course: only within the last day or two had the lead run into a drift of water which had flooded all the holes and completely damped Ralph's ardour. It was pronounced impossible to sink through this drift without the tiresome operation known as "puddling"; and that proved far too heroic a measure for Ralph Devenish, who was only happy when washing his two or three ounces a day. So one morning he was counting on making his three hundred up to five at least, and by the following night he had found out when the next ship sailed from Melbourne. It was at this juncture that Rackham brought word of a contrary turn in the affairs of Denis. The untimely news checked all Ralph's plans. He was not at all inclined to leave his rival with the ball at his feet, and nothing to stop him but the capricious persecution of a corrupt constabulary.

Ralph might have blushed to put it so even to himself, but that was his actual attitude as he sat smoking into the small hours, and so Jewson stole in and found him in the end. Ralph was not startled; the steward was regularly the last abed; but now his boots were yellow with fresh dust, and the perspiration showered from his peaked cap as he took it off.

"Where have you been?" asked Ralph, raising a morose face to stare.

"I thought you might like an extra drop to-night," replied the steward, winking and grinning as he produced a bottle, "so I've been getting you another of these from where the lieutenant gets 'em. You don't do your fair share, Captain Devenish, sir, and you may want to when you've heard my little report."

"Report of what?" asked Devenish. But the steward would only chuckle and shake a wicked skull until the grog was served out and the pair seated, pannikin to pannikin, on either side of the packing-case that did duty for a table.

"I heard what you were talking about, you see," began Jewson, wiping the gray moustache from which the dye had almost disappeared.

"You generally do."

"And you generally know it, so where's the harm? But when I hear you talking about the second mate that was," continued the steward, showing a whole set of ill-fitting false teeth, "I do more than hear—I listen—and listen I will whenever I catch his cursed name!"

"Well?"

"Well, sir, it's right."

"What's right?"

"What the lieutenant was telling you. He's fallen on his feet this time. I've been to see."

"You've been to Mr. Dent's tent already?"

The prefix was a mark which it would have been against Ralph's instincts to overstep with an inferior. It was incongruous enough to curve the corners of the steward's mouth.

"It ain't a tent," said he, chuckling. "It's one of the best huts I've seen on the diggings."

"It is, is it?"

"Once I'd found Rotten Gully, which isn't so very far from this, it was easy enough to find the only claim it could be."

"So it's as good as all that!"

"To look at," said Jewson, "on a moonlight night. But they'd their own light burning inside; you hadn't to get very near to hear their voices. They were sitting up yarning, same as you and the lieutenant. Only on tea," added the steward, in the absence of further encouragement.

"Poor devils!" remarked Devenish, raising his pannikin.

"You can't call 'em poor now, sir," declared the steward. "All's fair in love and war, and I had a look in on 'em like a mouse: they've proper crockery left 'em by the outgoing tenant, and a proper table to set it on."

"Anything else?" inquired Ralph, sarcastically.

Jewson leaned forward and lowered his voice as though they were being spied upon in their turn.

"Half a saucerful of gold-dust out of the hole!"

"Already!" exclaimed Devenish, dropping reserve in his astonishment.

"In the very first day's washing! They never began until to-day. That's what's keeping them up all night," added Jewson. "They've started looking ahead, you see. Let me fill up your pannikin, Captain Devenish. You don't get half a chance with Mr. Rackham, sir!"

Ralph Devenish was one who carried his liquor in a manner worthy of his blood. His worst friend had seldom seen him fuddled. He was so much the less proof against the deeper and more damning effects. His tongue did not slur a syllable that followed, but it ran away with him all the faster for that. It muttered degrading confidences; it snarled unscrupulous revenge; it revealed a man so different from the Ralph Devenish known of other men that it was as though the drink had gone to his heart instead of to his head.

"I will marry her! I swear I will! We were all but engaged before, and I'll marry her yet. He never shall. I'll see him in hell first—I'll send him there myself! An infernal snob out of the merchant service, and his infernal father's son all over! What's the matter with you, Jewson? What are you grinning at?"

"Only at the idea of you committing a crime, sir. A captain in the Grenadier Guards! Ho, ho, ho!" And the steward showed his horrible teeth again; but there was no mirth in the little black penetrating eyes that were fast to Ralph's.

"But I would!" he swore. "I mean to marry her, by hook or crook."

"You really do?" said Jewson, turning grave.

"Fair or foul!" cried Ralph, recklessly.

"It's all one in love and war," repeated the steward, with a shrug. "But if you mean what you say I'll tell you what to do."

"You will, will you? Well, let's have it."

"I should do as you were thinking of doing earlier in the evening. I should go home by the first ship, and marry her quick!"

"What! Leave him digging his fortune and writing her all about it every mail?"

Devenish had already vowed that he would never do that. He repeated the vow with an oath.

"But you don't know that she's getting any letters," remarked Jewson, calmly.

Ralph gave him a sharp look. "What do you mean by that?"

"Only that he may not be writing to her; he didn't in the beginning, you see; that letter I posted was his first."

"How do you know?"

"His mate told me so."

"You did post it, Jewson?"

The steward chuckled as he shook his head.

"That's tellings," said he, slyly. "You can think I didn't, or you can think I did. He deserved to have it posted, didn't he? He deserves so well of me and you, don't he? All's fair in them two things, you know; if it's the one thing with you, it's the other with me; it's bloody war between me and the second mate, and will be whether you stay or not!"

Devenish was revolted in spite of his worst self. But he was also relieved, and his conscience deadened as quickly as it had come to life again. If the letter had not been posted, it was through no fault of his, and even now he knew nothing about it. And if Jewson, for his own reasons, chose to stay behind on the diggings, in order to thwart the man who so richly deserved thwarting, neither had he, Ralph, anything on earth to do with that. Yet his nature shrank from such an ally, even as he began to appreciate the creature's value, and he frowned as he filled the Turk's head for the twentieth time that night. His hand was as steady as his speech. It was his better nature that was under eclipse. Meanwhile, the steward took the opportunity of surreptitiously replenishing Ralph's pannikin, and still more surreptitiously emptying his own upon the ground.

"So you propose to hold a watching brief on my behalf?" said Ralph at last, and forced a smile at the idea.

"I propose to keep an eye on him for you, if that's what you mean," replied the steward.

"But Sergeant Rackham's going to do that as it is. He says he'll be level with our friend in a month."

"A month!" echoed Jewson, scornfully. "He'll be a made man in a month, if he goes on as he's begun. He's tumbled on a jeweler's shop, or I'm much mistaken."

"Well, you can't take it from him, can you?"

"Perhaps not."

"You mean you can!" exclaimed Devenish, irritated by the confident subtlety of the man's manner.

"Oh, no, I don't."

Devenish tilted the pannikin and set it down with a clatter.

"Then what do you mean? Out with it, Jewson. I'm sick of beating about the bush!"

"So am I," said the steward, dryly.

"If you can't turn a man out of his hole, and prevent him getting all that's to be got out of it, what on earth can you do that's any good to me?"

"If you went home," said Jewson, slowly, "I could keep him here till it was no use his following you—till you were married!"

"Oh, so you think you could do all that?"

"I know I could, Captain Devenish."

"You know it, do you?"

"Of course, you would make it worth my while."

Ralph laughed harshly as he raised the pannikin once more.

"I was waiting for that, you old villain! I was waiting for that!"

But it did not disgust him. He did not even pretend to be disgusted. There were no scruples left in those reckless, heated eyes.

"You give me your promissory note for a thousand pounds, payable on your wedding day, or on demand thereafter, and you'll be married the month after you get back."

Ralph laughed more harshly than before.

"Go on, Jewson! You aren't drunk, are you? Then how do you think you're going to manage it?"

"Ah, that I sha'n't tell you; but manage it I can and will. You leave it to me. If you sail at the New Year—and there's two or three ships advertised—it'll be your own fault if you aren't married by midsummer. And if that isn't worth a thousand pounds I don't know what is."

"It's worth two!" whispered Devenish, hoarsely; "and you shall have two if—if—"

"If what?"

"If he—if he lives to see the day."

Jewson chuckled aloud.

"Of course he will!" he cried. "Where would be the fun if he didn't? Where would be my fun—that's been due to me ever since he had me disrated?"

"Then it's a bargain."

"What? Are you going to give me your hand on it, Captain Devenish?"

"My hand and word, and if I break the one may the other wither!"

"But you'll put it on paper, sir, won't you?"

"Whenever you like."

"One thousand or two?"

"Two if he lives to see it—nothing if he doesn't."

"A bargain it is."

CHAPTER XVIII

ROTTEN GULLY

Jewson had not exaggerated the manifest attraction of the claim in Rotten Gully. The hut was eighteen feet by ten, very solidly built, with a fireplace and a chimney at the inner end. Many neat contrivances in the shape of shelves and racks testified to the leisurely particularity of the late owner. He had settled down as on some desert island where a man might expect to end his days. There were refinements so superfluous in themselves as to suggest that the actual work had proved as alluring as the natural reward. In point of fact the Eureka Lead had been followed through the gully and lost on the flat beyond while this deliberate digger built him his hut and sank the hole which he was fated to abandon within a few feet of the gutter.

But the hole was by far the best and soundest in the gully, which deserved its name insomuch as it provided insecure sinkings as a rule. Some of the abandoned shafts had already fallen in; but this one was beautifully slabbed with timber from top to bottom, now some sixty odd feet, the depth of the lead hereabouts being something under seventy.

One of the first things Denis did when they were left in peaceable possession of the claim was to locate it in his last map; and a mark was duly made in the very middle of one of the red rivers.

"Right over the gutter!" he exclaimed. "The sinker said so; but he wasn't the man to sink anywhere else. Don't you remember him saying we were within a few feet of it? Jimmy, I'm going through some of those feet before I'm an hour older, and we'll try the first tub to-night!"

He went down at once in the bucket, armed with a spade—a complete plant had been thrown in with the claim—and for an hour he dug straight down, making the smallest and deepest hole possible, and finally filling the bucket from the bottom. But it was hard work. The red clay was so veritably rotten that again and again the little hole filled up. Denis's shirt was plastered to his skin when Doherty wound him above ground with the bucket, and the clay in the latter was still as red as ever. Denis took it to the creek, however, and tried it piecemeal in a tin dish, but did not get a grain. He returned to Doherty unruffled and smiling.

"It's no use, Jimmy; we've not got down to it yet, and we sha'n't get down to it like that. We must go on digging the whole shaft. But there's another good hour of daylight, and if you like to go down and do a trick I'll wind up the buckets as you fill them."

As the shaft went down by inches the sides had to be slabbed as heretofore; but the "sets of timber" stacked outside the tent proved to be cut to the size, pointed, and ready for fitting into the grooved uprights, which in their turn were found to have been driven into the four corners of the shaft to a depth of several feet beyond that of the shaft itself. So there was no difficulty there while the cut slabs lasted, and as the pair worked half the night in their excitement, by lantern light, and were at it again by sunrise, they had added some three or four feet to the depth by the following forenoon. Then Denis tried another little hole in the middle, and this time the third spadeful was different from the other two. Some particles of gravel trickled from the end of the spade, and even what was on it was of two colours and two consistencies. The next thrust grated to the ear. Denis roared for the bucket, and a head and shoulders stamped themselves upon the square envelope of sky overhead.

"I've struck it! I've struck it! Down with the bucket and stand by to wind up!"

A wideawake danced against the tiny square of blue; a shrill cheer came tumbling in echoes down the timbered shaft; then a leaping bucket, then a writhing rope; and the head and shoulders hung over the brink once more in motionless silhouette, while Denis filled the bucket with the gravelly substance, separating the inaugural spadeful with his hands. There was a difference even to the touch. The red clay was slightly damp, the gravelly compound perceptibly warmer, and so delightfully gritty that Denis could have sworn the grits were pure gold. But it took him some time to fill the bucket, for the red clay was not too damp to crumble, and it continually poured back into his advance hole, burying him sometimes to the thighs. At last, however, a homogeneous bucketful was got to upper air, and Denis after it in a mud-bath of clay and perspiration, but with his triumph shining through his filth.

It still remained to test the stuff and justify the triumph, but Denis did both without delay at the creek, which was far nearer here than on Black Hill Flat. They had no cradle as yet at the new claim, whose late methodical proprietor had not arrived at the stage of requiring one; but Denis took the tin dish once more, and came back beating it like a tambourine, on knee and head, but carrying the empty bucket at arm's length in the other hand. At least it felt as empty to Denis as it looked to Doherty, until the bucket was tilted, and what had seemed but a sparse deposit of rather yellow and sparkling sand formed a slender segment of palpable gold-dust.

They poured it from the bucket back into the tin dish, and from the tin dish into a smaller tin, and from the smaller tin into the saucer in which Jewson really did get a glimpse of about half of it that night. The trial "tub" had yielded upwards of two ounces, by the gold-scales of a friendly neighbour; before night Denis had spent quite half on a good candle, a pair of scales, and the wherewithal for a digger's supper of new damper, steaming chops, and scalding tea.

Thereafter the pair sat up planning, building, furnishing and inhabiting castles which were no longer altogether in the air; but with Denis, in any case, early hours would have been impossible after such a meal hurled into an empty stomach in the late evening of such a day; and the pernicious combination may be confidently traced in the view which he took of this very aspect of a situation otherwise surpassing all his dreams.

"It's all very well for a day or two," said Denis, "but you and I can never go on doing all the work and the cooking too. We couldn't even if we were born cooks. What we want is some fellow to look after us and the hut. Two all told are not enough."

Doherty was toying with the gold-dust in the saucer, picking it up in pinches, and letting it trickle through his fingers in fairy showers, playing with it, drawing in it, as children play and draw in sand. The game palled even as Denis spoke.

"Two were enough for the swell cove who was here before us, mister."

"I know: he took his time: so many hours a day, or so few, and not a minute more. What's the result? He isn't here to reap his reward, because he was in no hurry, and it didn't much matter after all. But I am here—I am in a hurry—every grain and every minute matters to me!"

"It would mean one grain in three instead of in two."

"Then the three would come quicker than the two do now. Not that we're obliged to take another partner because we want an extra hand; at two ounces to the tub we could afford to make it worth many a man's while to do all we want at so much the week."

Jimmy looked up quickly.

"Then you haven't heard from Mr. Moseley yet?"

"I have, Jimmy. I called at the post-office to-night, and the letter was there. Not he! Not for Joe! He wishes us all possible luck, but he has had enough of the diggings to last him a lifetime; and from what he says he ought to be out at sea by this time, homeward bound. Put the billy on the fire, Jimmy, and we'll drink him a good voyage in half a pannikin of tea before we turn in."

To all this Jewson stood listening, if not at the door, still within easy earshot of the unsuspecting friends; and as he listened an inspiration burst upon his crafty brain. He drew away in the moonlight, nodding and grinning to himself—a grotesque Mephistopheles if you will—yet deeper and darker than friend or foe imagined. His plan was matured on the way back to the Gravel Pits, and Captain Devenish was told just as much as it was good for him to know that night, but as we have seen, not a syllable more, and that modicum with the wary tact and infinite precaution of a Mephistopheles of higher class.

Next day was a great one at the new claim; from early morning to high noon the pair laboured in hourly shifts at lowering the whole shaft to the level of the precious wash-dirt. It was not to be done in the time. But later in the day they went deep at one corner, and at last uncovered an angle of the gutter which they had only probed the day before. They took up several bucketfuls to try in the new cradle before dark. The yields were uneven, but the lowest was an ounce, the highest three ounces ten pennyweight, and the day's aggregate just under one pound, or upward of forty pounds sterling.

Yet they were less excited than they had been the night before. The gold was there; it was only a question of getting it out, a question of time, ways, and means. They had taken turns at the creek as well as in the hole, and the friendly neighbour who had lent his scales had kept an eye on the new cradle in their absence, which was intermittent owing to the necessity of one always remaining on the claim. "You must find another mate," said he to Doherty, who no longer disagreed as he toiled back to the hut. They must find another mate, or they must greatly reduce their hours of labour. A reduction of profits would result in either case.

To-night they were too tired to cook. Denis made tea, and each took a pannikin to his couch, and spread himself prostrate in the dusk.

"In another hour or two," said Denis, "we'll go out one at a time, and have the best supper that money can buy on Ballarat. We can afford that; but we can't afford to go on using ourselves up at this rate."

A slumbrous sigh was the only answer from the other bunk; but Denis was too much exercised in his mind to close an eye. Should they seek a mate? or should they restrict their hours? Could they get a respectable hireling to look after them if they tried? The last plan was the most desirable for obvious reasons; and Denis desired it on other grounds as well. He was naturally anxious, for his own sake and for one other's, to make as much money as possible in as little time; and he had tasted blood, at last, in an intoxicating draught. He had begun making up for lost time; that was what he must go on doing. It was not so with Doherty, however, and this time Denis had quite decided to respect the prejudices of the lad who had stood by him so loyally through so many luckless weeks. After all, in the beginning they had actually started for the diggings, they two, to sink or to swim together. The importation of Moseley had been as unfair as it had proved unwise; the ignorant lad had found himself at a continual disadvantage between the two educated men; they could talk in parables beyond his comprehension, and Moseley invariably did. Doherty had been bitterly jealous of him, yet had striven finely to suppress his chagrin, and never stooped to backbiting or tale-bearing under its stress. And his devotion to Denis had never wavered; that was at once a touching consideration and a clear claim. No; there should be no more partners if Denis could help it, but if he could not, then the newcomer should be a man after Jimmy's heart rather than his own.

It was moonlight when Denis came to this conclusion of the matter, though he had lain down in daylight not long before. He did not lie many minutes more. A shambling step came to his ears, came nearer and nearer; he jumped up in time to meet a tottering figure at the door.

CHAPTER XIX

NEW BLOOD

"Jewson!" exclaimed Denis in cold astonishment. "What in the world do you want—with me?"

"You may well ask, sir," replied the steward, in an abject whine, "but on all the diggings there was no one else that I could turn to—little as I deserve at your hands, sir—little as I know I deserve! But you look at me, Mr. Dent, and you'll see the way I've been used!"

He turned his face into the level moonbeams; an eye was closed and discoloured; a lip was swollen and cut, and the coat was almost torn off the steward's back, hanging in ribbons from the shoulders only.

"Some one's been knocking you about," remarked Denis, dispassionately.

"Some one has," the steward agreed, grimly: "some one as ought to have known better—some one not half as old as me, and more than twice as strong! But it was my fault. I might have known! I seen it coming from the first; it was bound to come when the luck gave out. You'll have heard about the water on the Gravel Pits, likely? It's flooded us out altogether; and this is the way the Captain's used me, with his own hands, after two months' faithful service!"

"You've probably been getting drunk," said Denis; but there was no sign of drink about the man; and Denis accepted his denial with some regret for the suggestion, for he was already more sympathetic than he seemed, because readier than he knew to believe ill of Devenish.

The steward's story was that for some trifling omission he had been visited with a torrent of intolerable abuse, and on remonstrance, with the personal chastisement of which he bore marks which never struck Denis as other than genuine. The wretch was clever enough to make excuses for his late master, whose behaviour he attributed entirely to irritation caused by the ruin of his claim; but as Jewson said, that was not his fault, and he could not stay another hour with a gentleman who used him so. So he had turned to Denis in his distress—little right as he had—and he hoped the past at least would be forgiven and forgotten—if only for the sake of the season.

"Why, what is the season?" asked Denis; for in the incessant excitement of the last few days, and the unaccustomed surroundings of blue sky and blazing heat, he had quite forgotten that Christmas was upon them; but he remembered as he spoke, and could quite believe the steward's statement that it was already Christmas Eve.

"And to think you had forgotten!" added Jewson, who was fast recovering a careful kind of confidence. "Why, I expected to find you starting to keep it in the good old style—roast beef—turkeys—plum-pudding and mince pies! What's the good of being a lucky digger unless you keep a high old Christmas like the rest of 'em?"

"Who told you I was one?" asked Denis, suspiciously.

"Who told me? If you asked me who hadn't told me, Mr. Dent, I might be able to answer you, sir. You don't keep a thing like that to yourself in a place like this. Captain Devenish told me, for one; it was one of the things that helped to make him mad."

"Well," said Denis, "you must come in, steward, but I'm sorry there's nothing to offer you. We were going out to get something before we turn in. There's nothing in the place but the remains of some mutton we had last night and this midday, some stale damper, and some dried-up cheese."

"Call that nothing?" chuckled Jewson. "You might let me see what's left, Mr. Dent; it's wonderful what can be done with what, by a bit of a cook; and I'm all that, sir, though I say it. I might be able to save you turning out again, and I'd be proud to do it after your kindness, Mr. Dent, which I have done so little to deserve!"

Denis was not the man to refuse; he did not like the fellow's whining tone, but it was not his only tone, and he did appear to have been roughly handled. He did not impose upon Denis altogether, but only as much as was necessary, which was characteristic of his craft. He was admitted, a lamp lit without disturbing Doherty, and the remnants of the mutton fetched from an outside safe. Jewson sniffed it suspiciously.

"Sweet enough!" said he. "I see you knew enough to salt it. And are them taters I see in that sack? Then down you lie like your mate, and shut your eyes, and see what the king'll send you! Stop a bit, though; didn't you say there was bread and cheese?"

"Yes, but they're both as hard as nails."

"Never mind; they may make into something soft. Any mustard?"

"Yes; they left us some."

"No beer, I suppose?"

"No."

"Well, never mind. You leave the rest to me. Thank you, I see where everything else is, and in twenty minutes to half-an-hour there'll be something for you to see and taste too!"

Already he was crouching over the fire, blowing upon the red embers, coaxing them into flames; and in the growing glow his cunning face looked kindly enough, and his grin but that of an artist bent on triumphing over materials which only put him on his artistic mettle. Denis watched him a little from the door. Then he sauntered to and fro between hut and shaft; and presently there came to his nostrils the most savoury and appetizing smell that they had yet encountered on the diggings. Something was hissing on the fire; at the table Jewson was preparing something else. On his bed Doherty still slept the sleep of exhaustion; and down upon the bark roof of the hut, on the black hieroglyph of the mounted windlass, and on the white tents further along the gully, shone a moon of surpassing purity and splendour. And Denis thought of a Christmas hymn, and then of Father Christmas himself, as he peered in and watched the elderly evil-doer with the once-dyed beard preparing his miraculous and momentous meal.

Momentous as the sequel will very soon show, at the time it was indeed little less than a miracle, and nothing less to Doherty, who was roused from a castaway's dreams of plenty to find them true. The remains of the mutton had been changed as by some fairy wand into a spiced ragoût swimming in rich gravy. The cook apologized for the potatoes, which he had only had time to fry; but the other diners had forgotten that potatoes could be fried, and their appreciation was proportionate. But the greatest success came in the Welsh rarebit which a master hand had evolved from the stale damper and the dried-up cheese. It lay steaming in its dish like liquid gold—a joy to the eye, a boon to the nose, and to the diggers' hardened palates an inconceivable delicacy and treat.

"And to think," said Denis, "that we had the material by us; that we've had it ready to our hand any time these two months!"

"And much good it was, or would have been," echoed Doherty, "to our hand! It's the hand that matters, not the material. Mr. Steward, give me yours!"

"His name is Jewson," remarked Denis; and his heart sank in spite of him as he saw the young hand join the old across the empty plates.

"But you called me steward, Mr. Dent, and I like to be called steward," rejoined Jewson, adroitly. "It reminds me of times you may think I'd like to forget; but I wouldn't and shall I tell you why? Because I'd like to make up for 'em, sir, if only you'd give me the chance. I'm out of a job. Wild hosses wouldn't take me back to Captain Devenish. I was only his servant, not a partner, and I'll be your servant, Mr. Dent, and a good one, sir, if you'll give me a trial. Pay me what you like—I ain't partic'lar."

And the old rogue lapsed into a living heap of humility; but he had gone just one sentence too far.

"I'll pay you well if I take you," said Denis, shortly, as he sipped his tea. Yet even the tea seemed a better brew than they had managed to achieve for themselves.

"I don't want you to make up your minds to-night," resumed the steward, reducing the humility a degree or so. "I don't care about hotel work. I certainly shouldn't start work at any of these here shanties on Christmas Day. They have approached me, you understand, through Lieutenant Rackham, who has been kind enough to say a good word for my capabilities. But that's not the kind of place I'd like so well as this. Let me camp outside to-night, and cook your Christmas dinner to-morrow, while you think it over."

But Denis said he would prefer to think it over at once, and lit his pipe, and went out to do so then and there, with a troubled face which Jewson could understand and Doherty could not.

"He never liked me," said the steward with a sigh. "And it was my fault," he added self-reproachfully.

"But if you see that you could soon make him like you."

"If he gave me the chance, perhaps."

"He shall!"

Denis was leaning in the moonlight against the windlass staging. There he listened to the lad's strenuous and enthusiastic plea.

"We've never had a mate like that since we've been on Ballarat," urged Jimmy; "and all done in half-an-hour out of our own odds and ends! Why, mister, that steward of yours would make a man of me and a new man of you in less than no time. And he doesn't even ask to be a partner; he's the very man we want, dropped from the stars on to this blessed claim! If we don't snap him up, others soon will, and we deserve to lose the second-best chance we've ever had."

Denis puffed his pipe in silence.

"I know him, you see," he said at last.

"Of course you do."

"But I never liked him."

"So he says."

"And it was his own fault."

"He says that too. He's said enough for me to see he means turning over a new leaf if you give him this chance."

Denis wavered. If he was going to give the man a chance (and he could always watch him, and get rid of him at a moment's notice) it would be perhaps unfair to let the lad know all he thought about their prospective companion.

"Do you really want him to have the job, Jimmy?"

"I do so, mister. He's the very man for us. I want him bad."

"And you never wanted Mr. Moseley at all, eh?"

"No, mister, I never did."

Denis went on smoking for another minute. The moon was high now, and as pure as ever. The tents further down the gully shone white as from a fall of real Christmas snow; and sounds of real Christmas came faintly from them, and more faintly from far beyond. Denis, however, was not thinking of the morrow, but of many a morrow—of long days of unremitting labour—of short nights when the spent body would be fit but for rest and for refreshment. He felt the better already for this single evening meal. And the man could be watched—the man could be watched.

"Well, mister?"

"It's all right, Jimmy. He shall have his trial—to-morrow—the day after to-morrow—and as many days after that again as he suits us and we him. But never let him know the half of what we take, and never you leave him on the claim alone."

CHAPTER XX

THE JEWELER'S SHOP

Dent and Doherty became the heroes of one of those fairy-tales in which the times were rich. For eight consecutive days, after laying the gutter bare from wall to wall of the shaft, and slabbing the latter down to the last inch, they washed their twenty tubs a day, and averaged rather better than four ounces to the tub. The daily yield only once fell below £300 at current rates; but more than once it impinged upon £400. Altogether the eight days realized upwards of £50; which was the aggregate amount handed over to the Commissioner, who forwarded it to Geelong by Gold Escort, which delivered it to a firm of gold-buyers whom the Commissioner could recommend, and who presently remitted some £2,400 in hard cash.

These wonderful days were also the most comfortable that the partners had yet spent upon the diggings. They were properly looked after for the first time. They had three good meals a day, to say nothing of coffee and a biscuit before they went to work in the early morning and afternoon tea with hot cakes or any other incongruous luxury which happened to occur to the steward's mind. Denis said it was a good thing they were working so hard. Doherty rolled his eyes and put on flesh. The pair were being spoiled and cosseted by a master-hand, and it did them more good than their success. They were the better workers by day, the better sleepers by night, and this despite the manifold excitements of every waking hour.

Jewson was excelling himself; but an outsider would have said it was well worth his while, for Denis had hit upon a scale of pay which made him after all a small partner, whose earnings might amount to several sovereigns a day, and could not fall below five pounds a week. As prices went, the bargain was not extravagant, and Denis was the first to appreciate the blessing of better food; the steward's prowess was no small asset in the suddenly successful concern, and he must be kept in it by hook or crook; on that the partners were agreed. And yet Denis was as far as ever from trusting the man in his heart, though his original prejudice had abated not a little.

Jewson wore a shade over the blackened eye, which had only been exposed by moonlight; but Denis's distrust was not such as to make him want to lift it, because it never occurred to him to discredit the account of his cousin's violence; and therein is seen the working of another prejudice, on which a cunning brain had counted all along. A simple nature, on the other hand, is simple even in its suspicions; and the worst that Denis harboured were engendered by Jewson's strange practice of shopping at night only and usually being hours about it. Denis sometimes had a mind to follow him, but it was not in his nature to play the spy, and so the real spy went free.

The lucky pair took their luck very coolly, one because he did not understand the value of money, the other because he understood it too well to estimate a thousand pounds at a penny more than a tithe of the ten thousand on which he had set his heart. In money matters, however, the point of view is everything, and in none is it more mercurial. A day or two served to inure the partners to the idea of dividing a couple of thousand a week, and Denis began almost to resent the fact that at this rate it would take ten whole weeks for him to reach his minimum; he was also annoyed that in all the gold they had got there was not as yet a single nugget.

"I promised to send the first one home to England," he said openly in the hut. "I would give a hundred pounds to have one worth fifty to send by the mail to-morrow night!"

Jewson was crouching over his camp-oven at the time; his back straightened, and for some moments he sat in an arrested attitude, his head thrown up in undisguised attention; but this was not noticed, and his face could not be seen.

That night the steward was so long upon his rounds that Denis did not sit up for him, but decided on a word of remonstrance in the morning. Yet when morning came, the coffee was so hot and aromatic, the biscuit so crisp, the fresh air so cool and so invigorating, that he found it difficult to complain just then. And in the first hour of the new day that happened which effaced all untoward impressions from his mind.

Denis had been lowered into the shaft to dig. Doherty had raised one bucket of wash-dirt, and was waiting for the next, when a loud shout brought him to the shaft's mouth.

"A nugget, Jimmy! A nugget in the nick of time! I nearly cut it in two with the spade!"

It was a very small nugget, much in the shape and size of a kidney-bean, but of singularly pure and smooth gold, and Denis declared that it was just the thing. With the point of his knife he removed every particle of earth, and then scrubbed it with soap and water until it was as bright as the last sovereign from the mint. It seemed to give him greater pleasure than all the gold-dust despatched to Geelong; and no more work was done before breakfast, which was taken with the nugget on the table in front of Denis, save when he pressed a piece of twine into the cleft made by the spade and tried how it looked round Doherty's neck.

"Half should be yours, by rights," he said; "but you won't mind if I credit you with the weight instead? Don't be a fool! Of course I'll do that! But it was almost my last promise—to send her my first nugget— and it's been such a long time coming."

"Funny it's coming just when you wanted it for the mail," remarked Doherty in perfect innocence; but the steward spoke up from his self-appointed place beside the fire.

"I only wonder it's the first," said he; "but you take my word it ain't the last. Talk about jewelers' shops! You've opened one of the best on Ballarat. Look at the men you're bringing back to the gully; there'd be a rush if it wasn't for the depth they've got to sink, and that you had all done for you. I sha'n't be satisfied till I see you put your pick into a bit like they took out of Canadian Gully twelve months ago."

Nothing could have been more consistent and withal less officious than the discreetly sympathetic encouragement of the steward; he also knew something about gold-mining, and his unobtrusive suggestions were often of value. Denis was indeed more and more unable to reconcile the useful landsman with the ship's steward who had broached the ship's spirits and misbehaved himself in other ways; but after all, a man might pull himself together, and having suffered from a bad master, might well desire to make the most of a good one. So Denis was imposed upon while still as much on guard against imposition as these engrossing days allowed.

And the eight days of harvest were almost at an end; that very morning there was a subtle change in the appearance of a bucketful that Doherty sent up, and Denis forthwith washed an almost wholly unprofitable tub. He then went down the shaft, and found as he expected that they had struck the bottom of the gutter, and were on the hard paleozoic floor. The difference was even more marked than that between the red clay and the auriferous drift, here only four or five feet thick. There were still some tubs to take before the corners of the shaft were cleared to the bed-rock.

"And then?" asked Doherty with a blank face.

"Then the fun begins."

"Tunneling?"

"Of course."

"But how do you know which way?"

"Down the gully; nothing simpler. But first of all we can try all round with trowels, in holes just big enough to take your arm, like tasting cheese; then where it's richest we shall tunnel for another three months, and if this is the gutter and not a pocket we shall be well enough off by that time to take a spell and talk things over."

They were for once down the shaft together, and as they stood discussing the situation the steward's small head appeared like that of a pin against the little square of sky high above.

"There's a Chinaman selling beer," he shouted down. "Would you like some?"

"Very much," answered Denis. "Draught or bottle, steward?"

"Draught."

"Then take three pints, and cool it in the gallon jar. It's an occasion," continued Denis down below. "The first of the nuggets before breakfast and the last of the gutter before noon; only, it's not the last; and even if it were, that little nugget would be some consolation to me."

When they regained the upper air there was still half-an-hour before the midday meal, and Denis spent it in finishing a long letter and packing the nugget with it in a small tin box unearthed by Jewson. This he tied up in brown paper, but was unable to seal for want of wax; and the parcel remained by his plate as the naked nugget had done at breakfast.

It was now the middle of January, and the hottest weather that Denis had ever known on land. The well-built hut was cooler than the open air, but to swallow a pannikin of tea was to have a warm bath in one's clothes. The beer was therefore a great and timely treat; each man made short work of his pint, and the little package was duly toasted on the eve of its travels. Denis intended taking it to the post-office himself, while the other two enjoyed the siesta which was a necessity of the digger's existence in the hot season. A pipe on the bed was all he would allow himself that day; the others were already asleep when he lit up and began puffing vigorously to keep his eyes open. The eight long days were beginning to tell on him. This one was also of an unbearable and inhuman heat.

Denis was the first to open his eyes. The pipe had dropped from his teeth. It could not have dangled very long, yet the bowl was the coldest thing Denis had touched that day. Well, it was lucky he had not set fire to himself; and since the others were still stretched in slumber, the steward on his blanket near the door, it could not be very late. Time enough at least to do what he had intended doing without disturbing them—and with a bound Denis was in the middle of the floor.

The packet was not on the table where he had left it. Had he left it there? He tore the blankets off his bed in the wild hope of finding it there. No; he remembered keeping his eye on it as he lay back smoking like a sot. In an instant the things were swept off the table in a vain search for the little brown-paper parcel. All this time Denis was venting his feelings in little involuntary cries, but now he called the other two by their names. They stirred uneasily without waking.

Denis began to guess what had happened. His mouth was dry and his head heavy. The light had altered. Outside the shadows had run like ink, and by the watch it was almost five o'clock. A three hours' sleep instead of one! And his packet gone with the time for posting it!

He searched further before finally rousing his companions; and there were signs that the whole place had been carefully ransacked, but none as yet that anything else had disappeared. Denis was equally thankful that he had got rid of the gold-dust and that cash payment was still to come; after all, the value of the nugget was chiefly sentimental; and there was some compensation in the thought that the thief could not have chosen a worse time for himself or a better one for his victims.

"Robbed!" echoed Doherty, sitting up stupidly at last. His eyes had lost all their brightness, and he was soon nursing his head between his hands. But Jewson was quicker to grasp what had happened—quicker than Denis himself.

"That yellow devil of a Chinaman!" he exclaimed, and sat smacking his lips with a wry face. "Opium! I thought so! I've known the taste too many years; but I'll know him when I see him again, and I'll string him up to the nearest tree by his own pig-tail. Draught beer, eh? I wonder who else he offered it to? See what comes of striking it rich and letting it get about that you have struck it! No, I know you can't help it, unless you've got a private river to wash your dirt in; but that's what's done it, as sure as I'm standing here."

"But you are not standing there," rejoined Denis, as the servant made for the door. "Where are you off to in such a hurry?"

"To lay my hands on John Chinaman!" answered Jewson with an oath. "To catch him red-handed with your nugget on him, and to ram his own pig-tail down his yellow throat!"

The partners were left looking at each other with rather different expressions.

"He'll do it, too," said Doherty, jerking his head toward the door. "Trust the old steward!"

"I suppose one must trust him," remarked Denis in a dubious tone.

"Trust him? Of course you must! Why not, mister? Hasn't he looked after us well enough so far? Hasn't he made all the difference in the world to us, and haven't you admitted it every day? I don't care what he was at sea; let's take him as we find him ashore, and then we sha'n't get wrong. You don't seriously think the steward's had anything to do with this, do you?"

"Not seriously," replied Denis; nor, on reflection, had he the smallest ground for any such suspicion.

"Because," pursued Doherty, triumphantly, "if he wanted to put up a robbery, it's a funny thing he should wait until there was hardly anything to rob—isn't it?"

"Of course."

"And you've lost nothing except the nugget, have you?"

"And the parcel it was in, and my letter!"

"Perhaps he's a chap like me, wot can't read," the lad suggested by way of consolation. "But are you sure that's all you've missed?"

He was looking very hard at Denis.

"I think so, Jimmy. Why?"

"If you undo another shirt-button I'll tell you."

There was no need for Denis to do that. His fingers were down his neck in an instant. And the lanyard of his beloved's hair, which had encircled it day and night for the last three months, was gone with the little ring that Nan had given him at their farewell on board the Memnon.

His rage and distress knew no bounds; the loss of a far larger nugget had been a bagatelle compared with this. A certain superstition was ingrained in Denis; it was one of the few things he had inherited from both the races whose blood clashed in his veins; and in a moment it was as though his star had fallen from the zenith. Apart from the loss of that which he held dearer than aught but Nan herself—her talisman—there was the utter ill-omen of such a loss. And Denis raved about both, bidding Doherty find another mate as quick as he could, for they were at the end of their tether and would wash no more ounces.

"And if we did," cried the distracted fellow, "if we took out a million between us after this, it would only be to go home and find her dead! You make a note of it, and then clear out of the sinking ship. My luck has ended this day!"

Doherty bore it as long as he could, then jumped up saying he was going for the police. "Not for you," he added, "though you deserve the Logs if ever a man did. I've heard a blackfellow talk like that, but not a white man, and may I never hear the like again! We'll have the traps on the track of that Chinaman, as well as Jewson; and we'll get back what you've lost for its own sake, not for what it can't alter one way or the other."

This bracing remonstrance was not without effect. Denis controlled himself by an effort, dashed away an unmanning tear, and was soon the severest critic of his own despair; but he would not let Doherty summon the police, neither would he go himself.

"It is too intimate—too sacred—her hair!" he whispered in a fresh access of misery. "Fancy furnishing a description of that, and letting them publish it broadcast! No, no; better lose it altogether; and may the thief never dream what it was he took!"

"Then where are you going?" asked Doherty, following Denis as he strode out of the hut.

"Down the shaft, to start the tunneling, and to try just one tub before six, to see if the luck has changed or not."

While he was down, Doherty, waiting at the windlass, received a visit from the friendly neighbour who had kept an eye on their cradle at the creek. He said that one of his mates was minding it still, but as no one had been near it all the afternoon, and nothing seemed doing on the claim, he had just come to see if anything was amiss. The man was a genial, broad-shouldered, black-bearded digger of a rough but excellent type, and on reflection Doherty told him of the drugged beer and the resultant loss of the nugget, but of nothing else. The digger seemed considerably interested, asked several questions, and good-naturedly lent a hand to raise Denis from the depths.

"I've just been hearing of your loss," said he, "and I congratulate you! It's not many lucky diggers whose luck attracts the light-fingered gentry and who only lose a four-ounce nugget after all! So that cook of yours has gone to look for the Chinaman?"

"Yes."

"I hope he'll find him," said the burly digger, and went off with a dry smile and a good-humoured nod.

But it was no Chinaman whom Jewson had gone to seek; it was a gentlemanly digger of peculiarly British appearance, with military whiskers which had never been allowed to meet upon the chin; and he was found waiting at the place where the special coach with the English mail was due to start for Melbourne at six o'clock.

"At last!" said he in an ungracious undertone. "What happened to you, Jewson? I had given you up altogether."

"I thought he'd never wake up," whispered Jewson as they drew aside, "and I dursn't run the risk of his finding me gone, as well as—as well as this, sir!"

"What the devil are you talking about, Jewson? And what's that?"

It was a small brown-paper parcel which the steward had produced.

"Something you're going to be so kind as to post and register in Melbourne, sir. In Melbourne, mind— not in London, Captain Devenish!"

"But it's addressed—why, damme, it's addressed to Miss Merridew!"

"I know that, sir."

"Who addressed it?"

"The clever bloke who thinks he's going to marry her," answered Jewson through his artificial teeth. "Clever he may be," he added, "and successful he is, but he ain't so clever that he's going to succeed in that!"

Devenish took heart from the cunning and confident face raised so slyly to his. Yet his heart of hearts sank within him, for it was still not utterly debased, and his compact with this ruffian was a heaviness to him. "What do you mean by asking me to post his presents to her?" he demanded angrily; but his anger was due less to the request than to the underlying subtlety which he felt he had far better not seek to probe.

"I'm not going to tell you, Captain Devenish. You said you'd leave it to me, sir."

"But it is something from him to her?"

"That I promise you; but it'll tell its own tale, and you'll hear it soon enough, once you get home safe and sound."

The driver had mounted to his place, the five horses had been put to. Devenish hesitated with the little brown paper packet in his hand.

"And she really ought to have it?"

"It's only due to her, poor young lady."

"But to me? Is it due to me, man?"

"It'll do you more good, sir," said Jewson, raising his crafty eyes, "than ever anything did you yet, in that quarter, Captain Devenish."

Ralph put the packet in an inner pocket. "Well, I'll think about it," said he. But he did not take the hand that was held out to him. He went from Ballarat with no more than a nod to the man whom he was leaving there to play a villain's part on his behalf. It was enough for Ralph Devenish that he had soiled his soul.

CHAPTER XXI

THE COURIER OF DEATH

Denis passed many days underground, in the fascinating pursuit of driving a tiny tunnel due south from the bottom of the shaft. That way ran the lead as traced already on its outer skirts, and that way burrowed Denis through its golden core. The miniature corridor which he made was but two feet wide, and not six inches higher than its width. Denis could just turn round in it by a series of systematic contortions.

He would have made the drive roomier but for an early warning as to the treacherous character of the red clay stratum immediately overhead. Thereafter he confined his operations to the lower half of the auriferous drift, which being gravelly, was more or less conglomerate, and formed a continuous arch corresponding with the brickwork in a railway tunnel. The drive was not timbered like the shaft which led to it, but at intervals props were wedged against the walls, with flat wooden caps to support the roof. Yet the task seemed to Denis too precarious to depute, and worming every inch of his way, it took him till February to penetrate fifteen feet.

Doherty was consoled by a position of much responsibility above ground: he had the washing of every bucketful which came out of the drive, and he also was single-handed, but for some help at the water-side from the friendly fellow with the black beard, whose offices he was able to repay in kind. The creek hereabouts was more populous now than the partners had found it. Their success had had the usual effect of attracting numbers to the gulley. Some had taken possession of holes prematurely abandoned the year before, and were working them out in feverish haste; larger parties with plant and capital were rapidly sinking their seventy feet on the very edge of the successful claim. "We'll be down on top of you before you know where you are," said one of the newcomers when they heard the direction in which Denis was driving. Thereupon he redoubled his efforts to such purpose that Doherty could not keep pace with the output, and a stack of untried wash-dirt grew up beside the shaft. In spite of this the average yield in washen gold was many ounces a day. And daily Denis took it, his revolver in his pocket, to the Commissioner for transmission to Geelong, where the accredited gold-buyer had turned out so well that the partners no longer received his payments in cash, but had several thousands standing to their credit in his books.

Jewson was much subdued. There was something uncanny in the way this fortune was growing under his eyes, in spite of him. But he had his own reasons for undiminished confidence in the end which an undying grudge and innate cupidity alike demanded; meanwhile his honest emoluments were not to be despised, and he continued to earn them by the consistent exercise of his one accomplishment. His cooking was as good as ever, his behaviour even better, since the nocturnal excursions were a thing of the past. This circumstance was too much of a coincidence to decrease Denis's suspicions; on the other hand, nothing occurred to increase them, and Denis was not sorry for that. The man was invaluable. So much labour underground must have been deadly in its effects without regular supplies of proper food properly cooked. And there the steward never failed. But Denis had his eye on him, and was wise enough never to betray whatever suspicion he had entertained with regard to Jewson's complicity in the theft of the nugget and the ring.

Jewson naturally thought that matter had blown over; but one morning, as he was happily occupied with the duties which he really relished for their own sake, the door darkened as a pair of broad shoulders jammed between the posts; and the steward found himself confronted by a blue-black beard which contrasted invidiously with the unwilling whiteness of his own.

"Well," said a voice of grim good-humour, "have you found him yet?"

"What are you talking about?" replied the steward, testily. "Who are you—and what do you want?"

"Never you mind who I am," said the big man at the door. "You've seen me afore, and I've seen more of you than you might think. What I want is to know whether you ever found the Chinaman you went lookin' for a month ago; and that's what I be talkin' about. So now you know."

The steward stood at the table with his wicked head on one side, considering rapidly while he affected to ransack his memory.

"You mean the Chinaman who sold the doctored beer?"

"I mean the Chinaman who sold you the beer that got doctored."

"No—I never could lay hold of him," said the steward, ignoring the pointed improvement upon his phrase.

"Well, I have," said the big miner in the doorway.

"You've laid hold of him?" the other queried in nervous incredulity.

The digger nodded a big black head that looked as picturesque as piratical in a knitted cap of bright scarlet.

"I'd been lookin' for him, too, you see. You weren't the only folks who had some beer off that Chinaman the day he come along first; me and my mates had some, and it did us so little harm that we've always wanted some more. So I've been lookin' for him ever since, and yesterday I found him at the other end o' the diggin's, away past Sailor's Gully. And why do you suppose he'd never been near us again?" asked the big black man without shifting a shoulder from either door-post.

"I don't know," said the steward, sulkily. "How should I?"

"How should you? Because you told him never to come no more!"

"He's a liar," hissed Jewson, with a tremulous oath.

"And why should you say he ever came at all?"

"Some other lie, I suppose," said Jewson, with another oath.

"Because you told him to: went to the other end o' the diggin's to find him; bought a bit of opium from him, and told him to bring the beer next day. Oh, yes, they may be all lies," said the big digger, cheerfully, "but then again they may not. It's a rum world, mate, especially on the diggin's. I've known worse things done by coves I wouldn't have thought it of; but by the cut of your jib I should say you was capable of a good lot. Boss down driving, I suppose?"

"Like to go down and tell him now—like me to let you down?" asked Jewson, with a venomous glitter in his little eyes.

The digger laughed heartily in his face.

"No, thank you—not without a third party handy to keep you from meddling with the rope! But I can wait, my friend, and I can come again. My claim's not so far away, and I'll be back at dinner-time if not before. Of course, they may be lies as you say; a Chinaman's a Chinaman, and that's why I come along now to have a quiet word with you first. But by the colour o' your gills, old cock, I don't believe they are lies. So now you know what's before you when your boss comes up. He may believe you and send me to the devil, but he's got to hear my yarn and judge for himself. So there it is. I like to give a man fair warning, and that you've got."

The hut doorway was no longer obstructed. It framed once more a vivid panel of parched earth and blinding sky with a windlass and a stack of wash-dirt in the foreground. But the hut itself held a broken ruffian whose ruin stared him in the face.

One thing would lead to another, and the motive for the crime be readily deduced from the crime itself. Jewson saw his elaborate plot falling asunder like a house of cards, and involving himself in its destruction. Devenish had not been a month at sea; letters would chase him round the Horn, and the truth would reach England almost as soon as the lies. That marriage would never take place. That £2000 would never be paid. That hold upon a young married man of means and of position would not be given to Jewson as a lifelong asset after all. On the contrary, the petty theft might be brought home to him, and he might go to the hulks off Williamstown instead of back to England with an assured competence for his declining years. He did not believe this could happen to him—he was a far-seeing rogue—but the rest would follow as surely as Denis came up from the depths and the informer returned to keep his word.

Flight seemed the only course; a successful flight would at least avert the most unpleasant possibilities of the case. But darker thoughts passed through the steward's mind, and took him stealthily to the mouth of the shaft. A dull yet distinct chip-chipping was audible far below and out of sight along the drive. If only that sound could cease forever! If only the maker of the sound were never to come up alive! Then everything would be simplified; and Captain Devenish need not know of his death for years. Besides, it was an accidental death of which Jewson was thinking; he had looked at the rope with the bucket hanging to it, but only to remember that one man at least was prepared for even that villainy at his hands. Jewson shook his head. He was not so bad as all that. He was really only a potential criminal, who had seldom put himself within reach of the law. He might wish that the shaft would fall in and bury his enemy, but he was no murderer even in his heart.

Suddenly he gave a start, and then stood very still; stepping softly to the far side of the shaft, he had come suddenly upon a huge snake curled up and basking on the hard hot ground. It was not the sight, however, that made Jewson shiver; that was not particularly uncommon or untoward; the chilling thing was the thought that had flown into the breast which had not been that of a murderer before. Now it was; but even now the mean monster did not realize that the temptation upon him was the temptation of Cain; and he yielded to it, villain as he was, with eyes shut to the enormity.

The dangling bucket was gently lifted from its hook, was nimbly clapped upon the sleeping serpent, and kept in position with one foot; striding with the other to within reach of the heap of wash-dirt, the steward filled his hat with this, and then reversing the bucket with equal courage and dexterity, had the snake buried in the stuff in an instant, and the bucket back on its hook in another. A quick swing over the side of the shaft, and down went the bucket of its own weight, with the snake already hanging over one edge. But Jewson let every inch of the rope run red-hot through his hands, to lessen the noise of the windlass; and yet when it reached the bottom, gently, very gently, there was the chip-chipping still to be heard in the bowels of the drift.

Jewson held the bucket, as near as he could judge, within a few inches of the bottom of the shaft; when it lightened he went to the handle of the windlass and turned it slowly, so slowly that it came up without a creak, but also so slowly that minutes passed in the operation. When it was up he flung out the wash-dirt, replaced the bucket on its hook, and craned his neck over the lip of the shaft, to listen, and to peer.

A very faint light came from the single candle which Denis took with him along the drive; it just glimmered upon the floor of the shaft, and on the wall opposite the drive; but in the glimmer nothing moved, and nothing shone.

The steward closed his eyes and put a hand to either ear. The chip-chipping had ceased. There was no sound at all. And then, but not till then, did the criminal realize his crime.

He drew himself up with an uncontrollable shudder, and looked quickly on all sides of him. The sun was high in the deep blue heavens. The white tents in the gully shimmered in its glare. No one was about on the next claim; all were underground, or at the creek; no human eye had seen the deed.

Yet the skin tightened on the murderer's skull, a baleful dew broke out upon it, and the little eyes for once grew large with horror.

CHAPTER XXII

ATRA CURA

There are few more attractive houses near London than one that shall be nameless in these pages: enough that it lends the beauty of mellow brick and sunken tile to a hill-top already picturesquely wooded, but a dozen miles from the Marble Arch, yet in the country's very heart, on a main road where the inquisitive may still discover it for themselves. They will have to choose, it is true, between several old houses of rosy brick, all of them overrun with the rose itself, and all standing rather too near the road. The house in question is the one that has no other fault. It is the house with the plate-glass porch, the wide bay on either side, the luniform bay behind; at the back also are a noble lawn, several meadows, and a singular avenue, so narrow that the tall trees meet overhead as one. Other features are a rose garden, enclosed in the ripest of all the old red walls, and a model farm.

To this pleasant English home Mr. Merridew and his daughter returned in the month of February, after a wearisome but uneventful voyage and a week or two at the St. George's Hotel as a corrective. A distinguished physician had prescribed a month; but in ten days Nan had all the new clothes she needed, had seen all the plays she cared to see, and went in such fear of a certain topic of conversation, forced upon her by the heedless, that it was anguish to her to go about. So one of the carriages came up from Hertfordshire, and on a clear but chilly afternoon father and daughter drove home together.

It was not a hearty homecoming. John Merridew had been many years a widower, whose only other child had died in infancy. But the old red house looked warm and kindly; the servants stood weeping through their smiles; the firelit rooms were all unchanged, save in their new promise of perfect privacy; and in her home it was grasped from the first that Miss Merridew could not bear to speak about the wreck of the North Foreland and her own romantic rescue by one of the officers. Thus she had no occasion to explain that she was engaged to him; and Mr. Merridew left the announcement to Nan.

"She has nothing on her mind, has she?" inquired old Dr. Stone after an early call as physician and friend.

"She has the wreck on her mind," replied Mr. Merridew promptly. "She can't even speak of it, as you may have noticed."

"I did notice, and that's why I ask. I saw the child into this world, my dear Merridew, and I want to dance at her wedding before I move on to the next. She didn't give her heart for her life, I suppose?"

"You must ask her that yourself, doctor," the discreet father replied, meeting a penetrating look with a laugh. And a firm old friend retired dissatisfied and rather hurt. But so the engagement was kept a secret from the first.

It is none the less safe to assert that there was not a waking hour of these early days in which the girl was oblivious of her new estate. It weighed on her mind far more than it had done at sea, though there she had missed Denis dreadfully, and sometimes with a resentment which she could not help. She had formed a habit of thinking in these moods of her last conversation with Ralph Devenish; it was the only cure. But fresh cause for displeasure awaited her in London. The voyage had been so long that certain Australian packets had given the Memnon a start and a beating; when Nan learned this she counted on a letter, but there was none. She studied the shipping news in the Times. More vessels arrived from Melbourne, but from Denis never a word. Sometimes the disappointment made her positively ill; always it left her tossing between the Scylla and Charybdis of terrible alternatives. Either he was indifferent, or else he was dead. And when she deemed him indifferent, there were things unforgettable that made her almost wish him dead; but when the terror of his death came over her in its turn, then she prayed less for his love than for his life.

So the days passed, and the sea-bronze soon faded from the piquant face, leaving it pale but petulant. Nan had not lost her spirit; she was one to chafe rather than to fret, but to do neither more openly than she could help. She kept herself up by exercise and fresh air. It was hard, bright weather, a little wintry still, yet with that promise of spring inseparable from the longer day and the lighter sky. There were even twigs with green tips to them, and the chestnut branches ended in sticky cones. But Nan thought of the spring before, when she had met with no adventures and had not become engaged; her obsession followed her to all her favourite places; and in her daily ride along the hard, clean roads, the black imp kept its perch.

Mr. Merridew was not the man to note all this and hold his peace, for he had small tact where his feelings were engaged; but he was so little at home that it was easy to deceive him; and his first conversation with Nan on the subject was really started in the city, where his partner, Ralph's father, had been inveighing against the Dents with the unbridled bitterness begotten of a family feud.

"To think of the son of that marriage sneaking into our line, under his own accursed name! It's so common; and I had no idea the fellow was at sea; but now I know how we lost our ship. You may shake your head, Merridew; wasn't she lost in his watch? You don't know the breed as I know it, and I suppose you're grateful to the fellow. But what good object could he have had in choosing our line of all others?"

"To rise in it," replied Merridew with some warmth: "to be revenged on you that way, not the other. And I happen to know, because he told Nan."

"Told her that, did he? After the wreck, I take it, when decency obliged you all to listen to the fellow? By the Lord, but you were lucky if that's all he told her! His father would have taken advantage of the situation, and married himself into the family before you knew where you were!"

It was no mere lack of moral courage that deterred John Merridew from the admission which rose naturally to his lips. He no longer regarded as inevitable the marriage to which he had consented in his agitation after the wreck, and to mention it to Ralph's father, when Ralph himself had evidently not done so in his letters, seemed an altogether needless indiscretion. He was, however, a peculiarly conscientious man, who would have much preferred to have stated the fact; not having done so, he had a curious desire to alter the fact to suit his silence; and so struck his first blow at Denis, more heavily than he intended, that very night.

"No," said Nan in answer to his question. "No, I have not heard from him yet."

"Not a word?"

"Not yet, papa. Surely you knew? You may be certain I shall not keep it to myself when I do hear."

There was a double reproach, of which her father felt his share, in the sudden bitterness with which the girl spoke. But John Merridew had now convinced himself that he had a parental duty to perform, that cruelty was the only kindness, and some little exaggeration justifiable to that end.

"It is most extraordinary," he murmured. "I never heard of a more extraordinary thing!"

"I don't see that at all," replied Nan, hotly. "You know what he is doing, and I know he is doing it with all his might. What time can he have for letters—digging all day—and what opportunity—living in a hut?"

"But that's what is so extraordinary," pursued Mr. Merridew. "That he should have elected to stay behind to do all that!"

"You know it was for my sake!" exclaimed the girl, tears in her eyes. "Oh, you are unkind to us both! He would not marry until he had something to marry on, something of his own; and there he was where people were making fortunes in a day! Whatever I may feel, you ought to respect him for doing what he has done. But it shouldn't have been necessary for him to do it, and you were the one to make it unnecessary."

"I?" cried Mr. Merridew, quite taken aback. "Why, my dear child, what more could I have done?"

"You might have taken him into the office; you might have promised him a partnership one day. If he doesn't deserve well of you, I don't know who does; and you know how clever he is, and how he would have worked to deserve all the more! It might have been an unusual thing to do," Nan added, with a sudden sense that she was talking wildly. "Nevertheless, I have always thought it a thing you might have done."

She had, indeed, thought it for some time; but, after all, the notion had first occurred to Mr. Merridew himself; and in all the circumstances he was not disposed to suppress the fact another moment.

"My dearest Nan," said he, gently, "it is the very thing I did!"

She looked at him with blank, unseeing eyes.

"What do you mean, papa?"

"I actually offered him that very opening, with every prospect of partnership that single partner could hold out."

"When?" asked Nan after a further pause. Her voice had changed.

"The first time I saw him after the wreck. It was too late. He had heard of the diggings, and he would hear of nothing else."

"Why did you never tell me before?"

"My dear child, need you ask? I thought it would hurt you," said Mr. Merridew; and the tender compassion in his voice was not unmingled with remorse, for Nan had turned very pale, and her lip quivered.

"It does," she said, simply. "No doubt that was why he did not tell me either," she added, and the quivering lip curled. In a minute she crossed over to her father's chair and kissed him without emotion. "I am afraid I have been very rude, besides misjudging you so strangely. But—but don't let us misjudge anybody else until we must—or speak of him again until we hear."

But it was harder now to believe the best, harder yet to look back without a passionate shame and indignation which in their intensity surpassed all that the girl had yet endured. She came down paler and paler in the mornings. It was because she had lain such a fiery red half the night—in the ti-tree thicket of her waking nightmare. She could not know how her feelings had been foreseen, nay, endured from the first on her behalf. She only knew that never in the morning was there the letter for which she looked— and almost loathed herself for looking—nor yet ever toward evening, when the postman came again, and Nan watched for him, openly or in hiding as pride or passion might prevail.

All this time, but now more than ever, the girl filled her life with a resolution which declared her calibre. She regained touch with her friends throughout the countryside. She visited the villagers, managed her father's house with increased capability, and no longer discouraged him from entertaining, as her inclination had been for a time. People who stayed in the house found its young mistress brighter in a way than they had ever known her. But that was the form of hospitality Nan relished least. As spring advanced she was more and more out of doors, on horseback or afoot; but in the open air she still preferred to be alone, and would advertise the fact by carrying a book on all her walks. She had taken to reading as she had never read before, in a way at once desultory and omnivorous. And it was in a tome from her father's shelves, to wit Southey's "Early British Poets," that a sudden beam of comfort and enlightenment shot into her soul from the immortal lines of Lovelace to Lucasta:—

"Yet this inconstancy is such, As you too shall adore; I could not love thee, dear, so much, Lov'd I not honour more."

Nan knew the lines as a quotation. Why, why had she ever forgotten them? Why had she never once thought of them in all these weeks of doubt and pain? They put the case for Denis in a nutshell; and the quatrains before the quotation were hardly less poignant in their appeal, though Denis's "new mistress" was not war but wealth. Ah, if it had been war! And war was already in the whole air of England; but on the gold-fields there was no reason to think him other than safe and sound.

So powerfully was she affected and inspired that Nan showed the lines to her father that night. It had often troubled her that he must think ill of Denis; that was a more hurtful thing than thinking ill of him herself—who had the right. So she showed the open book to Mr. Merridew, counting unconsciously on his sentimental side, and not in vain.

"There," she said, "that is what I have been wanting to say for him all these weeks. There speaks Denis himself. He has called to me from the other end of the world. I was thinking of him when I went for a book, and I put my hand on this one, and I opened it at this place!"

Mr. Merridew was full of sympathy—a quality in which he was rarely deficient when there was trouble in the air; besides, he cherished the most genuine desire for his daughter's happiness. If she could be happy believing in Dent, well and good, and it might all come right yet. The great thing was that despite her energies she had been pensive and wan for many a day, but that now she was flushed and bright.

"Believe in him, dear!" she whispered in her father's ear, her arm round his neck.

"I always did, Nan," he answered, stroking her hair.

"No, not always; but you did once, and you will again."

"Very well, Nan."

"From this moment!"

"No; not from this moment," said Mr. Merridew, characteristically seeking to justify his former asseveration, "when not for a single moment have I ceased to bless him for preserving my darling's life. How could I disbelieve in him in my heart after that? If I have ever done so it has been when I have seen you sad and sorry. But when I think of all he did for you—"

"Don't; please don't!"

Her face was hidden against him. He might have felt its heat. But it was in the plain troubles only that he was a sympathetic man.

"But I must," he rejoined cheerily. "We must not forget all he did, and I am afraid we have. Why, Nan, what is it?"

"I am going."

"But why? What have I said?"

"Nothing—nothing—only I wish he had let me drown—I wish that!"

And with this hard saying the girl was gone, with tears that puzzled John Merridew to his dying day, and flaming cheeks that dried them as they ran.

CHAPTER XXIII

BROKEN OFF

One afternoon Mr. Merridew came home in a state of suppressed excitement which was none the less manifest to Nan's first glance. It was late in April, and he found her on the lawn behind the house. Cuckoos were calling in the narrow avenue, now faintly dusted with palest gold; lesser trees had reached the stage of emeralds, and a horse-chestnut on the lawn was parading a thousand pairs of light-green gloves. The radiant afternoon sky changed into that of a serene evening as father and daughter stood face to face.

"Who do you think arrived in London this morning? Ralph Devenish!" he said, speaking the name in haste as her colour went.

"Indeed!" she remarked, and bit her lip to hide the hope that she had cherished for one instant.

"Poor fellow," continued Mr. Merridew, with his facile sympathy for the luckless, "he is terribly upset! The last English news he had on sailing was not later than last October; of course they touched nowhere, so he had no idea there was war with Russia until this morning. It is his battalion of the Grenadiers that went to the Black Sea with the rest of the Guards two months ago; and here he has been cooling his heels in perfect innocence at sea! Of course he reported himself without a minute's delay to the authorities, and now awaits their pleasure in a perfect fever of disappointment and professional ardour. He says he has been in the service all these years without hearing an angry shot, and now after all he may miss the fun! A gallant soldier, Nan, whatever else he may be!"

"I should hope so," the girl said, simply and without scorn. Her mind had not crossed the seas with Ralph. "Did he really go to the diggings?" she asked in a constrained voice.

"Yes, and did very fairly there; what is more, my dear, he saw something of Denis Dent."

The girl was galvanized. "Was he well?" she whispered in a breath.

"Perfectly, when Ralph left, which was only in January."

Nan filled her lungs, and for the moment her soul sang praises; but for a moment only. If he was well, why had he never written? Her indignation had free play for the first time in all these months; she could better have borne to hear he had been ill, if only he were well again; for then she could have understood, then there would have been nothing to forgive.

"He was not only well," continued Mr. Merridew, with outward reluctance, not altogether an affectation, "but he was doing uncommonly well—far better than poor Ralph!"

Doing uncommonly well! And yet he could not write.

"And where is Ralph?" asked Nan, in a hard voice, and with that old hard light in her hazel eyes.

Mr. Merridew stood covered with a guilty confusion.

"Nan, would you see him if he came to see you?"

"Of course I would. Why not? I should like to see Ralph particularly."

"My dear, he didn't know; he was greatly afraid it would be just the other way. But since you say that, I must tell you he is within a hundred yards of where you stand, waiting in the road to know whether you would see him or not."

Nan was annoyed at this; it was giving romantic colour to a meeting which should have been perfectly natural and dispassionate on both sides; and on hers it was too dispassionate, and not natural enough, in consequence. Yet she wore a flush which might have flattered a less vain man than Ralph Devenish; and as for him he looked nicer than she had ever known him, in the shabby suit which was the best that remained of his Australian outfit, with the deep bronze upon his sallow face, and with inches added to his splendid whiskers. There was also, in him, a strange absence of arrière-pensée, psychologically more interesting than she dreamed; it was he who told her of Denis, unasked, in perhaps his second breath.

"Oh, I did decently," said Ralph, "and might have done really well had I stuck to it. But that cousin of mine—that's the man! He had some luck, though no more than he deserved; but when I came away he was the talk of his gully, to say the least. If he has realized half the prophecies I heard before I left he must be a wealthy man by this time."

"Do you mean to say he has been lucky from the beginning?" asked Nan, her incredulity strangely tinctured with disgust; and she brightened as perversely when she heard the truth. For it was the truth about Denis, so far as he knew it, that Ralph told Nan this April evening. He was cast for he knew not what part of bold duplicity; all he saw clearly was the end, and to that he was prepared to plough his way through all dishonour, as a traveler steels himself against every obstacle between him and the one light twinkling through the trees. The light was very brilliant in this sweet spring dusk, before his eyes yet not within his reach. It dazzled him, the light of the face he loved; and love he did, the more passionately, not the less, for the sacrifice of his honour that he had made already in his heart. To look through the sweet English dusk into her eyes, to hear her voice through the evensong of the dear old English birds, was to feel a final hardening of every unscrupulous resolve. And yet honour dies hard in the type to which Ralph Devenish belonged; it was dying so hard in Ralph that he was glad to tell the truth while he might, glad to speak well and kindly of the man he was to thwart in life by fair means or by foul.

So Nan heard of Denis's early unsuccess, and was thankful; a proud silence she could understand and might learn to forgive. And she was only less grateful for the way Ralph spoke of him; yet be it remembered to Ralph's credit, or what was left of it, that his tone, if assumed, was no device to win Nan's gratitude as it actually did.

Her satisfaction diminished as she heard of the wonderful doings on the new claim. Yet, after all, he had only been there a fortnight when Ralph left, and so immediate a success would in itself account for much. It must absorb every energy and every hour.

"Hand over fist!" said Ralph, laughing genially. "That's how the fellow was taking out the gold when I came away; at least, so I heard."

"Then you didn't see much of him yourself?"

"No, not much."

He might have added "naturally"; but the word was implied in his tone, which itself was as natural as could be. Nan noted and admired it. She was becoming more and more impressed with the general improvement in her companion. But it was another thought that kept her silent as they strolled to and fro upon the twilit sward.

"I suppose it is all in gold-dust," she speculated. "I know it is not in nuggets."

"Oh, isn't it?" he said quickly. "Then you have heard?"

Nan bit her lip.

"No, I have not heard, and you know I haven't!" she exclaimed with more tartness than discretion.

"My dear Nan, how could I know?" he asked, and with the utmost readiness, though her father had lost no time in informing him of the fact.

"I thought you must know," she said with a sigh that touched him and yet rankled. "I beg your pardon, Ralph. As for the nuggets, he promised to send me the first one he found, for luck; and he never broke a promise in his life."

"Perhaps it was too big to send," said Ralph, with his new and kindly laugh. "Or perhaps," he added, stopping in his walk, "perhaps this is it!"

A parlour-maid was approaching with a small salver. Nan raised her downcast eyes, and at a glance stood rooted to the spot. There was no letter on the salver, but there was a very small brown-paper parcel, which Nan seized and held in the half-light to her dancing eyes. And then for one unconscious instant she pressed it with both hands to her bosom.

"Oh, Ralph!" she cried in a voice like the song of a lark. "Did you ever hear of such a coincidence in your life? It isn't one—it's a miracle! Look: his writing, the Melbourne postmark: the nugget he promised me, come as we were speaking about it, from the other end of the world!"

Ralph set his teeth grimly; he had brought these confidences on himself, and Heaven alone knew how much more. He had not tampered with the parcel which Jewson had given him before he left the diggings; here it was as he had posted it in Melbourne, as it had lain in its mail-bag between the same wooden walls which had been his own prison for the last three months. He had no idea what the parcel contained; from Jewson's face and manner, as he remembered them at the last, Ralph did not think it was the nugget. But with a villain like that you never knew: he might have gone straight over to the other side, the richer side even then.

Nan was too excited to notice Ralph's excitement, and yet it was greater than hers. In her heart there was no longer the least suspense. This was the nugget. She was alive once more; and the world she had maligned in her heart, it was a dear world after all. Neither was Ralph its least dear denizen. Here was his penknife, out in a moment, one blade open; she never noted how it trembled as it cut the string. She was even unaware that Ralph stood looking over her shoulder, for it was by pure instinct that she had turned away.

Nor was there much for Ralph to see: what he first perceived was the difference in Nan. She was standing as in stone or wax, as breathless, as motionless, as unbending, as unalive to the eye. Over her shoulder, as in a waxen palm, he saw the glint and glimmer of a ring with three small stones of different hues. Then something fell, and he stooped to pick it up. In an instant her heel was on it, crushing it into the soft grass, but not before he had looked upon a plaited guard of finest hair. The shade was her own dark-gold; it seemed to Devenish that the very curl of her ringlets was preserved in the plaited wisp which he saw for an instant in the grass. He had the tact to pretend he had not seen it, to turn away and search further afield. But in his heart he was raging and railing against the author of this unforeseen infamy. What a devilish dodge! What a cruel and what a dastardly deception! Had he known of it he never would have posted the thing; and yet, now that he did know, was he to tell her? If so, what was he to tell?

The parcel might have been made up by Denis, for all Ralph actually knew. Denis might be false for all he knew, the traditional sailor with the wife in every port. Ralph's heart lightened at the thought; after all, how could he know? It was the triumph of a diabolical genius that he could know nothing absolutely, that he could lay this unction to his soul at every step, if he lacked the pluck to look his villainy in the face. And for the moment his embarrassment made Ralph Devenish as mean a villain as crawled the earth.

Nan was speaking. She might have been yards away instead of inches. He heard her faintly as he groped.

"What are you doing? I found what I dropped. Thanks for troubling. I am going in, I think. There—there was no letter after all." So she explained the heart-break in her voice; nothing else would have betrayed her.

She found herself in her room. The candles were lighted. Yes, that was her face, and she could look in it calmly, more calmly than many a time in her suspense. Her shame was not deeper than it had been ever since the day of her deplorable escape from kindly death. To know the worst is often less terrible than to fear it. That is one of Nature's mercies, and Nan felt it in a moment. She was blessed with the strong heart and the clear eye. She saw everything that was to be seen of her case, and she flinched at nothing that she saw. Only, as she sat before her glass in the chilly candle-light, she seemed to be looking upon another person, and into another heart.

An hour later she was shining with a hard radiance at the little dinner-table. Fine wines were brought up in the wanderer's honour; for once Nan let them fill her glass. Her mood was not unlike that of Ralph. He was equally determined to talk and not to think. They rattled on together like the oldest and the warmest friends. She sympathized with his disappointment and anxiety about the war, but hoped they would not send him out too soon, and could have groaned when he told her with airy cunning that it was quite on the cards that they might not meet again. He took her out of herself; he also gave her an unreasonable sense of retaliation. She certainly desired to see him again, and told him so frankly when he left.

Mr. Merridew was too puzzled to enjoy the other sensations which knocked for admittance to his mind. Devenish had told him nothing of the garden incident, partly from instinctive discretion, partly from a reluctance to enlarge the circle of his dupes before he must; but no sooner was he gone than Nan beckoned her father into the drawing-room and shut the door behind them both.

"Here is a ring," she said. "I want you to keep it for me in your safe—at least, for Mr. Dent."

It was not the ring that had traveled back to her from Ballarat. It was his father's ring, that Denis had lent her. And she had worn it about her neck since landing in England, because that was the way he was forced to wear hers, and it was nearer her heart, but away from prying eyes. Mr. Merridew took it between finger and thumb.

"Mr. Dent!" he echoed. "What in the world has happened?"

"Nothing terrible; only our engagement is broken off."

"You have heard from him, then?"

"Yes, this evening."

"And this is how he breaks his insulting silence!"

Already the father was trembling with rage and indignation; the girl was curiously serene.

"He doesn't even break it," she said. "He simply does what we arranged that either of us should do if we ever changed. And he is quite right."

"Right!" cried Mr. Merridew. "Quite right? Is the girl gone mad? The heartless blackguard, the insolent snob! But you are well rid of him, you are well rid."

Nan recoiled, stricken but roused. "You hurt me once by reminding me of things," she said quickly, in a low and passionate voice. "Don't hurt me more by forcing me to remind you of them. We made our own arrangement in the after saloon on board the Memnon when we said good-bye. It has nothing to do with anybody else, and nobody else can say a word against him if I do not."

"And don't you?" he cried. "And do you mean to say you don't?"

"Not a syllable," said the girl. "He has done the honest thing."

"The honest thing!"

"He could not pretend if he would."

"And you don't despise him for it—you have no contempt for him?"

Nan looked steadily on her father's horror.

"I honour him for it, as I always have," she said.

CHAPTER XXIV

DEATH'S DOOR

Chip, chip, chip, rang the driving-pick along the top of the drive, as it pricked its way from left to right, leaving a chain of holes in the rude right-angle under the arch; and chip, chip, back the other way, between the holes, till they united in one curved crevice, wherein the fingers could be passed from wall to wall, and the continued stability of the roof felt with the knuckles. Then a spell of harder and less cautious hitting, an interval of falling chunk and showering gravel, a period of irritation to throat and eyes. Presently a downward stroke, with more power behind it the lower one got; and in the end an advance from top to bottom of as many inches as the introductory crevice had been deep. So slaved Denis in his drive; so was he slaving when Jewson just heard him from above, on the 7th of February, 1854.

It meant lying prone in the earth by the hour together, an elbow pillowed in the morning's débris, the body aching in every inch. It meant a complete skin of the mud of dust and dirt and copious perspiration. It meant an atmosphere heated and poisoned by the flame of a single candle, a tickling throat, a trickling eye, an intermittent rigour of the lower limbs, a daily foretaste of paralysis. But it also meant a continuous excitement and an enduring satisfaction which to Denis were worth all these evils at once and at their worst. The drift was as rich as ever; and now it needed neither pan nor cradle to tell him so. He knew it at a glance, knew it by the light of his solitary candle. So far the wash-dirt had yielded a little more or a little less to the tub; its outward characteristics had not altered; but they always might. At any moment, after the next blow with the driving-pick, or the next—or the next—a change might be observable. It could hardly be a change for the better; thus each unchanged handful was to the good, and the uncertainty of every minute its fascination. Leads and gutters were notoriously capricious, and Denis was prepared for any caprice but the one that he encountered this very morning.

He had prolonged the roof a few more inches; the new chain of holes had resolved itself into another semicircular crevice, and to the knuckles the fresh roof was as firm as the old. Denis was dealing the random blows which were always a relief to him after this niggling work, when suddenly nothing fell, but the pick-handle dragged at his hand. The point of the pick had stuck; he gave it a gentle unavailing tug, but it was high up under the arch, and he had to alter his position before he could pull with any power. By this time he was trembling like a leaf; and still the pick stuck fast.

He drew his legs up under him, left the pick embedded, and began prodding near it with his knife. Presently the knife stuck too; this was some inches under the pick, and he had to work the blade backward and forward to release the point.

Denis could hardly breathe.

It must be a nugget—it must—it must—and if a nugget then the largest found on Ballarat for a twelvemonth.

It might even rival the two giant nuggets, worth thousands apiece, got from Canadian Gully at the beginning of the previous year; the nuggets of which Doherty had spoken after the wreck; the nuggets which first inflamed them both!

With fingers and knife he scraped down to it, then felt it with his fingers, then scraped it with his knife; and the point of the knife, held close to the candle, showed a filament of virgin gold upon the steel.

Denis closed his eyes and breathed thanksgiving; then to the handle of the pick once more, to prize the great mass loose in its gravelly bed. A shower from the roof at once deterred him. There was no guessing the size of a nugget like this. Its incontinent removal might cause such a subsidence as to bury him alive in the moment of his triumph; cautious even then, Denis blew out the light, screwed himself round on his own acrobatic principle, and began a trip to the top for props.

What time was it? Had Doherty returned? Could he trust Jewson to raise him in the bucket? He was looking pathetically far ahead; but there was the mouth of the drive glimmering within a few feet of him, and as yet Denis had not noticed any novelty in the intervening ground.

Now he noticed it; there was a lump of something, and the lump was moving. Then it lay still, but strangely extended. And two glittering little eyes were gazing into his at not more than eighteen inches' range.

Denis knew them on the instant for the eyes of an enormous snake. The tapering tail ran back into the light at the tunnel's mouth, as a river reappears beyond its woods; it was beautifully marked to its gracefully writhing tip; its glossy scales, where the daylight caught them, were as a suit of silver mail. All this Denis noted without taking his eyes from the small malignant pair in the zone of darkness between him and the light. And he thought of everything; that he was stripped to the waist, and utterly unarmed; that he had left his very knife behind him, and why he had taken it out, and what else he was leaving for men to find beyond his body. What a death to die! What an inglorious end! Its bitter and gratuitous irony was a redeeming point rather than an aggravation to a mind already distorted by such a strain in such an hour.

His eyes still gazing into the eyes of death, he thought of the two pioneer prospectors of California who wandered finding nothing until one died by the way; the other had just strength to dig his grave; and in so doing his pick stuck into such a nugget as Denis himself had found, only to lose it with his life. He was not a very egotistical man. Yet it was a certain satisfaction to him to feel that he would pass into history with the other poor devil who changed places with the other nugget.

Whether minutes or only moments flew in such thoughts, Denis never knew; but at last the other eyes rose suddenly, as the serpent arched its neck to spring. Instinctively Denis followed suit, was felled to his face by the roof of the tunnel, and lay stunned as mercifully as beast for slaughter.

Much more mercifully; for the snake recoiled, first in fright, finally in disgust. The snake must kill its own. Denis owed his respite to that law of reptile nature; he seemed dead enough already.

But he was sufficiently alive long before he dared betray sign of life. Luckily he remembered everything in a flash; and so lay waiting for the last. One thing seemed certain: he had not been bitten yet. There was no sense of pain or swelling; no heavy coil oppressed his flesh; no jets of baleful breath played upon his skin; and in his near neighbourhood nothing stirred. But far away he fancied he could hear the slightest of sibilant sounds, and by degrees he opened his eyes. In his position he could not see many inches in front of him, but they were inches of bare ground. He raised his head imperceptibly: the snake was circling round the patch of daylight at the bottom of the shaft, gliding half its length up its slippery sides, darting its forked tongue out and in, and slowly moving its head as if seeking for some hole.

Denis considered without moving a muscle. If he were armed he would creep on his belly like the snake itself and trust to his dexterity to strike the first blow. But he was not armed. He had no weapon of any sort; the one good weapon in the drive was fast in the nugget—ah! The nugget! He had forgotten it; the remembrance was like a glass of spirit. There behind him, within reach almost of his feet, was the only weapon worth thinking about—worth an effort—worth a risk.

Very slowly, very laboriously, he crawled backward until his foot did touch the wooden haft of the driving-pick. The snake was still circling at the bottom of the shaft. Turning suddenly, seizing the haft with one hand, and the unburied end of the pick with the other, Denis twisted it as a gimlet, and had it out at one wrench. Simple though the expedient, it had only occurred to him as he crawled backward for his life.

Now he was crawling forward again, feeling his way with the pick, his open knife between his teeth; and he crawled with less caution, savouring the fight. The pick rang against a stone. The snake was aroused. Its body writhed in angry knots and circles, still in the square of daylight, but now with tongue darting and eyes piercing into the mouth of the tunnel at each contortion. Denis felt its body was about to follow, made the rush himself on hands and knees, frightened the enemy by so doing, and next instant had its neck nailed to the ground at one lucky blow; but as he scrambled out its folds flew round his leg, crushing it horribly and irresistibly drawing it towards its head. The blood ran down Denis's chin as he plucked the open knife from his teeth. Then the strong blade sawed through the slimy body a foot below the head. But for long the headless coils wrung the slayer's leg, while the forked tongue played in and out of the bleeding remnant on the ground.

At last he leaned lame but unencumbered against the side of the shaft. The sun was in the zenith; it lit the slabs on two sides half-way down. Denis knew the sunlight was there, though he could not lift his head to look on it again. He was sick, dizzy, and in pain; with more space or a less loathsome litter he would have stretched himself out where he was. As it was he hugged the slabs in a standing swoon until a voice came down to him from the mouth of the shaft.

"Mister! Mister! Dent! Denis!"

He reeled and raised a ghastly face.

"What's the matter down there?"

"Nothing; only I was nearly killed by a snake."

"A snake!"

"A carpet snake; but I killed it, thank God."

"A carpet snake!"

"Nearly eight feet long."

"Why, there's one up here about the same size, must be its mate. That one must have fallen down. I've killed this one!"

But the raised voice quavered; the lad was whimpering, shivering against the sky. Denis became himself.

"Let down the bucket, Jimmy."

"Oh! Oh! I haven't got the strength to draw you up, I know!"

"What's happened—what else?"

"It's Jewson," the boy's voice came blubbering down.

"What's happened to him?"

"The other snake was round him—and he doesn't move!"

CHAPTER XXV

BEAT OF DRUM

The imbroglio with Russia had at this time scarcely earned the name of war. Half-hearted hostilities there had been for months; but a halting diplomacy had not altogether abandoned its ineffectual functions, and even at the latter end of April a hope was breathed from the highest quarter that peace might still be restored between the contending countries. Little as yet was heard of the Crimea, much less of its invasion by the allies. But the Brigade of Guards was actually on its way from Malta to Scutari.

The uncertainty in the official mind was exemplified in the case of Captain Devenish, who, though unfeignedly eager to join his fortunate battalion on the Bosphorus, was provisionally attached to one of those remaining at Wellington Barracks. It is true that he was ordered to hold himself in readiness to embark at the shortest possible notice; but in the constant society of disgusted officers, who consoled themselves with the conviction that there would be no serious fighting after all, Ralph soon absorbed their views, and began to look upon himself as a permanent ornament to the streets of London and the lanes of Hertfordshire. It was only in Hertfordshire itself that he affected a different feeling, openly congratulating himself each week on his arrival, and seldom departing without some half-hopeful and half-heartbroken hint that it was very likely for the last time.

Not a week, in the beginning, without one of these visits; but erelong, scarcely a day. The extravagant fellow would arrive in hansoms at all hours, and go rattling back to barracks through the silent country in the middle of the night. Often he would stay; his room was always ready for him; but his goings and his comings were alike erratic, and that was part of their charm. In the very beginning he was never without some offering for Nan. She soon put a stop to that. The bustle and clatter and high spirits which he still brought with him, these were enough for the girl, who little dreamed of what nervous tension they were the outward and reactionary sign. Yet such was the explanation of the boisterous animation which so improved Devenish in her eyes, and it dated from the time when his visits became more frequent and irregular.

One lovely morning in early May, after a whole long Sunday spent with Nan, the visitor had been first abroad before breakfast, and by merest chance had met the postman at the gate. Without an evil thought, Ralph had taken the letters from him, only to behold one from Denis to Nan on top of the pile. He stood where he was until the postman's steps rang away into silence along the hard highway. It was Denis's writing, without a doubt: the superscription on the fraudulent parcel was written indelibly in Ralph's brain; this letter was directed in the same hand; it bore the new Ballarat postmark; and until the sight of it Ralph had almost forgotten there was such a place, or such a person as Denis Dent. He had been equally absorbed in town and in the country. The cloud of war had obscured the past; the sun of love had blinded him to its consequences. Even the soul-destroying thought of the packet he had posted—the packet with which Jewson had obviously tampered—the packet on whose changed contents he himself was trading every day—even the thought of that had quite ceased to bother Ralph. He was not a man of much imagination. Dent and Jewson were at the opposite end of the world, a hundred days' sail at a flattering average; what was the use of bothering about Jewson or Dent? Yet on Jewson he had been relying more than he knew until this moment. The dirty work had been left in Jewson's hands; but until now, when he saw an important branch of it neglected, Devenish had not chosen to realize what the dirty work would be. Here was a letter from Denis to Nan. It should never have been allowed to reach the post. Jewson was not to be trusted after all.

Standing there in the fresh May sunshine, his ears filled with the morning song of birds, his nostrils with the thousand scents of the countryside, Ralph Devenish, annoyed and nonplused as he well might be, was still a comparatively honest man. A certain element of self-deception lingered in his dishonour. At the worst he had been a passive traitor to this point: nor was the next step downward taken in cold blood. A window opened behind his back, and Nan's voice hailed him from her room.

"Anything for me, Ralph?"

He wheeled about, but approached the house slowly, shuffling the pack on his way.

"I'm afraid not; but there's one for me."

And he pocketed her letter under her eyes.

"A bothersome one?" she asked, looking down from her window upon his bent head and rounded shoulders.

"I'm afraid so, Nan."

He had not looked up.

"But you didn't open it, did you?"

"No—that's why!" he cried grimly; and pleased with his own readiness he could look up now and meet her eyes. "They sha'n't badger me down here," said Ralph. "It can keep until I get back to town."

But it kept as insecurely as skeleton in open cupboard; not a moment was the letter off his mind. He lodged it in his innermost pocket, yet could not restrain his fingers from feeling if it were there; he buttoned up his coat, only to feel outside. A bank-note for a thousand pounds would have burdened him less; for his embarrassment went beyond the moment; the worst part of it was undoubtedly to come. But he must know the worst, and to get at it he must glance at the letter first or last. That was an absolute necessity of the situation, and the exigency itself was to Ralph Devenish the worst of all. Was it not written that his honour was dying hard? It was not quite dead yet.

He must get back to town first thing, so he told them at the breakfast-table; but Nan, seeing his trouble, inveigled him into the garden for a last turn (it might always be the last indeed), and in the narrow avenue, now nearly covered in for the summer, abruptly asked him if he had opened his letter.

"Not yet," he answered hoarsely. "It can keep till I get back."

"But it is bothering you."

"I know."

"It may not prove as unpleasant as you imagine."

"That is unlikely."

"If I were you I should prefer to know the worst; and if I trusted any one as you say you trust me—"

"Trust you! Nan, I—"

He had halted abruptly; but it was her face that stopped his tongue.

"Hush!" she commanded. "I have heard enough of all that, enough to last me all my life; but if you trust me as a friend, as you've said you do and promised you will, you might take me into your trouble, open your letter, and let us face whatever it contains together."

His tongue clove in his head; with a ghastly laugh he managed to refuse at last. Her curiosity was now on fire. And to gratify the sudden passion she stooped to a level of which she was very soon and very bitterly ashamed.

"If you ever want me to feel differently toward you—ever, ever, when we are both middle-aged people—you must begin by trusting me now!"

So spoke Nan, as unworthily as she was prompted, on the spur of a moment which marked an epoch in her life; but even the immediate effect was sufficiently sensational; for with a cry that was almost a sob, the conscience-stricken wretch broke away from her, and fled through the checkered sunlight of the narrow avenue, like the madman her words had made him.

Nan was puzzled and displeased, first with him, afterward and more seriously with herself. She remembered and deplored what she had said. If she had given him ground for hope! That would be terrible—unpardonable—an offense against God and man. And yet the evidence of his passion displeased her least; and least of all the indirect evidence contained in a few lines of explanation which a private messenger brought her during the day; for while they accounted for his conduct of the morning, they displayed an intention so in accordance with her wishes as to relieve her mind of many misgivings.

"I made sure it was my orders to sail," wrote Ralph, with a wise brevity. "I was wrong, but I made sure I was right, and yet I could not trust myself to know it for certain without telling you, or to tell you and then say good-bye as you would have me say it! Forgive me if you can. It was a sudden madness, and as it turns out there was little or no justification for it. Still, as a matter of fact, they do talk of sending me out with a draft next month. That will be soon enough. Yet in one way you know it could not come too soon for me. Oh, Nan, I am torn two ways!"

And yet this glib liar had not then summoned up the moral or immoral courage to open her letter; part of the glibness sprang from that last grain of virtue. He might not open it after all, could not all that day, with officers and gentlemen jostling him at every turn. It was only late at night, in the privacy of his own quarters, that the absolute necessity presented itself with fresh force, and with a sudden oath the envelope was ripped open; but even then the letter itself was glanced at rather than read.

Endearment and protestation this reader could indeed afford to skip; but what he could not help seeing in this kind at once hardened and inflamed his heart. He called her his. His, forsooth, his! Ralph ran a blazing eye over all that, tried another page, read a little, caught his breath, read backward and then forward in a skin of ice. Jewson was dead, killed by a snake! That was bad enough, but it was a trifle to what followed; for much had since come out, and more was suspected of the dead man. He had drugged some beer and stolen a nugget which Nan should have received a month ago. That much was proved. The nugget had been found; there could be little doubt that he had stolen the letter which was to have accompanied it. And here Denis reproached himself with having written so seldom, not once a month as yet; but in the first few weeks of abject failure he had never had the heart to write, but once, and for reasons given he could not be sure that even that letter had not fallen into the same dead hands.

Devenish held his breath. Was he suspected also? Yes, he could see that he was; he could read it between the lines; and his heart reviled the writer for suppressing his suspicions. There was no generosity in Ralph, and he wanted none from Denis.

"You will be seeing something of Ralph Devenish," the innocent could write. "You might ask him whether Jewson, to Ralph's knowledge, ever called at our first camp. He never did when I was there, but I remember thinking of him when Moseley told me a strange digger had offered to take our letters. He bore me a grudge as you know. But I can still hardly think he bore me such a grudge as that, or you any grudge at all. I should be glad if you had an opportunity of speaking to Ralph Devenish on the subject.

The wretched man was his servant at the time, so perhaps he could enlighten us a little. If he can I am sure he will."

Sure, was he? Sure of Ralph? What was the use of such transparent lies? Ralph himself was only enraged by them; they accentuated his meanness and the other's magnanimity. He forgot that they could not have borne such significance to Nan, that she would have suspected nothing, and that the letter after all was written to her. He read on as though it had been written to himself; and the end left him icy sick. Not because Denis had already made several thousands out of his fabulous claim, and upward of £2,500 by a single nugget found in the hour that was so nearly his last. He was welcome to his filthy gold. It was neither record nor assurance of monetary success that froze Ralph's blood; it was Denis's promise to make amends in the matter of correspondence, to write in future by every possible ship, and to post his letters with his own hand.

Ralph felt easier when he had destroyed this one; he was only thankful he had read it now; to have destroyed it unread would have been his ruin. But it was only the first. What of all the rest? Could he hope to intercept a series? Was there no postman or postmaster whom he could suborn to intercept them for him?

No—that was far too dangerous. No more assistant rascals for Ralph! Henceforward he would do his own dirty work; he approached it forthwith without a qualm, but, on the contrary, with the spirited intelligence of a bold nature and an educated brain.

His first care was to arrange with Lloyd's for immediate advice upon the signaling of any homeward-bound Australian packet at the Lizard or other Channel station; in each case, separate post-office inquiries were the next step; and it was from this point that Ralph's appearances in Hertfordshire became as delightfully erratic as the Merridews found them. So far everything was plain sailing. It was the actual interception of the letters which was fraught with inconceivable difficulty and incessant danger.

Its unforeseen variety was its greatest curse. If the letter came in the morning, well and good; but once it was only due by the evening delivery, and then Devenish fetched all the letters from the village post-office on some impudent pretext. He always met the early postman at the gate.

"You see they know where to put their finger on me now," he said to Nan, in presumed reference to the War Office. "Since that one fright I got down here I want to know the worst at the earliest possible moment. Yet but for you it would be the best, and even in spite of you I can't tell you how I burn to go. If only you would let me leave you on the one footing which would make me a happy man!"

For it had come to this: he had proposed repeatedly and gained the stage of receiving a fair hearing and some faint encouragement. "Some day—perhaps!" she said, with a stress which indicated a very distant day indeed; and that, of course, was no promise; nor was the pale prospect accompanied by any hope on Nan's part that she could ever love him as she should. Her heart was dead or numb; he heard it again and again, without loss of confidence in his power to quicken it in the end. And this self-confidence stood Ralph in equal stead with Nan and with his own soul: not from the first, yet in a very few weeks, he was playing a winning if a waiting game. He learned from her lips how he had improved in her sight; and though unable to believe there had been so much room for improvement, he was careful to keep the ground thus won in her regard. It was so at every point of his advance. Here and there the gain was trifling, but he never lost an inch.

Ralph had an open and yet silent ally in Mr. Merridew; of old he had always wanted this marriage, and now he wanted it more than ever. Nan was not happy; it was the one thing to make her happy. He would have told her so every day but for a plain word in the beginning from Ralph himself. "Din me in her ears," said he, "and I am done; leave it to her, and there is a chance for me. But never another word against Denis Dent; if his name comes up, make excuses for him. You don't know women as I know them, sir, or I wouldn't presume to offer you such advice."

It was followed, however, with all loyalty and devotion to their common cause. Not for weeks did the father venture to express any further opinion in the matter; and when he did break silence the occasion justified him. Captain Devenish was ordered out at last. Typhus, dysentery and ague had descended upon the Guards' camp at Aladyn close to Varna; thither Devenish was to sail before the end of June, in charge of a draft to replace those fallen in this unfair fight.

It was Mr. Merridew who brought the news home from the City, and capped it with the conviction, now indeed general, that there would be hard fighting somewhere before the end. The resolution to attack Sebastopol was not yet taken, but the probability had long been in the air, and Mr. Merridew spoke of it as an absolute certainty. It might be a short campaign; but from the character of a map which he spread out Mr. Merridew was not of that opinion. Nan took but a perfunctory interest in the map; she knew very well what had been in her father's mind for weeks, and she was entirely prepared for what was coming now.

"Whatever may be before them, you may depend the Guards will be in the van," said Mr. Merridew, grandly. "The chances are that many of them will never come back; but we won't think of that. Suppose they are away a year. Think of Ralph and of yourself. Imagine his torments all that time, fighting for his country, and yet uncertain of you! How can you expect him—not to do his duty, for that we know he will—but to be as efficient as a soldier with a single and a settled mind?"

"He is certain enough," said Nan, sulking sweetly, "if he can wait."

"But nothing is so uncertain as such a future!"

"Well, I can't marry him before he goes, can I?"

It was said flippantly, yet with a certain feeling far back in the mind.

"I don't know about that. Would you if you could, Nan?"

"It might save complications, if he is to be away a year! Suppose some one else were to come home during the year, you know!" added Nan, with undiminished flippancy; yet this was the thought at the back of her brain, and she was entertaining it in bitter earnest.

"Ah, poor Dent!" said Merridew, advisedly, as he grasped her meaning.

"You needn't pity him; he will come back rich, if not with a wife," said the girl whom Devenish knew so well.

Mr. Merridew came back to his point, after a pause intended to break the thread of painful association, as it did.

"But would you marry Ralph if there was time?"

"There isn't time."

"I don't know. I wish I knew the date he sails. It may be later than we think."

And the budding strategist dropped the subject with a tact which was growing on him with the conduct of this affair. But first thing next morning Ralph and he were closeted in his private office.

"Splendid! splendid!" cried the younger man. "Another word from you might have spoiled everything. I will run down this minute and say the rest for myself."

"But is it possible, Ralph?"

"With a special license it would be possible to-morrow."

"And how long have you?"

"I hope a month. Time enough for banns, if you like. We can get them put up this Sunday."

John Merridew looked at the young man sitting before him, his dark face flushed, his dark eyes sparkling—handsome, eager, and exultant—without a misgiving or a qualm for mortal eye to see.

"You are very confident, Ralph!"

"I am."

CHAPTER XXVI

HOMEWARD BOUND

That very month of May saw Denis deep in an orderly determination of his Australian affairs. These were in a state scarcely credible, but for the fact that his case was not unique. Denis was not the only lucky digger of his day, but he was one of the few who made the most of their good fortune. Half the blood in his veins was averse from squandering, but every drop was on fire for his reward. Suffice it that the sweat rolled off him until he had his ten thousand safe, and enough over to carry him home; there followed civil strife between the two distinct natures whose union in one body made Denis what he was. He must sail by the first ship. He must stay to set his house in order. He could not do both. Yet half the house was his, however come by, and it went against his Yorkshire grain to give it up altogether. The claim was still paying handsomely. A second tunnel had been driven north; and it was to be a longer tunnel, since that good neighbour with the black beard had pegged out on the northern boundary of the claim, to obviate a hostile encroachment back and front, on the very natural understanding that he should join Doherty when Dent was gone. And yet Denis was loth to go.

It was not for the financial sacrifice, though he was sufficiently alive to that. What was ten thousand pounds to take to Nan? It seemed almost criminal to go to her with so little when in a few more months he might have doubled it. Yet there was more to urge on the other side, and it was not the gold that he was grieved to leave. It was the work of his hands. The claim was largely that; the two tunnels were that and nothing else. Much had been given him, but it had been given into the right hands. Denis had carried on an excellent and shrewd bit of work with a thoroughness and an intelligence at least worthy of his predecessor; they were alike in this, that both had a soul aside from the mere gold; and Denis took as much pride in every inch of his two drives as the sinker had taken in every slab of his splendid shaft.

The others realized how much was due to the outgoing partner, and it was they who first begged him to retain a share. At first he refused. "Very well, mister. Then I come with you," said Doherty; and that was an argument; for Denis did not want the lad in England, much less at first, strongly attached as they had become. He had to listen after that, and at last consented to reap a small profit till the year's end, "in case," he said to Doherty's new mate, "things are not as I expect to find them in the old country, and I should want to come straight out again. Then I should be back for Christmas; and it would be like coming home." He said it with a smile, yet it was significant that he did not say it in Doherty's hearing; and the mere possibility of the thing he voiced, however remote, turned Denis sick at heart at the very time when Ralph Devenish was most confident in London.

His arrangements were concluded with some abruptness, but they showed a sound foresight in every detail. He had a draft on the Rothschilds (from the Montefiore then in Melbourne) for his entire savings of nearly eleven thousand pounds; one duplicate he took with him in the ship, another was to follow in the next vessel carrying mails. And there was now no dearth of ships, for Melbourne in these seven or eight months had evolved from the colossal encampment into the rudimentary city.

Of course Doherty came down to see him off, which he did with the liveliest lamentations; but already Denis had his eyes fixed on the old world, and his chief trouble was the time that it must take to get there.

"I'll follow ye, dear old mister!" whimpered the lad. "I'll be after you before the year's out—unless I hear as you're on your own way back!"

He stood on the quay, but a ragged young boor—unlettered child of felons—unshriven son of the soil—yet worth twice his weight in gold in all senses of the homely phrase. And the troubled face, with the tears rolling grotesquely over the tan, was the last that Denis looked on in a land as rich in such contrasts as in the precious metal itself.

The voyage took a hundred and thirty days, and was the longest Denis had ever made; but it must have seemed so to him in any case, for the gold-fever had passed its crisis, and now there were more sailors than enough to man the many ships, so that he found himself a passenger perforce for the first time in his life. And after a fortnight of heavenly rest, the idleness became more irksome to his temperament every day. Instead of reveling in the luxury of seeing others staggering in dripping oilskins, of hearing the starboard watch piped on deck, and of turning over on the other side, Denis would sooner have paid the second officer to change places with him. He missed the crowded hours, and the sense of responsibility so long associated with the sea; they had made his former ships fly their latitudes like hurdles, where this one crawled and climbed.

The voyage was quite uneventful, but of petty incident there was the usual supply. Denis himself incurred the displeasure of the captain by his professional interest in every move, but in a rough-and-tumble round the Horn he made certain amends, and won further favour in the tropics. There they were becalmed three weeks. The ship was full of returning diggers, mostly unsuccessful, and discontent in the steerage was fermented by the harsh treatment of offenders upon whom the thwarted skipper wreaked insensate vengeance with the irons which are a snare to so many of his kind. It was Denis who remonstrated in the captain's cabin and reasoned between decks, and it was Denis who forthwith initiated the various interests which redeemed the remainder of the voyage. Here, however, he received valuable aid from a hard-bitten old sergeant of the Black Watch, named Thrush, who had thus far been an unpopular advocate of steerage discipline. From organized games these two worked up to a daily drill, owing a plausible existence to the pirates with which the seas were still infested in those days, and a corporeal to the valuable money-prizes which Denis put up. This passed a lot of time. The captain looked on approvingly from the poop. Sergeant Thrush bellowed and swore in his old element. Denis drilled humbly with the rest. In the channel he was thanked by the captain in a public speech, and so cheered by every throat on board that he must have stepped ashore in a glow, even with no Nan Merridew in the world.

As it was he was naturally anxious, more nervous than he could have believed, yet full of simple-hearted faith and trust. God had been very good to him: disloyal and impious to anticipate aught but goodness at His hands. And yet—it was eleven long months and more! And yet—not a letter from his love in all that time!

This, however, was his own fault rather than hers; there had been no time for answers to the few letters he was justified in hoping she had received. No one therefore was to blame, except himself. But yet much, only too much, might happen in eleven months.

Denis went straight to Rothschilds' (for it was a Saturday morning), presented his draft, and was still wise enough in his excitement to open an account then and there. Fifty pounds he drew in cash, and the business was concluded in ten minutes. But it took Denis some hours, driving about in a cab, to render himself temporarily and approximately as presentable as he burned to be; and the afternoon was advancing when he stopped the cab on a country road, to jump out a new man, whose beard was trimmed beneath his changeless tan, but all else about him only too fresh from the shop.

In his heart he regretted his comfortable rags, his old hat, his easy boots, even his flowing beard; but he felt it would have been the greater affectation to go out to Hertfordshire just as he had left the diggings; and so you see him well upon the road, yet with a three-mile tramp still before him, deliberately chosen to calm his soul.

It happened to be the last day of September. The countryside lay porous but peaceful under a delicate film of mist and chastened sunlight. Trees showed to less advantage in limp leaves of a lacklustre shade between living green and dying glory; but to Denis the hour was still worthy of his dreams; it was for him to prove worthy of the hour. The rich scent of decay was not only perfume in his nostrils; it braced the brain like strong salts; and the sharp touch of autumn in the air had the like effect upon his blood. He strode out with the greater gusto for his long confinement aboard ship; the day could not well have been more restful, more reassuring, more inspiriting withal.

Presently a village—a village so utterly English in its great length, its red roofs, and the signs and archways of its many inns, that Denis could have tarried there merely to gloat over his native land. But he only inquired the name of the place, and was off with a nod on hearing it was Edgware. It could only have been Edgware; he knew where he was to a mile and less, though he had never before been there in the flesh. The spirit had atoned. Was it not Nan herself who had taught him the road she knew so well? Had she not told him exactly how to come, the very next time he was in docks? Ah, that was in the early days, in tropic nights on the North Foreland, yet how well he remembered one and all! How he could see the fresh young girl, so far from her home, but so full of it! Not Nan to him then—only Miss Merridew! It seemed a great many years ago.

But she had told him how to know the house, by its plate-glass porch and its dear red bricks; she had prepared him for the first sight of the sacred spot, the line of trees to be seen against the sky from a certain dip and sudden bend in the road. Great heaven! Could those be they? Denis was standing in such a hollow at such a bend. A file of trees ran into the sky like a giant hedge: even so had Nan described the first prospect of that narrow avenue in which Denis had done everything but walk.

Somehow his legs carried him up the last hill, and so to the low wall which made no pretense of shielding the front of the house from the road. Of course it was the house; the old red brick glowed as softly as in his dreams; the distinctive porch reflected a gentle sunset with all the sharp fidelity of plate-glass. Denis was glad to lean on the low wall, to peer through the shallow shrubbery on its inner side; he felt as though the muscles had been drawn out of him.

But as he leaned the reflected sunset was momentarily disturbed, and the next moment a figure stood in the doorway, gazing toward the west itself. It was Nan. The sunset lit her ringlets to warmest gold. It gave her some colour, too, yet still her face was paler than of old, as it was certainly far thinner and older. Its appeal to Denis was all the more potent and instantaneous. His muscles tightened almost with a twang. No running round by the gate for him! He vaulted the wall, burst through the bushes, stood panting at her feet.

Nan's hands clutched post and door; the sunlight turned ghastly on her face; but she could look steadily down on him from the step, she was so much the calmer of the two.

"I have been expecting you so long!" she could say with but a break in her voice. "Oh, Denis ... Denis!"

And her right hand lay cold in his.

"Come in!" she cried, wrenching it from his lips. Something rang on the flags of the porch as she pushed him before her. "No, no, through into the garden," she went on. "It's stifling in the house."

Yet firelight flickered in the rooms they passed, and it was really chilly on the lawn where Nan had walked with Ralph, also toward dusk, at the break of the leaf now floating back to earth.

"I found the house in a minute," he went on as they trod the soft turf together. "We only got ashore this morning, and I drove out nearly all the way; but I felt I must walk the part I seemed to know so well. This time yesterday we were off the Isle of Wight: such a voyage, a hundred and twenty-nine days from pilot to pilot! I'd have given a thousand pounds to knock off the twenty-nine!"

That was his only allusion to his success, and it was unintentional. She was sadly embarrassed; he saw it with some pain, but supposed it natural after so long a separation. After all, they scarcely knew each other; they only loved; but Denis was not going to force the love upon her all in a moment. His instincts did not fail him in his great hour. Yet the hour was not quite as he had foreseen it. He had foreseen two extremes: to be chatting in this fashion and ignoring all that mattered to him in life struck Denis at the time as scarcely credible in himself. Yet he kept it up for several minutes, in a tone light beyond his nature, with a heart cooling into solid lead. He would not even ask if she had got his letters; it was not for him to remind her of anything that had ever been, to take the continuance of anything for granted. He might have to begin all over again. That was nothing. In less than a minute he was resigned to that.

"And I seem to have found you alone," he remarked at last. It was his first wistful word.

"Papa is remaining in the city," replied the girl. "He has been asked to the Sheriffs' Dinner at the London Tavern. So I suppose I am alone."

She glanced over her shoulder at the firelit windows overlooking the lawn.

"That avenue!" exclaimed Denis standing still. "It was my first landmark, as you said it would be. You might let me see it before it's dark!"

Nan pointed to the screen of trees beyond the kitchen-garden.

"There it is. You do see it."

"But properly!"

"Very well."

She led the way. His voice had trembled; a deep compassion softened hers. In a minute they were in the avenue. It was narrower even than he had thought. The trees in their autumn tatters still met above their heads. But it was a place of premature twilight, where faces were already hard to see. Figures are often more eloquent. He stood in front of her with his arms unconsciously flung wide, and she stood drooping just beyond his reach.

"Nan!"

His voice choked with doubt and apprehension.

"Yes! I suppose you may call me that," she said, sadly.

"Call you that? Call you Nan?" His arm flew round her at last, but the bright bowed head forbade a kiss. "My darling, what in the world has happened?"

An alien voice came from the hidden lips.

"I am not your darling, Denis."

"No; that I have seen!" he cried bitterly, releasing her. "You don't love me any more. I saw it in a moment ... is there anybody else?"

No answer.

"Are you engaged to some one else?"

"No—no."

"I must have the truth."

"I dare not tell you the whole truth."

And she drooped to break it to him.

"You have nothing to fear, Nan."

"I don't know how to tell you...."

"I am ready for the worst."

"Then ... I am married."

CHAPTER XXVII

THE GREAT GULF

The words died away in the still air. They had been but faintly whispered, and now for many moments there was no sound at all in the quiet shelter of the trees. Then for a little the absolute silence was broken by short and laboured breathing through clenched teeth; then it became absolute as before. Denis was mastering himself as best he might; his whole being was as a knotted muscle; but by degrees that also relaxed, and he stood once more like a thing of flesh and blood, only swaying a little on his feet. But Nan had neither stirred nor made a sound. It was as though her dress supported her, as the dresses of those days almost might, yet there was never a rustle from its silken dome. And in the narrow avenue it was almost dark.

"Devenish, of course?" he said at last, but so hoarsely that he had to say it twice.

It was worth the effort. It made Nan look up; it brought her back to life.

"Yes," she whispered in simple horror. "Yes—I am married to that villain!"

Their eyes met through the dusk, as in a lane of light. His face reflected the unmixed horror so remarkable in hers. Yet already some bell was ringing in his heart.

"What do you mean by that?"

"I loathe him!"

"Yet you are married?"

She spread out her hands in a gesture that was no answer to his incredulity. Quick as thought he caught her left.

"Where's the ring?"

"Yours is quite safe."

"But the wedding-ring—your wedding-ring?"

"I took it off the moment we met. It dropped in the porch. I couldn't let you find out that way."

Her hand also dropped out of his. He turned heavily away from her. It was as though for a moment he had cherished some mad hope; now he stood broken and aloof, shaken with sobs that never reached his throat; oblivious alike to the rustle of the silk dress behind him, to the fluttering featherweight of her hand upon his arm.

"Oh, Denis, Denis, if I could die ... if I could die! It is worse for me. You are not married; you are not tied for life. But I deserve it all, all, all.... There's no excuse for me, none. Yet there is some explanation—poor enough, God knows! Won't you listen to that? Won't you listen to me at all?"

He turned slowly round, and looked upon Nan with the unseeing fixity of the blind. "Go on," he said. "I am listening, and will listen."

"He cheated me!" she cried, passionately. "He took your letters, and he told me lies. But I allowed myself to be cheated," she added, miserably, "and I believed the lies; so I deserved not to find him out till it was too late; and I deserve this, Denis, I deserve it all. If only, only I could die!"

He soothed her as best he could, taking her hand in one of his, and stroking it mechanically with the other. The action might have reminded them of something long past; but the present absorbed both their minds. It was all that they would ever have together. It was their life.

"Don't tell me unless it helps you," he said, gently. "I begin to understand. And it was my fault—mine—for leaving you as I did."

"Your fault! Yet if you had written—if you only had written!" she cried, loudly exonerating him in one breath, softly reproaching in the next.

"I know. That was pride," he said bitterly. "I was so desperately unsuccessful up to Christmas! I did write in November, but I was always afraid that letter never went."

"I never got it. Not a word of any sort, dear," she said, simply, "did I have from you till nearly May. And then—"

"And then?" he repeated as she paused.

"Have you no idea what I am going to tell you?" she asked, a new twinge in her tone. She could scarcely have explained her feeling, but the least inkling in him would have implied some slight excuse for her, would in any case have helped her to confess the climax of her late credulity.

"None whatever," said Denis.

"Yet it was your writing. I can show it you, for I have it still."

"What writing do you mean?" he inquired, quite in the dark.

"The address on the parcel."

"What sort of parcel?" he exclaimed, as the truth flashed across him. "Quite small? Brown paper? Quick! Quick! I want to know!"

"Yes—yes—and you don't know what was in it! Oh, Denis!"

"I know what should have been," he said, grimly: "my first nugget—according to promise. But it was stolen, and afterward found."

"And you don't know what was put in instead? Did you lose nothing else?"

Denis stood stock-still in the deepening dusk. No, he had never thought of that; even now his simplicity could not credit it until he had drawn every detail from Nan's lips. The ring had possessed intrinsic value. He had always looked upon that as an ordinary theft. The discovery of the stolen nugget on Jewson's body had puzzled him, but it was partially accounted for by another strange fact which had come to light after the man's death, namely, that the nugget had been purchased by Jewson in the first instance, elsewhere on the diggings, and deliberately planted at the bottom of the shaft where Denis found it. And not till this moment, months afterward, had Denis penetrated the dead man's design.

"You have indeed been cheated," he said, bitterly. "Yet to believe me capable of behaving like that without a word! To have known me as little as all that! Why, there was trickery on the face of it. But how can I talk? They took me in, too—decent people don't dream of such villainy—so I was fair game at one end, and you at the other. I begin to see the whole thing. Do you remember when we said good-bye on board your ship?"

"Do I remember!"

"It was then you gave me what I wore night and day until it was stolen and sent back to you."

"Oh, Denis!"

"And it was then you made me promise to send it back to you if ever—Oh, what a fool I was!"

"It was my doing—all. You didn't want to promise; it vexed you and hurt you, and it was all my fault."

"But I promised, and I was overheard, by the villain who is gone," said Denis. "He was in my cousin's cabin at the time, for I distinctly remember seeing him there as we went on deck. And he repeated every syllable to a ten times greater villain than himself, who is alive to answer for his crime!" and he ground his teeth, little dreaming that he had done the living criminal a double injustice in one breath.

"I am not sure that he is alive," faltered Nan, above her breath, but that was all.

"You are not sure?"

"I have not seen him since our wedding day!"

Denis was dumfoundered, but enlightened.

"So you found out just too late," he groaned.

"Yes; and the hard part was that I might have found out in time," she said sadly but only sadly, as if telling of some other person. "There were such a lot of letters for me that morning," she went on, "and there was so little time. I didn't even look at them; I said I would read them in the train; but after all I looked through the envelopes as they were dressing me to go away."

He heard her shuddering, and his lips moved. It was black night in the avenue now, and deepest twilight through the trees on either hand. So he never knew how meekly she stood before him in this bitter hour; even the striking humility of a voice so memorable for its spirit was lost upon a mind too absorbed in the sense to heed the sound.

"Your letter was among them," she went on. "Which letter I cannot say; it was the first that ever reached me, and I was in two minds whether to read a line of it or to tear it up unopened; but I could not bring myself to do that, nor yet resist just looking to see what you said. And there in the first few lines I saw it was but one of many letters that had gone astray! It was the letter in which you began by saying how often you had written lately, though you had never yet had a single word from me. But how could I write when I never had a line to tell me where you were?"

"I don't blame you for that," said Denis. "I never blamed you in my life before to-day; when I know all I may not blame you yet. I understand nearly everything as it is." There was a slight emphasis on one of the last words, but it was very slight: in their common misery he was now as unemphatic as she.

"It was the letter," continued Nan, "in which you told me how splendidly you were doing, and how soon you hoped to sail; I think it must have come in a much quicker ship than yours; but it was a long time before I read that part. I nearly fainted—not quite—but they sent downstairs for our doctor. It was a very small party—everything was hurried and quite private—but Dr. Stone has known me since I was born, and fortunately he was there. I told him everything, and what I suspected in a moment. He tried to talk me over, but I refused even to see my husband until my suspicions were set at rest, and appealed to him to stop a scandal. He did so—there is no public scandal to this day. He went downstairs and declared that the hurry and excitement had proved too much for me; that it was nothing serious, but I could not possibly go away that day. That emptied the house, and gave me time to think. But they all pressed me to see Captain Devenish, so at last I did see him. And in my misery I came down to his level, and pretended not to care if he would only tell the truth."

"And did he?"

"How can I tell? He told me a tale, and he brazened it out. I believe it was the truth. The fraud was not begun by him, but first he countenanced it and then he had to carry it on. He had taken your letters systematically for weeks; whenever a mail came in, here he was, on the spot, and ready for the worst. He boasted of it, gloried in it, said he would play the same game again for the same stake! That was the end. I never looked at him again, though he stayed in the house a week to save the appearances that were so dear to him and to my father; but it was I who saved them, little as I cared. Next day I was really ill, and before I came down again he was gone."

"Gone where?"

"To the Black Sea. You see, he had to go in a week, in any case."

"I don't understand."

"To the war—with a draft of the Grenadiers."

The war! Denis had never heard of it until the night before, when the pilot came aboard his ship, and since landing his own affairs and his own anxieties had filled his mind down to this cruel culmination. So Ralph Devenish, traitor and thief, had fled to fight his country's battles because he had not the pluck to stand and fight his own! Denis could not be fair for a moment to such an officer and such a gentleman; it was not in his allowance of very human nature.

"Now you have told me everything," he cried, "I can understand all but one thing. I can understand your disbelieving in me, your resentment of my silence, your failure to see that what you received without a line of explanation could never have been sent by me. It was your idea that I should send you back your ring if I changed—if I changed! You thought I would take you at your word without a word of my own to ask so much as your forgiveness. Well, you were at liberty to think what you liked of me; you little knew me, and it was a poor compliment to what you did know; but all that I can understand. What I cannot and never will understand is how you flew round the compass and married that fellow within two months!"

What had Nan to say? She had long been utterly unable to understand it herself. Ralph had never seemed so nice; she herself had been wretched, reckless, wounded, numbed; nothing had seemed to matter any more, except to show that she did not care; and that was her wicked way of showing it. Oh! she had been wicked, wicked; but see her punishment! See the shipwreck of her whole life! He who understood so much—Denis—dear Denis—could he not forgive the mad sequel?

"Forgive!" He laughed out harshly. "Oh, yes, I can forgive you; but that's the end. We must never see each other again. This is good-bye; and the sooner it's said the better for one and all."

He was actually holding out his hand. Nan caught it and clung to it with both of hers.

"Good-bye?" she almost screamed. "You are not going away like this? You wouldn't leave me more desolate and desperate than I was before? You'll stay, or at least come back to see my father—to see me?"

Denis did not hesitate for a moment. "No," said he, firmly; "no, it's not a bit of use my staying to see anybody or any more of you; and the sooner you let me go the better and easier for us both."

"But where will you go?" she asked, partly to gain time; yet the desire to detain him was not greater than the dread of sending him she knew not whither.

"God knows!" he answered. "Not to my death, if I can help it, and if that's what you mean, but very likely back to Ballarat. I was making a small fortune there. I might go back and double it, or lose it all. What does it matter now?"

Even while he spoke, the vision of his mates on the claim in Rotten Gully rose warmly to his mind; and yet, even before he ceased speaking, he knew that he could never go back to them now.

"Don't go!" she urged piteously. "Denis, Denis, don't leave me so soon. You are always so ready to leave me, and see what came of it before! I never could forget it—I never could—it made all the difference in the end. But now you are the only one I have to look up to in the world; stay and help me; be my friend. Oh, Denis, you once saved me from the sea. Stay—do stay, for God's sake, Denis—and save me from myself!"

It needed heart of flint and will of adamant to resist so wild and touching an appeal; but Denis had soon formed his own conception of his duty, and every moment since he had been subconsciously hardening himself to its performance. All his character came into his resolve: strength, promptitude, unflinching courage, undeniable obstinacy, and withal a certain narrowness, a matter of upbringing and of inexperience, in questions of right and wrong. She had married another man; there was an end of it, and let the end come quickly. It would be wrong to see more of her, wrong even to remain her friend. So he had argued in his heart; so he answered her now, kindly, tenderly, with much emotion, but with more fixity of purpose and finality of decision.

"But it isn't the end!" cried Nan, wildly. "It's only the beginning—because I was cheated into marrying him, and because ... I love you, Denis, and only you!"

It was long before Denis remembered how he broke away from her; how and where he left her came back to him slowly after hours. It was in the house. He had carried her there. She loved him. He could not leave her out there to creep in through the dark alone, even if she could have crept half the way unaided. But the struggle came before all that. The rest made no immediate impression on his mind. He was a mile on his road before his brain began to clear, on the crest of a hill, where a sudden night wind searched his skull. Under his eyes, and a rising moon, the road he had to traverse fell almost from his feet, to glimmer away into a flat and open country, and to remind him of the ship's wake on a calm night; only it was no longer the wake; it was his course. On the horizon the faint glow of the metropolis was just discernible, and to ears fresh from the incessant noises of the ocean, the hum of the great human hive seemed not absolutely inaudible in the young night's stillness. Yet every now and then there was a rattle of parched leaves, as if the quiet earth stirred in its sleep; for some minutes Denis also heard his own heart beating from the speed with which he had come so far; and as this abated, somewhere in the nether distance, on the way to London, a clock struck seven.

CHAPTER XXVIII

NEWS OF BATTLE

There was a fascination in returning stride by stride to the rattle and roar of the metal tyres upon London's stones. Denis felt it through the depths of his blank misery and impotent rage; he only wondered that the noise had never struck him in the morning. Now he picked it up plain at Hendon, and it reminded him of its miniature—the first far sound of Ballarat—as it seemed to rise with each ringing step he took. His body was bathed in perspiration; never had he walked so many miles at such a rate. But a vague object had developed on the way. By half-past nine he was in London's throat; and now he might have been walking on cotton-wool.

Never had he heard such an uproar: it was Saturday night. Edgware Road was a vast trench of stalls and barrows, lurid with naked flames, strident with hoarse voices, only Denis was not Londoner enough to know that it was Edgware Road. He had the vaguest ideas as to where he was, until, on asking his way to the London Tavern, he was invited to take his choice between the glaring illuminations of several London taverns before his eyes. After that he applied to a constable, and next minute sat cooling in a hansom cab.

The hansom beat up into the east in a series of short tacks, grinding endless curbstones as she went about, but at last emerging into latitudes less unknown to Denis. There was St. Paul's Cathedral, perhaps his westernmost landmark, though he had once or twice threaded Temple Bar: so the London Tavern was somewhere in the city. The sailor began to feel at home. The offices of Merridew and Devenish were in one of these silent streets. How silent and deserted they were! What a change from the Edgware Road! And this was London's hub, that he had imagined deafening and congested at all hours of the twenty-four: that sleeping palace was the Royal Exchange: this black monolith the Bank. At the first oasis of light and life the cab drew up.

"London Tavern, sir," said a voice overhead.

Denis dismissed the cab and found himself confronted by an overpowering Cerberus, who desired to know what he could do for him, but Denis scarcely knew himself. His impressions in the cab had been acute but superficial. The mind's core was still stunned. He had to think hard in order to recall the resolve which had brought him hither; a burst of applause through the tall lighted windows came to his aid in the nick of time.

"I want to see a gentleman who is dining here."

"What, now?" sniffed Cerberus.

"Before he leaves."

"I could take in your card," condescended the other, who had probably heard the thanks which Denis had earned from his cabman, "when the Lord Mayor's said what he 'as to say, if it's anythink very important."

"To me it is," said Denis, "and I pray that it may prove equally so to him; but it will be time enough after the banquet, and I can take care of myself meanwhile."

He crossed the street slowly, pondering his resolve, which was simply to impress his daughter's despair upon John Merridew's mind; to implore him not to leave her too much alone, but to find her some bright companion without a day's delay, to keep watch and ward over her from that day forth.

That was the motive of which Denis found himself aware; if in the bottom of his heart he yearned for a word of unforeseen sympathy, of inconceivable comfort, of wildest hope, the thought never rose to the surface of his mind.

But he was distracted from all his thoughts by cheer upon frantic cheer from the great hall across the road. This was no ordinary after-dinner enthusiasm. The lighted windows rattled in their leads. A crowd was forming in the street. A whisper was running through the crowd.

"The Lord Mayor's there," said a voice near Denis. "He came on foot not five minutes ago. It's something worth hearing, you mark my words!"

Denis marked them with the listless interest of one who had realized neither his country's peril nor his countrymen's excitement. It was impossible that he should. He had forgotten that England was at war.

"Here he comes back again!" exclaimed the same excited voice. "That's his lordship, him in the gold chain. See the papers in his hand; see the face on him! It's a victory, boys, and he's going to give us the news!"

The Lord Mayor wore a frilled shirt-front behind the massive chain of office, and between its tufts of whisker his well-favoured face shone like the sun. But he did not deliver his message from the steps of the London Tavern; attended by one or two members of his household, he led the way on foot toward the Royal Exchange. A handful of diners were at his heels, and the gathering street-crowd at theirs; but Denis did not think of joining them until among the former he recognized John Merridew, himself brandishing some missive and gesticulating to his friends.

It was Merridew alone whom Denis wished to keep in view, yet as he slowly followed in the civic train he experienced a reawakening of that impersonal curiosity which had possessed him in the cab. What had happened? What was going to happen now? The answer came in the blare of a bugle, even as Denis reached the steps of the Royal Exchange.

The bugle sounded again and again, waking the echoes of the silent streets, filling them with answering cries and the shuffle of hastening feet. Meanwhile the Lord Mayor had climbed the few steps, and taken his stand under the grimy portico, behind the footlights improvised by half-a-dozen policemen with their bull's-eyes.

"Fellow-citizens and gentlemen," he cried, "I have to announce to you the intelligence of a splendid victory obtained by the Allied forces over the Russians in the Crimea!"

A wild roar rose into the night, and the speaker himself prolonged it by calling for cheers for the Queen before going any further. Heads were uncovered and hats waved madly. Cheer after cheer rang to its height and dropped like musketry in single shouts. The converging streets were alive with running men. The blood was draining back into the City's heart.

Denis wondered to find a moisture in his eyes; it brought back the heart-break which had occasioned him less outward emotion, and he was carried away no more. The Lord Mayor, indeed, was departing from the point; he had paused to enlarge upon the delightful character of his duty before completing its performance. Some few months since it had fallen to his lot to announce that war had been proclaimed between that country and Russia; he had now the great satisfaction of making known to them that the Allied forces had taken the first step toward reducing to reasonable limits the barbaric Power against which they were engaged. He could not help adding that he considered the interests of humanity, and the happiness of the whole human race, were all deeply concerned in the victory.

Denis did not join in the renewed cheering. His brow was contracted, but not from want of sympathy with the excellent sentiments expressed. He was himself engaged against the sudden onslaught of an impossible thought.

"I will now read to you," continued the Lord Mayor, "the letter with which I have been honoured by the Duke of Newcastle. 'My Lord,' he writes, 'I have the honour and high gratification of sending your lordship a proof copy of an extraordinary Gazette containing a telegraphic message from her Majesty's Ambassador at Constantinople, by which the glorious intelligence of the success of the Allied arms in a great battle in the Crimea has been received this morning.—I am, my lord, your lordship's obedient humble servant, Newcastle.' And this, fellow citizens," the Lord Mayor proceeded in higher key, "and this is the text of that message: 'The intrenched camp of the Russians, containing 50,000 men, with a numerous artillery and cavalry, on the heights of the Alma, was attacked on the 20th inst., at 1 P. M., by the Allied troops, and carried by the bayonet at half-past three, with the loss on our side of about 1,400 killed and wounded, and an equal loss on the side of the French. The Russian army was forced to put itself in full retreat.'"

There was perhaps one second of profound silence.

"Fourteen hundred!" said an awed voice.

And then arose such a storm of shouting and of cheering as Denis had never heard in all his life; and he was roaring with the lustiest, roaring as if to expel his thoughts in sound. But in the first pause another voice said, "Fourteen hundred!" and the figure passed below the breath from lip to lip till one exclaimed, "The poor Guards!" Thereat the creases cut deep across Denis's forehead—so deep you might have looked for them to fill with blood—and he asked the man next to him if the Guards were in it.

"In it?" cried the man next Denis. "In the thick and the front of it, you may depend!"

The Lord Mayor had not finished. He was thanking one and all for their attendance. He was expressing a pious belief that this victory of the Alma would promote the civilization and happiness of the world more than anything that had happened for the last fifty years. He was bowing to the cheers that echoed his remarks. He was proposing the cheers for our soldiers. He was leading the cheers for the French. He was descending with dignity from the portico, with the policemen's lanterns still playing upon his great gold chain and rubicund face, a hearty figure in spirited contrast to the dark colonnade at his back.

But Denis bent glowering at the flag on which he stood. His neighbour's answer to his query about the Guards was still rattling in his head; he had heard nothing since with that part of the ear which communicates with the brain.

The group of gentlemen from the London Tavern followed the Lord Mayor down the steps; one of them passed close to Denis, waving a telegram as if it were a flag.

"He must have got it off with the dispatches," said he. "It has been delivered at my office this evening, but fortunately the housekeeper knew where I was."

"And your son-in-law has come through safe and sound?"

"Safe and sound, thank God!"

It was Mr. Merridew, still flushed and flustered with sentiment and satisfaction; as he passed, Denis scanned the smug, well-meaning face; but he had withdrawn deliberately from the path of the man whom he had driven across London to see. Talk to him about Nan!

"Now, sir, move on, please!"

The swollen crowd was streaming down Cheapside, shouting, cheering, and singing "Partant pour la Syrie," as it bore the great news westward. Already the sounds came faintly to the steps of the Royal Exchange, where Denis was the last man left to blink in the rays of the last policeman's lantern.

"All right, constable; but I only landed from Australia this morning, and I wish you'd tell me a thing or two first."

"Indeed, sir?" said the policeman. Denis felt in the pocket that was full of notes and gold.

"About this war," he pursued: "you see I never heard of it before to-day. Can you tell me which of the Guards have gone?"

"Coldstream and Grenadiers, sir."

"But not all of them?"

"The first battalion of the Coldstream and the third of the Grenadiers."

The man's prompt answer drew Denis's attention to the man himself. He was over six feet in height, and not an inch of it thrown away. But still more noticeable was a peculiar pride of countenance—some secret enthusiasm which added a freshness to the patriotic emotion to be found in any other face.

"An old Guardsman?" inquired Denis.

"An old Grenadier, sir!" cried the policeman. "And I would give ten years of my life to be with them now!"

"Do you suppose they have lost very heavily?" Denis was searching the old soldier's face.

"If the losses altogether are fourteen hundred I'll back ours to run well into three figures!"

"But they'll keep the regiment up to strength, I take it?"

"No doubt they'll send out a draft as soon as possible."

"Of course there'd be no chance for a recruit in such a draft?"

Denis had hesitated, and then forced a grin. The old Grenadier shook his head.

"I doubt it, sir; but a very good man, who knew his drill, they might take him over the heads of others. They want all the good men they can get in time of war. Why, sir, that's a sovereign!"

"It was meant to be; it's not a night for less. And now can you tell me where the rest of the Grenadiers are?"

"Wellington Barracks, sir."

Denis fell into his natural smile.

"I don't know London very well. Will you do one more thing for me before I move on?"

"That I will, sir."

"Will you tell me how to find my way to Wellington Barracks?"

CHAPTER XXIX

GUY FAWKES DAY

A company officer was making his round of an outlying picket of Grenadiers; the black hour before a drizzling dawn effectually shrouded moist features and sodden whiskers, as bearskin and greatcoat served to modify an erect yet incorrigibly casual carriage. It was Ralph Devenish, however, and he was performing his duties with some punctilio. The sentries stood their twenty paces apart, all but invisible to each other, sundered links waiting for the dawn to complete the chain. And at each link the officer halted and beat his foot.

"All's well."

"Except your rifle, eh?" muttered Devenish to one or two; from a third he took the man's dripping piece, and from the nipple poured a tiny jet of water into the palm of his left hand. "Keep it covered if you can, or it will never go off," was his audible injunction to that sentry and the next. One who knew him would have marveled at such zeal and such initiative in Ralph Devenish.

One who knew him did.

"All's well."

"Except your musket, I expect. Let's see it. You know my voice?" It had dropped with the question.

"I do."

"I suppose you thought I didn't recognize you?"

"I didn't know."

"Well, I did, and had you put on this picket on purpose to get a word with you; but don't you raise your voice any more than I'm raising mine," whispered Devenish in one breath, with a louder comment on the condition of the rifle in his next. "What are you doing here?" he added in his strenuous undertone. "When did you land in England?"

"The last morning of September."

"So it made you enlist."

"The same night."

"Yet you got out in the draft."

"I knew my drill. It's a long story."

"It must be! You've been bribing the sergeants, or somebody; but I don't blame you for that. Try to keep the nipple covered," said the zealous officer, returning the piece. "Why the devil did you choose my regiment?" whispered Ralph.

"It was the night the news came of the Alma—and—I hoped you were killed!"

"No wonder." Ralph chuckled harshly.

"It was one to me; but I couldn't help it, and I felt in every other battle it would be the same. So I enlisted that night."

"To make sure, eh?" sneered Ralph.

"To run your risks!" said Denis through his teeth. "The chances are that one of us will go back. The chances are less that we both will!"

The rain took up the whispering for the next few seconds.

"I see!" said Ralph at length. "The latest thing in duels! Well, my congratulations must keep till next round." And he marched on nonchalantly enough, with a final chuckle for Denis's salute; but the note was neither so harsh nor so spontaneous as before; and Denis was left to glory in his last words, to regret them, and yet to glory in them again.

The rain sank into his bearskin, pattered on his shoulders, and made quite a report when it beat upon a boot; the next sentry was to be heard answering questions about his rifle, and Denis wondered if he himself could be the sole cause of the unusual inquisition. The officer passed on out of earshot; other noises of the waning night returned to recapture the attention. The dismal watches had long been redeemed by a series of exciting sounds from within the enemy's lines. The belfries of Sebastopol had first united in discordant peals; and from that hour the outposts had heard low rumblings, distant, intermittent, but now more distinct than ever, and something nearer to the ear. A dull gray light was beginning to weld the links in the chain of bearskins and greatcoats that stretched across the soaking upland. And by degrees the dark night lifted on a raw and dripping fog, almost as impenetrable as itself.

A patter of invisible musketry sounded in the direction of Inkerman heights, increased to a fusillade, but came no nearer; the Grenadier outposts were withdrawn, and in the misty dawn the company fell in with other two of the Guards Brigade. As they did so a level rainbow curved through the fog, and some one shouted "Shell!" Every man stood his ground upright, but as the shell skimmed over their heads, and sank spinning into the soft ground beyond, a number flung themselves upon their faces, and lay like ninepins until it burst without hitting one.

"Stand up, stand up!" cried a sergeant with a cheese-cutter on the back of his red head. "You're not in the trenches now, and that's sugar-plums to what you're goin' to get. Look over there!"

On the plain beneath the high plateau occupied by the three companies, the Russian cavalry could be seen below the rising fog, advancing obliquely on the northern heights, preceded by a cloud of skirmishers. Nothing threatened the outpost of Guards; no more shot or shell fell among them; and word came for them to march back to camp in order to draw cartridges and exchange their dripping muskets for dry.

It was no welcome order to the picket, already further from the action than their gallantry could bear. Heavy firing on the northern heights convinced them that the bulk of the Brigade were already hotly engaged. Yet a whole company of Grenadiers and two of the Coldstream had to start the day by turning their backs upon friend and foe and din of battle.

"Never mind, boys," cried the sergeant in the cheese-cutter. "It'll be your turn directly, and meanwhile you can say your prayers, for you'll be smelling hell before you're an hour older!"

Denis, for one, would have given a good deal to have been spared this delay before battle of which he had heard so much. He found it as trying as report maintained. He could not but think of his last words to Ralph Devenish, and as Ralph marched aloof he looked as though he might be thinking of them too. Denis began to suffer from a sort of superstitious shame: he deserved to be the one to remain upon the field. He was grateful to his rear-rank man, a Cockney, and a consistent grumbler, for a running commentary of frivolous complaint.

"I 'ope they'll give us time for a cup o' cawfee—if yer call it cawfee," said he. "Green cawfee-beans ground between stones—I call it muck. But 'ot muck's better 'n nothink w'en you've 'ad no warm grub in yer innards for twenty-four hours. But wot do you 'ave in this God-forsaken 'ole? Not a wash, not a shave, no pipe-clayin', no button-cleanin', no takin' belts or boots off by the day an' night together!"

The deserted encampment was far from an inspiring spectacle. Denis kept outside his tent; the idea of a farewell visit was not to be resisted; but a tough biscuit munched in the open air, and a dry rifle handled as the rain ceased falling, were solid comforters. At last the companies fell in, and swung out of camp with a cheer, greatcoats and bearskins, red plumes and white, as briskly and symmetrically as through the streets of London.

"'Remember, remember, the fifth o' November!'" said the red-haired sergeant. "So you never knew Guy Fawkes was a Rooshian? You hark at 'em keepin' the day!"

Indeed, the firing was growing louder every minute. It was still nearly all in one direction, on the heights where the fog clung thickest, and whither the three companies were now tramping through the fog.

"I wish they'd remember the seventh day, an' keep it 'oly," grumbled Denis's rear-rank man. "I s'pose you godless chaps 've forgot it's yer Sunday out? I don't forget it's mine, darn their dirty skins!"

A horse's hoofs came thudding through the fog, a scarlet coat burst through it like the sun.

"The Duke says you're to join your battalion," cried the staff-officer to Devenish. "They're hard pressed at the two-gun battery up above."

Devenish wheeled round, and his handsome face was transfigured as he waved his sword.

"They want us with the colours!" he shouted. "They can't do without us after all!"

And with a laugh and a yell the men sprang forward, the sergeant's face as red as his hair, even the grumbler pressing on Denis's heels, and perhaps only Denis himself with a single thought beyond coming at once to the rescue of the regiment and to grips with the shrouded foe. But Denis had been near Ralph when he turned, near enough to note the radiant look, to catch the smiling eye, and his country's enemy was blotted out of mind by his own. Had he done Devenish justice after all? Was his behaviour as base as it had seemed? Was that shining and fearless face the face of a bad man and a coward? Handsome, joyous, and brave, as strangely ennobled as some faces after death, could any woman have seen this one now, she might rather have forgiven it any crime!

So thought Denis to himself as he marched in chill silence among his yelling comrades. He had not been with them at the Alma. It was his first battle, and as yet it had only begun to the ear; not a man had been hit before his eyes, not a flash had penetrated the pale mist ahead upon the heights. Yet the mist was paler than it had ever been; and to the right, over the green valley of the Tchernaya, whence it had risen in patches, there was a faint round radiance in the pall. None noticed it; all eyes were straining through the haze in front of them; but of a sudden, as the bearskins breasted a ridge, the sun broke forth upon an astounding tableau.

Under a canopy of mist and smoke, belt-deep in sparkling bushes raked by the risen sun, a thin line of Guardsmen were holding their own against dense masses of the enemy. Between the Russians and the lip of the plateau in their rear, over which they were still swarming by the battalion, rose the dismantled redoubt whose empty embrasures were open doors to the attacking horde. Weight of numbers had wrested the work from the British—but that was all. Instead of pressing this advantage, the enemy had set his back to the parapet of sandbags, overlapping it in dense wings, and so standing at bay in his thousands against a few hundred Grenadiers. The lingering mist and the smoke of battle were doubtless in favour of the few; only the remnant of their own brigade, approaching obliquely from their rear, could see how few they were; and for an instant the sight appalled them. It was a hedge of bearskins and cheese-cutters against a forest of muffin-caps and cross-belts, and between them a road narrowing to a few yards at the end nearer the relieving handful. Rifles flashed and smoke floated along either line; uncouth yells were answered by hoarse curses and by savage cheers; and Guardsmen who had fired away their sixty rounds were hurling rocks and stones across a lane so narrow that there was scarcely a yard between the sprawling dead of either side.

Such was the grim gray scene upon which the three companies appeared. The rank and file were in their greatcoats almost to a man; but here and there were a scarlet tunic and a flashing sword; and in the centre of the line, in the swirl of smoke and mist, staggered a crimson standard and a Union Jack.

"Our colours!" screamed Devenish, racing ahead of his men. There was no need for him to tell them. The gray pack were yelling at his heels, and Denis saw but dimly as he ran roaring with the rest.

The thin line heard them; a couple of officers glanced over their epaulettes, saw the red plumes of the Coldstream outnumbering the white plumes of the Grenadiers, and tossed their swords in a sudden passion of jealousy. "Charge again, Grenadiers!" they roared, and leaped into the lane with the whole gray wave rolling after them. And with bayonets down and wild hurrahs the battalion drove straight into the redoubt, trampling the dead, and driving the living through the two embrasures as a green sea is emptied through lee scuppers.

Simultaneously the mass of Russians to the north of the battery were routed by a charge of the Scots Fusiliers at the far end of the line of Guards; and now the Coldstreamers blooded themselves upon the companion wing extending from the southern shoulder of the redoubt; but Devenish and his Grenadiers had followed their own into the redoubt itself, and Denis was leaning with his back against the parapet, brushing the sweat from his forehead and cleaning his bayonet in the earth.

There was no more moisture in his eyes. The emotional effect of the spectacle had yielded in an instant to the ferocious frenzy of the deed. Yet, as he leaned panting in the momentary pause, there was enough still to be seen, and more than enough to do. A quartermaster-sergeant arrived with a tray of refreshments on his shoulders, and a Grenadier in the act of helping himself was shot down as though by one of his own comrades. An officer wheeled round and fired his revolver in the air, whereupon a dead Russian came toppling from the parapet with a fearful thud almost at Denis's feet. But the fierce fellows struggling for the biscuits took no notice of either incident. Stained with powder, caked with blood, bearded, tattered, torn, they fought with their rough good-humour, for their first food since the night before, and with their mouths full rallied each other on their appearance.

"You ain't fit for Birdcage Walk," panted one. "I'd like to let them nursemaids see you now!"

"It's about time I fired a round," said another, snapping caps to dry his nipple. His bayonet was bloody to the muzzle. A third was replenishing his pouch from that of a dead comrade, with grim apologies to the corpse. There was less levity among the officers. It was at this period that Lord Henry Percy twice scaled the parapet,—a simple slope to the enemy—in order to clear it with his sword. Each time a well-aimed fragment of rock threw him backward over; the second misadventure left him senseless where he fell; and Denis, who was now reloading, sprang with others to his assistance.

"Get yourself something to eat," said a brother officer of the fallen Colonel, brushing the private aside.

"Thank you, sir, I had plenty in camp. I'm waiting for the next charge!" said Denis, with his cartridge between his teeth; and he bit off the end, dropped the powder into the muzzle of his piece, reversed and rammed home with no other thought in his heated head. He had been speaking to the gallant officer who had led him into his first action. He did not realize that it was Ralph Devenish. He had forgotten that there was such a being in the world.

CHAPTER XXX

THE SANDBAG BATTERY

Denis had not long to wait. There was a sudden agitation at the northern shoulder of the redoubt. Shouts and shots rose in an instant to the continuous din of desperate combat, as the strokes on a gong ring into one. A sulphurous cloud brooded over the struggling throng, worked its way down the inner wall of the battery, and clung to the angle of the first embrasure; inch by inch the bearskins were overborne, and between them pressed the cross-belts and the infuriate sallow faces in the peaked caps. Just then Denis saw a handful of his comrades, not actually in the path of the Russian avalanche, forming for a flank attack upon the intruders; in an instant he was one of them, and in another they had leaped upon the enemy with ball, butt, and bayonet. The Russians were pinned against the wall of the work. Those whom they had been driving rallied and drove them. Murderously assaulted in front and flank, the invading battalion turned and fled as they had come, leaving the ground thick with their dead.

Again Denis stopped to breathe. His bayonet was bent nearly double; he put his foot in the crook, detached it with a twist, and was about to replace it with the bayonet of a ghastly Grenadier when he found the butt of his own piece plastered with blood and hair. So he exchanged muskets with the dead man, but wiped his hand without a qualm. He remembered whirling his Minié by the barrel when the bayonet bent; he could remember little else. Of his life before the fight, of his own identity, he had lost all sense; his ordinary being was in abeyance; he was a fearless and ruthless madman, smothered in blood and gasping for more.

Comparatively calm intervals he had throughout the fight, intervals in which for one reason or another, he was a momentary spectator of the scenes in progress all around him. It was these scenes that lived in his memory; even at the time they moved him more than those in which he had a hand. Once the Guards were fighting on the other side of the Sandbag Battery, between it and the long lip of the ravine; he had to wait for accounts of the battle long afterward to learn how they had got there, or what relation this phase of the action bore to the whole. At the time he was one of a handful of furious Grenadiers, fighting for their lives in the fresh fog which their powder had brought down upon them, and a moment came which Denis felt must be his last. He had tripped headlong over a dead Russian, and a quick Russian stood over him, aiming his bayonet with one hand while the other grasped the stock high above his head. But a British officer flung out his revolver within a few feet of the deliberate gray-coat, and it was the sensation of being shot from behind at such a moment that Denis anticipated more poignantly than that of being transfixed where he lay. The man fell dead on top of him. Anon he saw his friend the red-headed sergeant, being led captive down the hill by two of the enemy, suddenly wrest the carbine from one of them, club them both with it, and bayonet one after the other before they could rise. That also made Denis shudder. And yet he was biting a cartridge at the moment, having killed with his last, at arm's length, a splendid fellow who had grasped his bayonet while he poised his own.

Now the Sandbag Battery seemed out of sight, because it was quite another thing from this side, and now they were back in it, sweeping the Russians out once more. Denis did not know that the work had changed hands, half-a-dozen times before his company came into action, but even he saw the uselessness of a redoubt from which our soldiers could only see one way, and that in the direction of their own lines. The dead, indeed, now lay piled to the height of any banquette. No wilful foot was set on them. It was only the living for whom there was neither shrift nor pity on that bloody field.

This was the last that Denis saw of the Sandbag Battery; he was one of those who, led by a bevy of hot-headed officers, incontinently scaled it as one man, flung themselves upon the ousted enemy, and hunted him down-hill in crazy ecstasies. A hoarse voice in high authority screamed command and entreaty from the crest where the Grenadier colours drooped in the haze, deserted by all but a couple of hundred bearskins. It was as though the curse of the Gadarene swine had descended on this herd of inflamed Guardsmen. Down they went, if not to their own destruction, to the grave peril of the remnant up above. An officer in front of Denis was the first to recognize the error; he checked both himself and a rough score of the rank and file; and together these few came clambering back to the colours on the heights.

Breathless they gained the edge of the plateau, to swarm over as the Russians had so often done before them, and to find matters as grave as they well could be. The crimson standard and the Union Jack swayed in the centre of a mere knot of Guardsmen, already sorely beset by broken masses of the enemy. And even now a whole battalion was bearing down upon the devoted band, marching to certain conquest with a resolute swing and swagger, and yet with the deep strains of some warlike hymn rising incongruously from its ranks. In a few minutes at most the little knot of Grenadiers must be overtaken, overwhelmed, and those staggering and riddled colours wrested from them for the first time in the history of the regiment. But the officer whom Denis was now following was one of the bravest who ever wore white plume in black bearskin; and he had the handling of a team of heroes, some of whom had fought at his side against outrageous odds at an earlier stage of the battle.

"We must have a go at them, lads," said he; "we can keep them off the colours if we can't do more. Are you ready? Now for it, then!"

Denis had come to himself; here at length was certain death; and for the last moments of conscious life he had turned his back upon the battle's smoke and roar, while his eyes rested upon a clear and tranquil patch in the green valley of the Tchernaya, with tiny trees and a white farmhouse set out like toys. His thoughts were not very clear, but they were flying overseas, and as they still flew the officer's voice rang in his ears. So this was the end. A few Russians in loose order led the column; they were soon swept aside; and into the real head of the advancing multitude the twenty hurled themselves like men who could not die.

Denis never knew what happened to himself. He remembered his captain being bayoneted through the folds of his cloak, and cutting down two Russians at almost one stroke of his sword; he remembered longing for a sword of his own, as his piece was wrenched from his grasp by a dead weight on the bayonet. Yellow faces hemmed him in, their little eyes dilating with rage and malice; he remembered striking one of them with all his might, seeing the man drop, being in the act of striking another.... His fists were still doubled when he opened his eyes hours later on the moonlit battle-field.

A great weight lay across his legs, so stiffly that Denis thought the dead man a log until his hand came in contact with damp clothing. His own throat and mouth were full of something hard and horrible. His moustache and beard were clotted with the same substance. One side of his face felt numb and swollen;

but his sight was uninjured, and the pain not worse than bad neuralgia. He got upon his hands and knees and looked about him.

The day's haze had vanished with the smoke of battle; it was a still and clear night, brilliantly lighted by the moon. The Tchernaya lay like a tube of quicksilver along the peaceful plain whereon Denis had gazed before the end; he could see a light in the white farmhouse. The heights of Inkerman twinkled all over with scattered weapons, and all over were mounds more like graves than bodies waiting for the grave. The Sandbag Battery rose sharply against the moonlit sky. Denis was not near enough to see the fearful carnage there, but he remembered what it had been quite early in the day, and he had only to listen to hear the groaning of the wounded who had yet to be disentangled from the dead in the shadow of those ill-starred parapets. The night was so still that a groan, nay, a dying gasp, could be heard even further than sight could penetrate through the rays of that glorious moon; and yet it was so light that the glimmer of lanterns round about the fatal battery was not at first apparent to the eye.

When Denis saw the lanterns, he got up and tried to stagger toward them, but collapsed at once, and had to lie where he fell until they came to him.

"Come on, boys, I see a Rooshian!" called Linesman, holding his lantern level with his shako.

"Wait a bit, here's one of our chaps," replied a voice that Denis knew. "S' help me if it ain't our old sergeant. I'd know him by his ginger nob a mile off! And him in such a stew to get at 'em this morning! It's more'n ever I was, though I'd as lief be on that job as this ... ugh!"

Denis soon attracted their attention, and in a few more moments his original rear-rank man was stooping over him.

"Why, you're stuck through the face!" he cried, screwing up his own behind the lantern. "But the glue seems set, and don't you go for to move and melt it. There's a wounded officer wants to see you."

Denis whispered something inarticulate. It was his first attempt to speak.

"What's that? Yes, it's our captain," said the other, "and he's waitin' to hear if you're alive. If you're sound below the teeth we can give you an arm apiece and take you to him in ten minutes. He's on'y in one o' the Second Division tents."

Denis could ask no questions, but he had strength enough to act upon this suggestion, and in a few minutes he was among the lighted tents. They put him vividly in mind of his first night at Ballarat. That was the last time he had spoken to Ralph Devenish until the morning of this dreadful day.

Now Ralph was lying in a military tent, a candle and a tumbler of champagne on the service trunk at his elbow, and an army surgeon on a camp-stool beside the bed.

"Is that the man you want to see?" asked the surgeon, but bundled Denis from the tent next instant, and made his conductors hold both lanterns to his face. "Don't you try to speak!" he went on to Denis. "Your wound has practically frozen; and we must keep it so as long as we can. Hold this wad to it till you come out. I oughtn't to let you go in—but he's worse than you."

The caution was repeated to Ralph; then Denis took the camp-stool, and the two were left alone.

"I am glad to have seen you again," murmured Ralph in hollow tones. "Do you know when I saw you last? I never thought of it till this moment. It was on the far side of the battery. Some fellow was going to bayonet you where you lay, and I—I was just in time."

Denis was nodding violently. He also had remembered. He stretched out a trembling hand. But Ralph drew his beneath the blanket.

"Wait a bit," he whispered. "You see, I never thought of its being you; but I'm rather glad it was. Badly hurt, I'm afraid?"

Denis shook his head.

"I am. Lungs. I'm afraid it's a case. Do you remember this early morning?"

The disfigured face made a ghastly protest. Devenish only smiled.

"It was a good sort of duel," he whispered. "And you see, you've won!"

He stretched out a deathly hand for the champagne. Denis reached it for him.

The surgeon stood in the opening of the tent, advanced a step, shrugged, and retired unseen. Ralph had not hidden his hand again. Denis held it in both of his.

"Ask her to forgive me," gasped the shallow whisper. "No.... I can't ask you.... I don't. But you might tell her—when it came to this sort of thing—"

And the deathly face lit up with such a smile as it had worn that morning, when Ralph Devenish waved his sword, and led his company to the succour of their comrades before the Sandbag Battery.

CHAPTER XXXI

TIME'S WHIRLIGIG

John Dent was a Yorkshire yeoman, born in the last years of the eighteenth century, of that hardy northern stock which is England's biceps to this day. As a very little boy he was sent to Richmond Grammar School, and there eventually educated beyond the needs of his vocation, which was to live all his days upon the land of his fathers. John Dent was quite prepared to do so when he had seen something of the world; and by thirty he had not only seen more of it than was usual in those times, but had fallen in love on his travels with a young Irish girl of a social station indubitably above his own. What was more important, the young Irish girl had fallen in love with John Dent, who was handsome, huge, and gentle, with no great sense of humour, but of tenderness and strength compact.

Being what he was, John Dent came to his point with startling directness, was accepted, left the party which he proposed to deplete, and traveled like the crow to Dublin, where a perfect old gentleman sent him about his business in the sweetest imaginable brogue. John Dent returned to Yorkshire with hardly a word, set his affairs in order, ascertained his income to a nicety, chartered a little ship at Whitehaven, and landed in Dublin with his business books under his arm and certain family documents in his wallet. This time he sent a note to Merrion Square, and was content to beard the perfect old gentleman in his official quarters. But to no purpose; he was not even suffered to produce his books or his papers; neither deed, document, nor yet banker's reference, he was smilingly informed, would recommend the match to which he aspired. John Dent replied that he was sorry, as he certainly meant to realize his aspiration, and since his beloved was of age, at the earliest possible moment. Dogged as could be seen, but more enterprising than was supposed, he went straight aboard his vessel, where Nora Devenish actually awaited him; and in two or three days they were leaving Gretna Hall as man and wife when a Carlisle coach rattled over the bridge and up the hill with the perfect old gentleman screaming curses from the box.

Such was the story of the marriage of Denis's parents in the last days of George IV. Right or wrong, justified or unjustifiable, it led neither to long life nor to prosperity. Nora Devenish had the spirit to cut herself off from her own flesh and blood, but Nora Dent had neither the heart nor the health to bear a permanent severance. They never forgave her, and it broke her heart. Meanwhile the perpetual care of an ailing wife combined with the new Corn Laws to impoverish John Dent's estate. He did not live to see the repeal of the measures which had helped to ruin him; and he too died unforgiven, not only by his wife's family, but by himself for her early death. And the last thing that John Dent foresaw from his deathbed was the reunion of his name with that of Devenish in the very next generation.

Nevertheless, just as John Merridew had himself foreshadowed in a moment of emotion on the Australian coast, the place that was made for Denis in his firm led almost at once to a junior partnership. But the new partner was now enabled to bring in a little capital, and that at a time when the growing need of steamers was involving every line in large expense; his few thousands, however, were as nothing compared with his practical knowledge of the sea; and so, still in the 'fifties, a Devenish and a Dent were hand-in-glove.

Denis and Nan were not married until the winter before the Indian Mutiny, because Denis made a quick enough recovery to abide by an impulse, as he had always done, and to fight through the rest of the Crimean War. He was a sergeant of that ragged remnant of the Guards Brigade which marched through London on a midsummer's day and which the Queen welcomed from the balcony of Buckingham Palace. Thereafter Denis had quickly and quietly bought himself out, and it was as a civilian, once more shorn of his picturesque tatters, that he drove down to Hertfordshire for the second time in his life. He looked several years older. His habitual expression was a little grim and wary, the movement of head and eyes something staccato. But that wore off. And many people never noticed that the curve of one nostril was much deeper than the other, though it was there a Russian bayonet had been driven through his face.

They lived in London, if the part that was still Old Kensington could be so reckoned at that time. But in summer they took a cottage near Mr. Merridew, partly because it was called The Fortune, and was yet one of the smallest fortunes in the world, and partly because Nan loved roses, which grew on that rich soil as on no other. Shortly after Mr. Merridew's death his house, being sold, was turned into a school; after some years it became a great school; and their boys, the grandsons of the old red place, went back there on the way to Harrow.

Denis kept in touch with his first partners on the gold-fields, though it was some years before he saw either of them again. Doherty did almost as well as ever for some time after his departure, but the life was no longer what it had been, and the lad gave it up on hearing from Denis that there was no chance of his return. He went back to the station on the craggy coast where the North Foreland had met her doom. Denis next heard of him as a pioneer squatter in the Riverina country, and a partner of his former master, the kindly Kitto; and when they did meet in after life the younger man happened to be the richer of the two. His career was checkered but honourable, and his memory is one of the few green things in the district of his adoption. Denis saw more, however, of a bland clergyman who called on him in the City one fine May morning: he had come in for a family living in East Anglia, where the Dents found Parson Moseley as great a success with his crass parishioners as he had proved a failure among the quick and energetic diggers of the early days.

There was one other figure of those days whom Denis encountered twice in the 'fifties, once for a minute in Pall Mall, when an ill-advised expression of gratitude on the part of Denis curtailed an interchange of much interest, and a few years later at a social function of some magnitude to which Nan enticed her husband. She recognized the tall and lazy-looking gentleman who recognized Denis; in point of fact he was a public man, and far less lazy than he looked; but as Nan did not know him she withdrew to the nearest ottoman, where she looked very beautiful under the glass chandelier of the period (in spite of its unregenerate skirts) during the little conversation which Denis was careful not to cut short again.

"I hope you saw the news?" said the tall man, as though he and Denis had been meeting every day.

"The news from where, sir?"

"Black Hill Flat, if you happen to recollect such a place."

"I should think I did!" cried Denis. "But I haven't seen anything about it in the paper."

"I knew you had a good memory," said the tall man, smiling a little over his beard. "I suppose it doesn't by any chance hark back to what I told you would some day happen on Black Hill Flat?"

"Rather!" cried Denis again. "You used to say that gold would be found there sooner or later."

"It was found the other day, within a few feet of the top."

"You said it would be!"

"On the Native Youth side, and plenty of it, including a solid lump nearly as big as the one you got out of my old shaft. They call it the Nil Desperandum Nugget, which amuses me, because I never met another man who didn't despair of the place. I'm surprised you hadn't heard of it," said the old deep-sinker, and with his old nod passed on.

Nan was immensely excited under the glass chandelier; and excitement and bright lights still became her; but Denis had never known his wife so bad a listener.

"But you know who it is?" she asked him both at beginning and end.

"Indeed I don't."

"You know that man to speak to, and you don't know him by name?"

"No; who is he?"

And she told him with bated breath.

E. W. Hornung – A Short Biography

Ernest William Hornung was born on 7th June 1866 at Cleveland Villas, Marton, Middlesbrough. He was the third son, and youngest of eight children, to John Peter Hornung and his wife Harriet née Armstrong.

By the age of 13 Hornung had joined St Ninian's Preparatory School in Moffat, Dumfriesshire before enrolling at the exclusive Uppingham School, in Rutland, in 1880.

Hornung suffered from a general state of bad health, including asthma and poor eyesight but managed to be well-liked at school and to develop a life-long passion of cricket. He loved to play despite the obvious fact that his talents were rather limited.

At 17 his health worsened, and he left Uppingham to travel to Australia, where a sunnier climate was deemed to be better for his various ailments.

Upon arriving he worked as a tutor to the Parsons family in Mossgiel, in New South Wales. As well as teaching he spent time working in remote sheep stations in the outback and began to contribute materials to the weekly magazine; The Bulletin. It was also at this time that he began work on his first novel.

After two years of very valuable life experiences Hornung returned to England in February 1886, a few months before the death of his father, in November, whose deteriorating business interests had become a constant worry.

Hornung found work in London as a journalist and story writer. In 1887 he published his first story under his own name, 'Stroke of Five', which appeared in Belgravia magazine. His work as a journalist coincided with the reign of terror brought about by Jack the Ripper's grisly murders. From this Hornung developed an interest in criminal behaviour.

He had completed the manuscript of the novel he brought back from Australia and, between July and November 1890, the story, 'A Bride from the Bush', was published in five parts in the respected Cornhill Magazine. It was released later that year in book form. This, his first novel, was well received by critics.

Hoping to further his talents in cricket Hornung, in 1891, became a member of two cricket clubs: the Idlers, whose members included Arthur Conan Doyle and Jerome K. Jerome, and the Strand club.

Hornung knew Doyle's sister, Constance ('Connie') from when he had visited Portugal. Connie was described as attractive, "with pre-Raphaelite looks ... the most sought-after of the Doyle daughters".

They were married on 27th September 1893, although Doyle was not at the wedding and relations between the two writers were occasionally difficult. The Hornung's had their only child, a son, Arthur Oscar (but always called just Oscar), in 1895.

In 1894 Doyle and Hornung began work on a play for Henry Irving, on the subject of boxing; Doyle was, at first, eager to begin and paid Hornung a £50 advance but then withdrew before the first act had been completed: the play was never finished.

Like Hornung's first novel, 'Tiny Luttrell' had Australia as a backdrop and the device of an Australian woman in a culturally alien environment. This theme ran through his next four novels: 'The Boss of Taroomba' (1894), 'The Unbidden Guest' (1894), 'Irralie's Bushranger' (1896), in this Hornung introduced the character of Stingaree, an Oxford-educated, Australian gentleman thief. In 'The Rogue's March' (1896) Hornung began to show a growing fascination with the motivation behind criminal behaviour and was sympathetic to the criminal hero as a victim of events. It was different thinking but caused some consternation for others.

In 1898 Hornung's mother died and he dedicated his next book, a series of short stories; Some Persons Unknown, to her memory.

Later that year Hornung and Connie spent six months in Posillipo, Italy. An account of this trip was published in the May 1899 issue of the Cornhill Magazine.

The fictional character Stingaree was re-written to become his most famous creation; A. J. Raffles; the gentleman thief, first used in six short stories published in 1898 in Cassell's Magazine. Modelled on George Cecil Ives, a Cambridge-educated criminologist and talented cricketer who, like Raffles, lived in the Albany, a gentlemen's only residence in Mayfair. The first tale of the series 'In the Chains of Crime' was published in June that year, titled 'The Ides of March'.

Another account adds to the richness by asserting that Raffles and his sidekick, Bunny Manders, were based not only on Doyle's Holmes and Watson but also on his friends Oscar Wilde and his lover, Lord Alfred Douglas. Whatever the exact amalgam the characters were warmly embraced by the reading public who turned it into both a popular and financial success, although some critics echoed Doyle's own fears of the dubious nature of a criminal being used as a hero.

In early 1899, the Hornung's returned to London, and resided in Pitt Street, West Kensington, for the next six years.

After publishing two novels, 'Dead Men Tell No Tales' (1899) and 'Peccavi' (1900), Hornung published a second collection of Raffles stories, 'The Black Mask', in 1901. The critics again complained about the criminal aspect. The public who bought them had no such qualms.

In 1903 Hornung collaborated with Eugène Presbrey to write a four-act play, 'Raffles, The Amateur Cracksman', which was based on two previously published short stories, 'Gentlemen and Players' and 'The Return Match'. The play was first performed at the Princess Theatre, New York, on 27th October 1903 and ran for 168 performances.

In 1905, after publishing four other books in the interim, Hornung brought back the character Stingaree. Later that year, in response to public demand he published a third collection of Raffles stories in 'A Thief in the Night', in which Manders relates some of the earlier adventures he had had with Raffles.

In 1909 the final Raffles story was published, the full-length novel 'Mr. Justice Raffles'. It was poorly received. The Observer reviewer asking if "Hornung is perhaps a little tired of Raffles".

It seems not. That same year he partnered with Charles Sansom for the play 'A Visit From Raffles', which was performed in November that year at the Brixton Empress Theatre, London.

Hornung turned away from Raffles thereafter, and in February 1911 published 'The Camera Fiend', a thriller whose narrator is an asthmatic cricket enthusiast and his attempts to photograph the soul as it leaves the body. This was followed by 'Fathers of Men' (1912) and 'The Thousandth Woman' (1913) before 'Witching Hill' (1913), a collection of eight short stories in which he introduced the characters Uvo Delavoye and the narrator Gillon. In 1914 his fictional works ceased with 'The Crime Doctor'.

His son, Oscar, left Eton College in 1914, and was due to proceed to King's College, Cambridge later that year. However, the terrors of WWI were about to unleash themselves all over Europe. Oscar volunteered, and was commissioned into the Essex Regiment. He was killed, aged a mere 20, at the Second Battle of Ypres on 6th July 1915.

Although heartbroken Hornung edited and issued privately a collection of Oscar's letters home under the title 'Trusty and Well Beloved', in 1916.

Around this time Hornung himself joined an anti-aircraft unit. He also joined the YMCA and did volunteer work in England for soldiers on leave. In March 1917 he visited France, writing a poem about his experience afterwards—something he had been doing more frequently since Oscar's death—and a collection of his war poetry, 'Ballad of Ensign Joy', was published later that year.

In July 1917 Hornung's poem, 'Wooden Crosses', was published in The Times, and in September, 'Bond and Free' appeared. A few months later he was accepted as a volunteer in a YMCA canteen and library just a few miles behind the Front Line.

Hornung was concerned about support for pacifism among troops and wrote to Connie about it. She spoke to Doyle and, rather than discussing it with Hornung, he informed the military authorities. Hornung was naturally angered by Doyle's action and relations between the two men were further strained as a result. He continued to work at the library until a German offensive overran the British positions and he was forced to retreat, firstly to Amiens and then, in April, back to England. He stayed in England until November 1918, when he again took up his YMCA duties, establishing a rest hut and library in Cologne.

In 1919 Hornung's account of his time spent in France, 'Notes of a Camp-Follower on the Western Front', was published. Doyle later wrote of the book that "there are parts of it which are brilliant in their vivid portrayal". That year Hornung also published his third and final volume of poetry, 'The Young Guard'.

Hornung finished his YMCA work and returned to England in early 1919. He worked on a new novel but was hampered by poor health. But Connie's was of greater concern. In February 1921 they took a holiday in the south of France to recuperate. Whilst travelling there on the train Hornung fell ill with a chill that progressed to influenza and finally pneumonia.

Ernest William Hornung died on 22nd March 1921, aged 54.

He was buried in Saint-Jean-de-Luz, in the south of France, in a grave adjacent to that of George Gissing.

E. W. Hornung – A Concise Bibliography

Periodicals
Stroke of Five (1887, Belgravia)
Spoilt Negative (1887, Belgravia)
Nettleship's Score (January 1890, Cornhill Magazine)
A Bride From the Bush (5 Parts. July-Nov, Cornhill Magazine, 1890)
Thunderbolt's Mate (4 Parts. March 1892, Chambers's Journal)
Kenyon's Innings (April 1892, Longman's Magazine)
The Burrawurra Brand (November 1893, The Idler)
The Unbidden Guest (6 Parts. May-Oct 1894, Longman's Magazine)
The Governess at Greenbush (4 parts. February 1895, Chambers's Journal)
After the Fact (3 Parts. January 1896, Chambers's Journal)
The Ides of March (June 1898, Cassell's Magazine)
A Villa in a Vineyard (May 1899, Cornhill Magazine)
No Sinicure: More Adventures of the Amateur Cracksman (January 1901, Scribner's Magazine)
A Jubilee Present: More Adventures of the Amateur Cracksman (February 1901, Scribner's Magazine)
The Fate of Faustina: More Adventures of the Amateur Cracksman (March 1901, Scribner's Magazine)
The Last Laugh: More Adventures of the Amateur Cracksman (April 1901, Scribner's Magazine)
To Catch a Thief: More Adventures of the Amateur Cracksman (May 1901, Scribner's Magazine)
An Old Flame: More Adventures of the Amateur Cracksman (June 1901, Scribner's Magazine)
The Wrong House: More Adventures of the Amateur Cracksman (Sept 1901, Scribner's Magazine)
Chrystal's Century (June 1903, Atlantic Monthly)
Charles Reade (June 1921, London Mercury)

Novels and Short Story Collection
A Bride from the Bush (1890) Novel
Under Two Skies (1892) Short story collection
Tiny Luttrell (1893) Novel; two volumes
The Boss of Taroomba (1894) Novel
The Unbidden Guest (1894) Novel
Irralie's Bushranger (1896) Novel
The Rogue's March: A Romance (1896) Novel
My Lord Duke (1897) Novel
Some Persons Unknown (1898) Short story collection
Young Blood (1898) Novel
The Amateur Cracksman (1899) Short story collection
Dead Men Tell No Tales (1899) Novel

The Belle of Toorak (1900) Novel; published in the US as The Shadow of a Man
Peccavi (1900) Novel
The Black Mask (1901) Short story collection; republished as Raffles: Further Adventures of the Amateur Cracksman
At Large (1902) Novel
The Shadow of the Rope (1902) Novel
Denis Dent: A Novel (1903) Novel
No Hero (1903) Novel
Stingaree (1905) Novel
A Thief in the Night (1905) Short story collection; republished as A Thief in the Night: Further Adventures of A. J. Raffles, Cricketer and Cracksman
Raffles: The Amateur Cracksman (1906) Short story collection; stories taken from The Amateur Cracksman and The Black Mask
Mr. Justice Raffles (1909) Novel
The Camera Fiend (1911) Novel
Fathers of Men (1912) Novel
The Thousandth Woman (1913) Novel
Witching Hill (1913) Short story collection
The Crime Doctor (1914) Short story collection
Old Offenders and a Few Old Scores (Published posthumously) Short story collection

Plays
Raffles, The Amateur Cracksman (27th October 1903) By Hornung and Eugéne Presbrey; first performed at the Princess Theatre, New York
Stingaree, the Bushranger (1st February 1908) First performed at the Queen's Theatre, London
A Visit From Raffles (1st November 1909) By Hornung and Charles Sansom; first performed at the Brixton Empress Theatre, London

Non-Fiction
'Trusty and Well Beloved', The Little Record of Arthur Oscar Hornung (1915) Privately published
Notes of a Camp-Follower on the Western Front (1919)

Poetry
Ballad of Ensign Joy (1917)
Wooden Cross (1918)
The Young Guard (1919)